Strange Moves

by Cheryl Yax

with Lil Barcaski

Strange Moves
By Cheryl Yax
with Lil Barcaski

ISBN: 978-1-7336929-1-5

Book Cover Design by LongBar Creative Solutions
www.LongBarCreatives.com

Printed in USA

This book is dedicated to my beloved husband who has
faithfully believed in me...
always!

Table of Contents

Introduction: Jordan and Angelique - 1972 7

Chapter 1: 1995: Tampa Florida.............................19

Chapter 2: Jordan and Angelique – 1974 26

Chapter 3: 1995 Ura Dances 31

Chapter 4: Tampa 1995 – 96.................................39

Chapter 5: Jordan and Angelique and Heaven 1977.........48

Chapter 6: Chapel Hill 1996.................................53

Chapter 7: Waking Up in Tampa 1996 60

Chapter 8: It's Only Dinner.................................66

Chapter 9: Angelique and Heaven 1985 - 1988 77

Chapter 10: Tampa 1996-97 80

Chapter 11: Chapel Hill 1997.................................93

Chapter 12: Angelique goes to work 1989.....................99

Chapter 13: Chapel Hill 105

Chapter 14: Portland 1997.................................110

Chapter 15: Rain, Rain, and Scooters.............................118

Chapter 16: 1990 Angelique Gets Caught 128

Chapter 17: Portland 1997.................................137

Chapter 18: 1990 Changing Tides 148

Chapter 19: Leaving Portland.................................161

Chapter 20: An Unexpected Detour - 1998.....................169

Chapter 21: Designs, Designs, Designs 98 - 99 Chapel Hill
.................................181

Chapter 22: 1991 The Year Everything Changed............189

Chapter 23: Tillie 1999 197

Chapter 24: 2003.................................208

Chapter 25:Ura Returns 2003.................................217

Chapter 26: 1991.................................230

Chapter 27: 2009 - 2011...239

Chapter 28: 1992...248

Chapter 29: 2012...256

Chapter 30: Jordan and Heaven – 1994 – 95 268

Chapter 31: 2013...275

Chapter 32: 2015 – 2018..290

Chapter 33: Arriving Back in Tampa............................307

Chapter 34: Answers 316

Epilogue 328

Heaven Turns Fifty - 2027 328

Acknowledgements...330

About the Author 331

Introduction

Jordan and Angelique - 1972

Jordan was standing off to the side watching nervously as the models took their paces down the runway. His assistant, Grace, was in back dressing the girls that had been sent from the agency for the fundraiser. Normally, Jordan would be in back helping, but this was a sorority alumni charity event and he was the only male designer, in fact one of the only males, in the room. He was debuting a brand-new line of women's summer and beach wear and he had volunteered to be part of the event to get some notoriety for his designs. One of the board members of the charity was a buyer for Macy's and this was a great way to get in front of her. The women attending the fashion show and luncheon paid $250 each to be there. A few of them had made a $5,000 donation which allowed them to choose a designer to custom make them an outfit with half the money going to the charity and the other half to the designer they chose.

He had a lot riding on this and was chewing softly on his thumbnail as his clothing began to take center stage. First, a good looking brunette sashayed down the runway wearing a flowing caftan of bright orange and salmon tones. When she hit the top of the walk, she turned and slid the outer garment off her shoulders to reveal a stunning white one-piece bathing suit with tiny gold accents across the waist and neckline. Applause and even a couple of gasps! Good start.

For the next five minutes, the models brought his work out one piece at a time. His final piece in the show was his favorite. A tunic top of azure blue with three large dark blue snaps down the front accompanied by a wraparound skirt in sweet corn yellow. He closed his eyes as they announced that this was his final piece. He heard the audience's murmurs of delight and approving whispers and slowly opened his eyes.

He couldn't focus on his design. All he could see was her. Her hair was the color of summer wheat and her eyes were so big and so green that he literally stopped breathing for a moment.

She reached the top of the runway, turned, and unsnapped the blouse, tossing it over one shoulder and with the other hand, deftly pulled the wrap around skirt from her waist to reveal the deep blue bikini beneath. She slowly paced the runaway back to the exit dragging the skirt seductively behind her as if she was floating.

The women cheered and he heard the announcer call his name. He hopped up onto the stage and waved quickly. Pictures were snapping even as he rushed backstage. He had to meet that girl.

"Excuse me," Jordan said as he tapped Angelique lightly on the shoulder.

She turned to face him and smiled. "You're Mr. Kenny, aren't you?"

"Yes," he managed, trying not to stare. It was if he'd known her his entire life. *Is there such a thing as love at first site?* he thought.

"I love your designs. I'm hoping to study design at FIT. I've been working on some lingerie designs on my own."

"Really? I'd love to see your lingerie… I mean lingerie designs." *Awesome Jordan, get your foot out of your mouth.*

Angelique giggled. "I would love to show them to you."

"Have you had dinner?" Jordan asked.

"It's two thirty in the afternoon, Mr. Kenny," Angelique replied, suppressing a laugh.

"Oh, yes, of course. Jordan by the way."

"Excuse me?"

"Mr. Kenny was my father. Call me Jordan and you are… Besides stunning that is?"

"Angelique."

"Real name or modelling name?"

"Guess."

 Real. Wait, no! Stage name." Jordan locked eyes with her, his sea blue and hers the color of emeralds. At 42 he still retained his boyish good looks and was often mistaken for being much younger. "Either way, it suits you."

"It's my real name. My parents were hoping for an angel. Sadly, I disappointed them on that one."

"Well, probably just as well." Jordan laughed. "Angels are overrated. But I will say, you looked like an angel in my designs."

"Not hard to do. Your work is lovely. I love the outfit Grace chose for me."

"It's my favorite from this line. You really made it sing. You should keep it."

"Seriously?"

"Yes, but only if you'll have dinner with me tonight."

"You could be dangerous," Angelique, smiled.

They stood and chatted like old friends for nearly an hour and finally, Angelique agreed to meet Jordan for dinner at 7 pm that night at a small French restaurant on the lower east side of Manhattan. The food was wonderful, and they laughed and talked as if they had known each other for a lifetime.

Jordan asked Angelique how old she was and came to find out that she was twenty-four.

***

"Really?" he replied. "Me too… backwards."

"You are not forty-two years old. Not possible," the joke becoming clear.

"Have I scared you off?"

"Not a chance. I have daddy issues."

Jordan nearly spit out his wine, laughing loudly. "Then we're a matched set."

After dinner, Angelique convinced Jordan that they should go dancing at little club in midtown. It was a smoky little place with a dance floor and a small stage where a four-piece band was playing R&B and funk.

She pulled Jordan onto the dance floor and was immediately taken by the rhythm. Jordan had never seen anyone dance the way she did. Her eyes were closed, and it was as if she was an extension of the music itself. She wound the fingers of her right hand with those on his left hand and pulled and pushed him away and toward her, back and forth, round and round, sometimes spinning, then dipping down near to the floor. Suddenly she let go and was moving on her own, as if he wasn't there. Her hips rotated, her arms moved flowingly above her head and then her hands found her own breasts and rode down her chest to her belly and around her waist.

Jordan backed away till he was nearly off the floor, watching her every move. He began to realize he wasn't alone in that voyeurism. Every man and most of the women were watching her movements. The only word that came to mind was exotic, like something you would expect to see in a ritual or tribal dance on a remote island in the pacific.

Jordan felt the oddest mix of pride and jealousy as he watched her, completely enthralled. *What have I gotten myself into,* he thought? *And how will I ever get out?*

The band extended the song a little longer. Angelique had cleared the floor of all other dancers and was on her own. Suddenly, she opened her eyes, seeking Jordan and the band brought the song to a close. Jordan stepped back toward her just in time to take her in his arms as the music changed as the band began playing Al Green's popular hit, "Let's Stay Together."

And that's exactly what they did.

They stayed out till dawn and then went back to her tiny one room studio in Brooklyn.

"Well, this is it," Angelique said suddenly nervous at being with this older man she admired and was completely smitten with.

"It's…" Jordan stammered.

"Miniscule?" Angelique finished his sentence.

"I was going to say charming, but that works."

"It's a glorified closet but it's affordable and the neighborhood is great. I love it here," she said. "I would live here the rest of my life. In a bigger apartment, maybe."

"Who know. Maybe that'll happen."

There was just enough room for her twin bed, a nightstand with a lamp and clock radio on it and one small desk and chair with some sheets of art paper with half-finished drawings strewn about on the desk. There was a tiny bath with a very small shower stall and what one could call a kitchen in the corner that amounted to a hotplate, small refrigerator, and counter with a half-sized sink. But the little studio was clean, and Angelique had done all she could to make it warm and cheery with soft colors on the walls, where she'd hung some prints of her favorite artwork. The bed was covered with a soft, stark white comforter.

Jordan sat on the edge of the bed and kicked off his shoes. Angelique moved to sit next to him, but he put a hand up.

"Not yet," he said.

"No?" she asked a quizzical expression crossing her face.

"Dance for me," Jordan demanded. "I love the way you dance but I want you to only dance for me now. Tonight, watching all the other guys watching you, all I could imagine was you dancing only for me. You taking your clothes off, only for me."

"Don't you mean your clothes?" Angelique replied.

"What?"

"I'm wearing the bikini you gave me under my dress," she replied provocatively. "I thought there was a chance you might want to take it off me if the evening went well."

"And did it go well?" Jordan asked smiling.

"What do you think?" Angelique reached over and turned the radio on. A song was just ending and as luck would have it, the next song began and Bill Withers began singing his hit song, "Use Me Up." She laughed and started to move with the sexy rhythmic bass line of the funk song.

"Perfect," Jordan said as she slowly started to slip the straps of her sundress off her shoulders as she moved to the music. She lowered one strap, then the other and slid the top of her dress down just enough to give Jordan a view of the top of her soft white perfectly rounded breasts. As the music continued, Angelique slowly removed her dress, wiggling out of it, letting it fall to the floor. She moved toward Jordan and began to straddle him, lowering herself onto his lap but he pushed her away.

"Not yet! Keep dancing. I want to watch you strip," Jordan said.

Angelique stepped back and started to remove the top to the beautiful bikini that Jordan had designed.

"Slower," Jordan said and as she did, he removed his own shirt button by button in time with her movements and the music. Angelique undid the clasp in the front of the bikini top. She slid the material lower and lower till she was barely covering the hardened nipples of her breasts.

Jordan unzipped his pants and lowered them to the floor. As Angelique revealed one perfect breast then the other, Jordan kicked away his designer jeans and stood to meet her. His erect penis pushed the material of the black boxer briefs he wore. He pulled her to him and ran the thumb of his right hand around the front of the waist band of her bikini bottoms. She moaned softly in his ear feeling his hardness against her. Painfully slowly, he began to remove the bikini bottoms while locking eyes with hers. With his left hand, he grabbed a handful of her beautiful hair and pulled her head back to kiss her hard on the mouth.

Jordan stopped suddenly, then spun Angelique around and in one swift movement lifted her to place her on the middle of the bed. He removed her bikini bottoms and tossed them to the floor, kicked off his underwear and slid down on top of her. He began kissing her neck and throat moving to take each of her breasts in his mouth kissing the space between them. He worked his way down her belly kissing and licking her soft, slightly salty skin. When he got to the triangle of soft blond hair between her legs, he spread them apart and flicked his tongue over her swollen clitoris. Angelique cried out with desire as he began to use his tongue and fingers to pleasure her. When she was seconds from exploding, he lifted himself up and entered her, moving slowly as she lifted her hips to meet his thrusts.

He increased the speed of his movements and moment later, they both climaxed in white hot ecstasy. Jordan leaned on his elbows and stared at the beautiful young creature beneath him for a moment before rolling to her side. They both lay spent for a little while then Angelique turned lay her head on his chest.

"That was amazing," she said.

"Yes, you are," he replied.

After that night, they became inseparable. Within a month, she had given up her apartment and moved into Jordan's loft on the lower east side where he lived and worked.

They went out dancing often and Jordan began to bring a sketch pad along. Her dancing inspired a whole new line of clothing that mimicked her dance moves. He used soft, flowing materials that swirled with her movements. Different shades of sky blues, warm gold tones, and cream colors that highlighted her golden hair and wild green eyes. His work had always been good, and he made a decent living as a designer, but he'd never done work like this before. This was a whole new level and he knew it. He contacted the buyer from Macy's who had been involved with the fashion show and asked her to come to the studio for a private showing of the new line. Angelique modeled every piece, one at a time while Jordan poured wine and explained each garment.

"I liked the work from the fashion show, but this is different. You've outdone yourself," the buyer said after seeing the entire collection. "How soon can you have the line in production?"

"Which pieces?" Jordan asked excitedly.

"All of them, the whole line. We can offer you an advance for production. I'll have my assistant draw up the paperwork and get a check cut. We'll have to discuss sizes and quantities. It will be an exclusive for Macy's New York store, of course."

"Of course."

"By the way, what are you calling this new line?" the buyer asked.

Jordan took a deep breath and looked at Angelique. "Angel Wear."

"Perfect. I'll get marketing moving on some promotion."

Once she left, Jordan looked at Angelique and howled like a crazed animal!

"Let's get very, very, very drunk!" he said.

Chapter 1

1995: Tampa Florida

"This is ridiculous. Why would I want to invest my hard-earned money in a bar this dingy and, well…" Dennis Brooks surveyed the room, "…empty?"

"It's not empty. There are at least fifteen guys in here," Tony said just as an older man walked out of the bathroom. "Make that sixteen. So, what if it's a little underwhelming right now. A little paint, some better lighting for the stage.

"More attractive strippers," Lenny chimed in.

"They're not so bad," Tony replied. "This from a guy that hasn't been laid in three months."

"Five, but who's counting?" Dennis laughed.

"Four and why are you guys monitoring my sex life? Gay much?" Lenny Thompson sneered at them. He was the least attractive of the three young men, a skinny nerdy guy with dirty blond hair that was thinning on top already despite that fact that he was only 28 years old.

"We don't care about your sex life, or lack there-of but you have to admit, your chances with the ladies will increase exponentially if you're a part owner of a bar," Tony replied.

They had all gone to college together and remained friends ever since. Dennis was a computer whiz and was making a ton of money creating software as a consultant for big firms. He was tall, with chestnut brown hair and blue gray eyes that women often referred to as smoldering. Tony Paglione had a mop of black hair that fell over his deep brown eyes. He was Italian and proud of it. His Grandfather passed away just a few years before and left him with a decent inheritance and part ownership of an import business he "dropped in on," two or three times a week, mostly to make sure his income stream was safe. Tony had heard that the *Where the Girls Are, Gentlemen's Club* was in dire straits, and could be bought for a song. He convinced his two buddies to check it out in hopes of talking them into joining him in the venture. It was a Wednesday night in November and the bars on the North side of Tampa weren't all that busy in general, but this was particularly dismal attendance.

"You know I don't have any money to invest in this," Lenny said. "So, as for clout with the ladies, I'll have to hope that they find assistant manager of an Outback Steakhouse sexy."

"Yeah, that'll happen," said Dennis.

"You're gonna be the manager," Tony said. No money down and far better than hawking mediocre steaks for shitty money. Maybe we'll add food here in the future and you can put those Outback skills to better use."

"I don't know, Tony. I mean who doesn't like a strip club now and again, but as a steady diet, it's not really my scene," Dennis chimed in.

"That's why we have Lenny. We keep working at our regular jobs and he holds down the fort. Lenny, you dig that idea? C'mon old ladies eating steak or hot chicks on poles? It's a no brainer if you ask me."

"Will you match my salary?"

"Play your cards right and we get this place up to speed and you'll double that miserable pay in a few months."

"Not with these girls." Dennis shot a look at the stage where a nondescript young woman was gyrating mindlessly. She moved around the edge, playing up to each man sitting front and center at the little tables that lined the stage, collecting the dollar bills they tucked into her G string. She was topless but had little bright pink tassels covering her nipples. The fringe that hung from them swung with her movements and was more comical than sexy. "This is plain pathetic."

***

Ura drove the big gold Caddy past the neon signs on Busch Boulevard. She was looking for something but not sure exactly what. She needed to eat, her stomach growled a low empty moan, but she needed something more than food. She would know it when she saw it. Up ahead, a sign with a dancing girl in bright red caught her attention. "Yes, that's it. That's it exactly," she said and swung the Caddy into the big parking lot to the right of the building. There were only a few cars. *Perfect,* she thought and pulled into a space near the door.

Just as Dennis uttered the word pathetic, the door to the bar swung open and a young woman in flowing clothes of muted purple and greens slid into the room. Dennis was the first to turn his head and see her arrival. *Is she gliding in slow motion or is it me,* he thought? He nudged his companions who turned to see the gorgeous young woman. Her hair was golden blond and fell in waves down her back. She went directly to the DJ booth and spoke to the him. They were near enough to hear her say, "I would like to dance now."

The DJ looked like he'd been struck by lightning. "Sure," was all he could manage. He scurried over to the stage and motioned for the listless young lady to vacate. She looked confused but walked off and over to the bar to get a drink.

"What should I play," he said to her as he passed her on the way back to the booth. She was directly in front of the guy's table now and as she turned, they could see her eyes, emerald green and glowing in an unearthly manner.

"Something sexy and slow," she murmured, then step up on to the T shaped stage to take her place. "Can you play, Let's Stay Together, by Al Green?"

"Sure," he said again, as if it were the only word he could manage and cued up the song.

Ura began to slowly move around the stage, as if she were examining her space and how to use it. The back wall was all mirror and she looked at herself as she slid down, opening her legs in an almost frog like stance then slowly coming back up to slide her hips back and forth. She put her hands against the mirror and bent forward, her ass jutting out toward the men who were moving in around the stage to fill in every available seat. Dennis, Tony, and Lenny moved to a table at the top of the T shaped stage never once taking their eyes off Ura as they did so. She swung her hips and moved her body like a snake then slowly turned to face the crowd. She knew they were there, but their faces were a blur. All that mattered was that they were watching her, needing her, wanting her; her body, her soul. She could feel the heat rise in the air around her and could hear the audible gasps and heavy breathing. She slid the cloth material of her flowing dress off her shoulders and let it slide down to reveal her breasts in a tight corset that made them jut out, the nipples barely covered by top of the white lace material. She moved over to the pole in the center of the stage and wrapped her legs around it, her skirt still attached at the waist but with one simple movement, she yanked, and it fell to the floor revealing her lower body in nothing but a tiny white lace G String. The men in the room groaned as if in unison, feeling the ache of desire. Ura matched her movements with the slow and heartbreakingly sexy music coming from the DJ booth. He had abandoned his post and was standing directly behind Tony, watching this miracle on the stage in front of him. Tony, feeling his presence behind him, leaned back, and without taking his eyes off Ura, asked him, "Who the hell is she?"

"I have no idea. An angel maybe. Do angels dance like that?"

As the music built to a crescendo, Ura slid to the floor and rolled and gyrated with the cacophony of sound as if she were the music itself. She moved on all fours around the edge of the stage like a tigress and made eye contact with each man as she passed them, never once taking the money they offered but rather letting them toss it onto the stage as she passed. Twenties and fifties, even a couple of hundred-dollar bills rained on to the stage behind her. When she got to Dennis's table, she stopped and locked eyes with him for what seemed like an eternity, though it was only a few seconds. Then she moved on and as the song ended, she rose to her feet and walked off to the backstage area passing the other girls who, stunned, had gathered there to witness her performance.

Tony sprang into action. He jumped from his seat and turned to follow the DJ back to the booth. "Hey, man! Is the owner here tonight?" he asked the dizzy young man.

"No, he only comes in on Fridays, but I need to call him and tell him about this chick. He needs to hire her. She could save this joint."

Tony pulled out his wallet and took out two crisp one-hundred-dollar bills. "Tell you what," he said waving them at the DJ. "How about you forget about calling him. These two Benjamins and I would appreciate it and if you play along, I think we could arrange a raise in salary. Deal?"

"Sure," he said and plucked the bills from Tony's hand. "I don't really like Roger much anyway. He's a prick. I like the girls here though. They deserve a better place to work."

"Let's make that happen. You got a phone I could use?"

"There's one in the office. I'll let you in… boss!"

Once the door to the office was closed, Tony pulled a number from his wallet. "Hey Greg, sorry to call so late, but I need you to meet me at 9 am sharp at the office. We're buying the club. Get the papers ready, my buddy and I will be down to sign them. I want to move on this right away.

As Tony approached the table, Dennis looked up at him and said, "I guess this means we're going to own a strip club."

"The best strip club in Florida. Let's go talk to that girl."

"So long, Outback, hello strippers," Lenny sighed.

"Are you complaining?" Tony chided.

"Not on your life."

Backstage, Ura sat at one of the little mirrored stations along the wall of the dressing room staring at the very young woman looking back at her. One of the dancers had taken the stage but two others remained and were sitting across from Ura, confused and more than a little jealous of this strange creature who had simply landed in their midst. Finally, one of them got up the nerve to speak. "Who are you?" she asked.

"I wish I knew. Best I can tell you is, my name is Ura."

Chapter 2

Jordan and Angelique – 1974

"Mr. Kenny," the nurse called out.

Jordan jumped out of the hard metal chair in the hospital waiting room like someone had lit a match under his seat.

"Here, right here!"

"Congratulations, it's a girl. You can see your wife now."

Jordan pushed open the door to Angelique's hospital room and rushed to her side. She was holding their newborn baby in her arms. The tiny little creature was swaddled in pink coverings and was as wrinkled as a raisin. "Look at her," he said as he stood over his wife and child. He reached out and brushed a lock of Angelique's damp hair from her forehead. "She's beautiful, and so are you."

"Liar!" She responded with a raspy laugh. "She looks like a little old man and I look like death warmed over, or at least I feel like death warmed over."

"You're both perfect. My little goddesses. Speaking of which. Are we cool on the name?"

"Artemis, if it was a boy." She said.

"Helena..." Jordan continued.

"… If it was a girl, and it is a girl. Pink, see," she responded touching the soft pink cloth surrounding her baby girl. Yes! Right, Helena? Do you like your name?" she said bringing the baby's face closer to her own.

"Beautiful one," Jordan said. "Her beauty will make all humans jealous."

"I just hope they don't call you Hell for a nickname." Angelique sighed and pulled the baby closer to her chest.

The first six months of Helena's life were trying for Angelique and Jordan. The baby was colicky and cried a great deal. They were lucky to get three hours uninterrupted sleep on any given night. But just after Helena turned seven months old, she suddenly became calmer. It was as if she'd resigned herself to her mortal life and she began sleeping through the night like a champ. She giggled and made gurgling sounds until one morning she said the unexpected word, "Dada."

"Okay, little girl. I see how this is going to go," Angelique mused.

"I told you she was going to be very smart," Jordan laughed.

True to form, Helena became a daddy's girl. She followed Jordan around the studio, never more than three steps behind him. She curled up on his lap for story time and he read to her constantly. She loved her mother but from an early age seemed to know that Angelique had a distance about her. Jordan began to notice some disturbing things about Angelique. She didn't seem to be bonding with her daughter. She started taking long walks in the evening, saying she needed to get out of the house and get some space. Angelique and Helena didn't have the strong bond that Jordan had expected to happen between mother and child. He had heard that often daughters were closer to Fathers and sons closer to Mothers, but this was different.

The day before Helena's first birthday, Angelique developed a severe migraine and took to her bed. Jordan had a cake and toys for Helena and a few close friends came by, some with their children. Angelique never came out of the bedroom. After that, she had episodes like that more and more frequently. Angelique's moods began changing as well. She was often sullen and sometimes very short tempered with both Jordan and Helena. Once, when Helena was not quite two, Angelique pressured her to eat her vegetables.

"But Mommy, I don't like these funny looking green things on my plate," Helena moaned.

"Those are lima beans and they're good for you. Stop complaining and eat them. If you don't clean your plate, no dessert for you."

Helena loved ice cream and knew that there was mint chocolate chip to be had so she forced the last of the pale little kidney shapes down her throat. After a minute, her face was a similar color to the lima beans. "I don't feel so good," she managed just before hurling lima beans, chicken, and mashed potato bits all over the kitchen table.

"Jesus! Look what you've done," Angelique screamed at the child.

"Ang! Please. I've got this. It's not her fault." Jordan replied sharply as Helena's little face scrunched up, tears rolling down her cheeks. "It's okay, little one," he said to his daughter and went for a wet cloth to wipe her eyes and mouth. Angelique quietly stood up and left the table. She went to their bedroom and didn't come out till morning. Jordan cleaned up the mess, put Helena to bed and worked on designs till dawn.

***

"I think I'm pregnant again." Angelique stood over Jordan's drafting table where he was working on a new dress pattern.

"What? Are you sure?"

"Pretty sure. I mean I should see Doctor Bill, but I peed on one of those little sticks, actually twice to be sure, and both times it said, pregnant."

Jordan sucked in a deep breath. He was a little shocked. They hadn't had a lot of sex over the last year but there was that night a couple of months before where Angelique had suddenly turned on the charm and made it clear that she wanted to be with him. He had been a little surprised at her sudden amorous attitude but let himself believe that maybe she was settling down; that maybe a page was turning in their favor. Helena's third birthday had been just a month earlier. Now that she was going to be a big sister, maybe things were going to be better.

"Well, are you going to say anything?" she asked.

"This is great news, baby!" Jordan said as he stood and pulled Angelique into his arms. He wasn't sure it was, but he was hopeful. "Maybe it's time we look at bigger apartments."

"Can we please move back to Brooklyn?" Angelique pleaded.

"It would certainly be cheaper than in the city. We'll start looking next week," Jordan answered.

Chapter 3

1995 Ura Dances

"She's not into you, man! Get over it," Tony chided Dennis. They sat at the bar in their newly purchased night club with cold beers in front of them.

"I'm not giving up that easily," Dennis replied. "I've never met anyone like her."

"Look. I like Ura fine. She's easy on the eyes and the way she dances would make most men fall in love with her, but we have a lot to do to shape this joint up. I don't want you getting distracted and more importantly, I don't want you to creep out our money-making machine. Ura is the big attraction and I have to say, in the three weeks since we took this place over, the other girls are starting to step up their game too. Ura makes them have to dance better to compete."

"That's not why," Dennis said.

"Sure it is, they want to make the money she makes… or somewhere in the vicinity of it. Jealousy is a great motivator."

"Yeah, but it's more than that. That's what I've been trying to tell you. Ura is not just some dancer. She's special."

"They're all 'special'," Tony said making little air quotes around the invisible word special as he said it.

"Ura has been teaching the other girls," Dennis replied.

"What? Teaching them what?" Tony asked.

"Style, moves, creating a character and taking their dancing from cheap stripping to exotic art. Have you been paying attention at all?" Dennis asked thumping Tony's head lightly with his index finger. "You in there? She brought in a sewing machine on Monday and has been making them costumes to match their new persona's. It's amazing."

"Well, I did notice the weird new styles on a couple of them. Ura did that?" Tony asked surprised.

"Yup!" Dennis said, proudly.

"Hey." Tony's eyes lit up. "Wait a minute. We can really market this. If we can pump this up, we can be way more than a strip club. We can be a high-end exotic dance club. Bring in the money crowd, couples even. Maybe we can do a women's night and get some of those Chippindale guys in to dance for the ladies."

"I guess. I just know I have to get her to go out with me. I can't stop thinking about her and I know she likes me. She's been through some shit, I bet," Dennis said.

"Okay, Sir Dennis, get off the white horse and get your head out of your ass. We've got a lot of work to do. This place can be a freaking gold mine. Let's get to work."

Tony pulled Dennis off his bar stool and yanks him toward the far wall of the bar which is half painted, the roller and pan still sitting with fresh paint. "Get back to work, partner.

I have some calls to make. We need a lot of publicity for our grand reopening.”

“Grand reopening?” Dennis asked.

“Just paint. I’ve got this,” Tony called over his shoulder and headed to the office.

“Dennis, can I speak to you for a moment?” Ura asked. Dennis was sitting in the office doing the books. His head snapped up at the sound of her voice. It was like little bells ringing or crystal glasses clicking against one another in a toast. *Get it together man,* he heard his own voice in his head. *She’s just a girl, right? Be cool.*

“Sure, come in, sit down.”

“Thanks. I hope you don’t think me pushy or anything, but I’ve noticed some things I think would help improve things with the girls. I’ve talked to Lenny and he said to come to you first then maybe we can all talk about how to help the girls and make the club a better environment for everyone; us and the customers.”

“I’m all ears,” Dennis said, leaning in toward her, his elbows on his desk.

“Well, I don’t think it’s any surprise that most of the girls have problems with substance abuse. They have problems making it to work on time, miss days, some have kids and can’t afford day care all the time. I’d like to help them. I think if they’re lives were less stressful and they had a little structure, they would be happier and more productive which is better for everyone.”

"Makes sense," he said nodding.

"I think we could start slowly by having rules they need to adhere to, posted backstage in the dressing room so they can remember the rules and try to follow them." She handed Dennis a sheet of paper with ten rules neatly printed out. "I think these are a good start. What do you think?" she asked.

Dennis took the paper and read from the list.

1. No drugs

2. No dating the customers

3. No leaving with customers/No prostitution

4. No ripped or dirty clothing

5. No foul language on the floor

6. No getting drunk (one drink per shift – after shift is over)

7. No bad attitudes in front of house or back of house

8. No stealing

9. No bullying

10. No chipped nail polish

 "Wow!" That's a great start," he said, really impressed by her. "Can we get this printed and posted today?"

"I think it would be good to have a company meeting with

them first. Go over the rules, answer questions. The first rule is going to freak some of them out. They need to get off the drugs but that may not be an easy sell. However, if you can make it a rule for while they're on the job, it might slow them down a little. At least it's worth a shot," Ura said.

"Agreed. I'll get Lenny to call them all and have them in for a meeting on Sunday when we're closed. Talk things through."

"That's great, Dennis. Thank you so much," she said and instinctively reached out to touch his hand. *No, Ura, he's adorable but he's your boss. No good can come from flirting with him,* she thought and quickly pulled her hand away.

Dennis felt a shock wave go through him from her touch, and all but shivered at it. "No, I need to thank you. I've never run a nightclub before much less a strip club... I mean exotic dance club. Tony's on my case to be sure and call it that," he laughed.

"He's right," Ura replied. "This place is really starting to come together. It's way classier than the night I first walked in here. You guys have moved a mountain in a month. I think the grand reopening is going to be a huge success," she said.

"Couldn't have done it without you," he said. *Wouldn't have done it without you,* he thought. *You're why I got into this mess,* he wanted to say out loud, but he just smiled as he locked eyes with her emerald green ones for just a moment longer than comfortable. Ura rose and smiled as she floated out of his site.

Over the next couple of weeks, as the grand reopening day approached, Ura had several conversations with Lenny and Dennis about how to improve things for the girls. Ura helped most of them create new stage names. She and Lenny created a strict schedule that included dance lessons, makeup lessons, and costuming. They were made to understand that they have to live by the rules posted by Dennis. As manager, Lenny was thrilled to put all this into action. He loved his job and genuinely liked most of the girls but secretly began to form a little crush on Ura. He informed the girls that there would be a meeting once a month and that he will provide food, but they would have to be there. Not all the girls loved the new deal and the ones who couldn't abide by the rules left quickly. Drugs was a factor with many of them and Ura tried to help them without pushing them further away which she found to be more difficult with some of them than others. *I've got to help them live a healthier lifestyle,* she thought.

The girls were excited to see all the changes and to be a part of it. No one had ever cared about them before. Some of them got onboard fast while others were suspicious, wondering why someone like Ura would help them. Most of them had worked in other clubs and had a little trepidation about the three buddies who ran the bar. It all seemed a little too good to be true.

Each day, Ura pushed for small changes. She set up a beauty station for the girls to use with different nail polishes and polish remover, a curling iron for their hair and hair spray. She always made more tips than they did, and this was a way to share in her good fortune.

She asked Dennis if the club could provide some healthy food for them. He got a small fridge and a list from Ura who suggested fruits, vegetables, protein bars, and juices. She told him they needed lockers so they could feel they had a safe place for their belongings.

"Some of the girls are pretty broke and the temptation to steal things from each other is understandable. Lockers would solve that in both directions. Less temptation, less cat fights over small items or a couple of dollars stashed in a purse and left out while someone's on stage," she told Dennis.

"I'll have them installed. Good idea, Ura."

"Most of these girls are in a lot of pain, Dennis. I don't know how to thank you for doing all this," she gushed.

"Dinner tomorrow night? I know a great little French place on the other side of town." He smiled broadly and waited for a positive reply.

"Please tell me you're not helping these girls because you want me to go out with you," Ura pleaded.

"No! Honestly Ura. It's the right thing to do but the more I watch you take care of them and go to bat for the things they need, the more I want to get to know you better. I've never met anyone like you. It's just dinner and chance to maybe find out more about you. That's not asking too much is it?"

Ura looked at Dennis and she felt her heart break a little. She wasn't sure why, but she couldn't give in on this, at least not now.

"I think we need to keep things professional, Dennis. I want this place, you guys, and all the girls to be a huge success. Let's not lose focus, for now okay? And besides, I'm more of a steak girl." She said trying to lighten the moment.

"Okay, but I heard two words in there that I really liked," Dennis said.

"What two words?" she said smiling.

"For now!"

Chapter 4

Tampa 1995 – 96

It was hard for some of the girls to accept Ura. To some of them, she was like a movie star... and yet like a little girl. Even if they wouldn't all admit it, they loved looking at her. They would go to the wings off to the side of the stage area and watch her dance. There was such a mix of jealousy, envy, and admiration in having her suddenly in their midst. Some of them were more seasoned dancers, others, beginners but each of them had a different reason for being there; for making this dubious choice. Some of them found it easy to open up to Ura. They could see that she understood them. For others not so much.

One of the dancers, Aiyana, just 21 had been dancing for a couple of years. The legal age to dance was 18-year old and she'd been working the clubs since her nineteenth birthday. She had tried working at the Indian resort in Tampa as a cocktail waitress, but the money was nowhere near what she could make dancing. She was mostly serving blue haired ladies playing the slots and killing time between rounds of bingo. A friend told her about a strip club that was hiring cocktail waitresses and she applied. But with her exotic looks, copper skin, and luxurious thick black hair, she was constantly being encouraged to dance.

"Trust me, Aiyana," the club's manager said. "You'll make three or four times as much dancing in half the time if you put down that beverage tray and hit the stage." One night, she got seriously stoned with a couple of the girls and the next thing she knew, she was topless and collecting five and ten-dollar bills from the excited patrons. She was a hit. She'd been dancing ever since.

She didn't know that Ura was actually two years her junior, though her ID said she was also 21, yet Aiyana didn't feel like she was on equal footing with Ura. Ura carried herself in a way that made her seem ageless, timeless, almost otherworldly.

"I love your hair," Ura said. "I wish my hair were thick like this. If I had a little girl and her hair was like yours, I'd sit and brush it every night. Can I brush yours?" Ura asked.

Aiyana hadn't had anyone brush her hair since she was a little girl when her grandmother would make her sit her on the floor in front of her to do so. She remembered the feeling of the soft brush and the strength of her grandmother's withered yet still strong hands. Aiyana's mother worked two, sometimes three, jobs to keep a roof over their heads after her father was sent to prison for selling drugs to minors. There was no time for hair brushing or bedtime stories, just work, and chores, and school. She had dreamed of going to college, but her grades were never that great and there was no money for higher education.

"Yes," Aiyana answered, surprised that she would allow this woman who was practically a stranger to do something so intimate. Ura sat Aiyana in a chair facing one of the dressing mirrors and slowly brushed through the thicket of her hair. Aiyana closed her eyes and, without realizing it a first, began to cry. No one had shown her such tenderness in a very long time.

Most of the girls started to get the feeling that they were part of a team, no longer just every woman for herself. They didn't bicker as much and were more encouraging to one another. They still had lots of problems, but they weren't drinking to excess anymore because the rules of the bar didn't allow for that behavior, and they seemed happier to be at work. None of them had ever had a boss, or bosses, try so hard to make a decent working environment for them before.

But one of the girls, Terri, was not buying the camaraderie bull she thought Ura and the new bosses were selling. She was leery of anyone being too nice or promising too much. Things just didn't work out like that for her. Terri was mad at life. All she ever wanted was a home filled with children and love. A series of bad choices in boyfriends and some drug abuse put her in financial jeopardy. She'd been a bank teller from right out of high school but that didn't cover the bills and mounting credit card problems she and her male companions had racked up. She had a great body and a reasonably pretty face, but she was no beauty queen and she was sexy though a little mechanical as a dancer. She didn't make the big bucks, but it was far more than she made counting change at Bank of America.

"Try loosening up your hips," Ura said grabbing Terri's hips in an attempt to help her move with the music.

"Hey!" Terri pulled away abruptly.

"I'm sorry, Terri," Ura responded with sincerity. "That was inappropriate on my part."

"Yeah, well," Terri shook off her bristling attitude. "I just don't like to be touched without warning. I over reacted. Show me what you mean... when you do it, I mean. I'll watch and try to copy you."

She knew Ura was just trying to help but Terri had had more than her share of unwanted touching, albeit from men. The men she dated didn't take no for an answer and had no trouble meeting her less than fabulous face with the back of their hands. She found herself jumping now when anyone touched her. But she liked being on stage. The men that came to the club knew what the limitations were. There were bouncers to keep them in control. They only got to touch her when she let them, and no one was going to hit her while she was dancing. She was in charge.

She watched Ura move like quicksilver, her hips swaying like they had no bones. Her entire body was connected to the music, to the rhythm and beat. She wanted to move like that. She wasn't sure she could, and she was both grateful to Ura for trying to show her and jealous that she would never look like her or perhaps be as kind.

The day before the grand reopening, everyone was nervous and excited. With Ura's help the girls had created a show rather than just a bunch of random girls dancing and stripping. They had even worked up some numbers where they danced together in pairs and small groups. They were proud of themselves and were ready to show off their new moves, costumes, and for some of them, whole new personas.

Aiyana had blossomed the most and had decided to use a stage name, Chayanne. She was a delicate, thin, and stunning young lady and was excited to create a new character for herself.

"I feel like a real performer for the first time in my life," she told Ura. "Thanks for helping me with all of this." She was practicing with the leopard skin cape Ura had made for her, twirling it around her body as she twisted and floated across the stage. When the music reached a crescendo, she let the cape slip off her shoulders and then slide to the floor to reveal her perfect 10 body beneath. She chose to incorporate some native American music and the DJ, Rory, was even getting into the action, creating mashups of music for the girls. He mixed a brilliant combination of native drums with pop songs for the new, Chayanne.

Even Terri had relaxed a little and was enjoying the hubbub and excitement of the opening. They had all helped paint and redecorate the club. The guys had called a caterer and there was going to be a whole buffet for the patrons to enjoy. Some new light fixtures, a top to bottom cleaning, and a little décor and the place was starting to really shape up.

An hour before the doors were set to open, Dennis, Tony, and Lenny asked the girls to come out to the bar area and have a quick meeting. When they were all seated, a couple of bottles of champagne were popped and everyone was given a small plastic flute for a toast.

"First, I want to thank all of you for pitching in to make this place as nice as it's turned out to be," Tony started the conversation. "We're three dumb dudes who appreciate the woman's touch you guys put into this. The three of us have known each other since college," he continued, pulling his two buddies to him and placing a burly arm around each of them. "We get loyalty. We reward and honor it more than most things and you guys have really shown us that kind of loyalty you only get from family. Yes. I'm an Italian boy so I will say this in my family's native tongue. Please raise your glasses. Buona fortuna… ala famiglia. Good luck! To the family!! And that's what you all are to me; family."

"We have one special person that no amount of thanks can do justice to," Dennis picked up where Tony left off.

"Please Dennis, you embarrass me," Tony said laughing and took a little bow.

"Not you, numbnuts."

"Me?" Lenny piped in.

"God no!" Dennis laughed. "Though you're a pretty damn good manager. I'm referring to the woman that is a generous as she is talented." He turned to Ura and raised his glass. "To Ura!"

"To Ura!" they all repeated.

"We know what a treasure we have in you. Thank you for everything," Dennis said. "Now, get the hell to work, we open in thirty minutes."

The opening was a smashing success. There were lines out the door and the class of people that showed up was a few levels above the old crowd. There were couples coming in wearing nice clothes and guys in suits and sports jackets. There was even a group of young people that came in for drinks after their engagement party.

The girls put on a real show and there was a buzz in the crowd that this was more like burlesque or something from the Flash Dance movie of the 80's. Tony overheard the crowd talking about how awesome the show was and he was determined to continue on that path. He planned to talk to his partners and Ura after the opening and step up their game even more. His marketing had gotten them this far and he knew if they played more on the show aspect and raised the performance bar, they could be something Tampa would be proud of.

Ura was having a blast. The girls were shining, and the money was flowing onto the stage. She knew for most of them it would mean a lot. They all had financial needs be it bills or family to support. For a couple it might mean they would waste it on drugs and alcohol, but she hoped that would improve for those women over time. They all had a little more hope and a lot more pride. She knew that could carry them through a lot of bad times.

Ura was dancing her last set when she started to feel dizzy. The sound of the crowd became louder and louder, almost deafening to her. The lights suddenly seemed to be getting brighter and brighter and her head felt like it might explode any minute. She stopped moving and stood stock still for a moment.

Where the hell am I? she thought. Nothing seemed familiar. *Who are all these people and why are they staring at me?* The music was pulsing in time with the throbbing in her head. Without warning, she rushed off stage just as the last notes of her seductive song finished.

She didn't pick up the money strewn all over the floor of the stage. She didn't go back out despite the thunderous applause and the voices yelling for more. She went to her locker and with her head pounding, grabbed her purse and keys and stepped out into the warm night air.

The next thing she knew, she was in the Caddy and headed north.

***

Heaven Kenny pulled into the quiet cabin she had purchased a few months earlier. It was on two acres of land, covered in trees and set back from the road a few miles outside Chapel Hill North Carolina, a college town she loved dearly. She set her bag and keys down on the heavy oak table she ate at and turned up the heat. It was a cool spring evening and she decided to throw a few logs on the fire to take the chill out of the cabin. She would eat the salad she'd picked up on her way there and then go to bed. She had a lot of design ideas swimming around in her head and for the next couple of weeks, getting them on paper and off to Helena and her brother in law Ryan would be her main focus. She could not remember where she'd been for the last several months, but she needed to work now. The designs needed to come to life. It wasn't a wish or a desire; it was a compulsion as it always had been since she was a teenager and began designing for Angel Wear. The designs had made her rich; they had made her whole family rich, even her father but that was not why she drew them. She had no choice. The designs, the ideas, the rich and vibrant concepts had to leave her head and become living things, or she felt her head would simply explode from holding them in too long.

She finished her meager meal while the logs burned to cinder and then dropped onto her feather bed in a heap.

Tomorrow. Tomorrow I will draw, she said aloud and feel into the deepest of sleeps.

Chapter 5

Jordan and Angelique and Heaven 1977

"Look at her, Jordan, she's perfect," Angelique cooed over the small baby in her arms.

"That she is," Jordan replied. He was so happy that Angelique was reacting this way. She'd been so sullen for the last few years. He had hoped that motherhood would somehow be a happier thing for Angelique, but she never connected with Helena the way he had. Their first born was more and more a daddy's girl and now this new child seemed to be getting the attention from his wife that he's hoped for.

"She looks so much like you," he offered. "No one will wonder who her mother is."

"She does, doesn't she? I'm going to spoil her rotten."

He hadn't seen his wife so happy in such a long time. They had found the perfect apartment in Brooklyn with two tiny bedrooms, one for each of the girls, as well as a large master suite for them and a room big enough for Jordan to have his work studio in the house. The next few months were pure bliss. For the first time in years he had hopes of being the family he always wanted. They would take the girls to the park. He and Helena would fly kites while Angelique and Heaven lay out on a big blanket in the grass watching. Heaven was a perfect child. She slept through the night, was never cranky, always smiling and laughing. She was so bright and happy.

Her first word was mama, as expected, and everything was wonderful. But as the baby grew, and the connection between mother and child grew into what was clearly an unbreakable bond, little things began to become apparent issues with Helena; little resentments. And the resentments became increasingly alarming. When Heaven was nine months old, Jordan was working in the studio with the baby monitor on. Heaven was sleeping a room away in her crib and he heard what sounded like her making choking sounds. He raced to her to find a napkin in her mouth. It had a little bit of chocolate icing on it. Angelique had made cupcakes for Helena's pre-school class the night before and had not let Helena have one after dinner saying they were for school and she would have to wait until school to share them with her friends. Helena had pouted and even kicked the leg of her chair as she got up from the dinner table.

Jordan called for Helena who had come home with the remaining cupcakes in her knapsack.

"Helena!" he called sharply. "Come here, please."

"Yes, daddy," she came running to the sound of his voice.

"Honey, did you try to give the baby a cupcake?"

"Yes, daddy. I thought Heaven would like one."

"There was napkin in her mouth, Helena. What were you thinking?"

"I gave her a little bit of cupcake and wiped her mouth after."

"But… you realize she's too little for you to feed her like that. She could have choked," he tried to explain gently. After all, Helena was only 4. She surely meant well.

"Oh! Okay daddy. I'll be more careful," Helena said in her small voice and smiled a crooked smile up at her father. "I love you, daddy," she said.

"And you love your baby sister too, right? We just have to be gentler with her. She's just a baby, not a big girl like you, sweetie."

"Yes, daddy. I understand. Can I go play now?"

"Yes, of course." He knew she understood him, but he had a bit of an uneasy feeling in his stomach, just a small butterfly of doubt.

Other little things happened over the next couple of years. Nothing you could put your finger on but overall it was obvious that Helena was less than thrilled at having a baby sister. The worst incident happened when Heaven was about four. Helena was nearing eight years-old, old enough to know better but still quite young.

Angelique was out shopping. Jordan was working in the studio. He'd left the kids in Helena's room having a little tea party. He was happy to see the little girls playing so nicely together. He'd become engrossed in a design he was doing. His business had been doing well but it was a constant struggle to stay relevant with his designs. They were comfortable but not well-off and he wanted so much more for his family. He didn't notice that the giggling had stopped or that the girls had moved from their room to the bathroom.

Angelique came in and gave him a peck on the cheek. "Where are the girls?" she asked.

"Playing tea party. I checked on them about 10 minutes ago. Nice to see them getting along."

"Good, I'll go crash the party," he said with a smile.

A minute later Jordan heard a blood curdling scream coming from the bathroom. He sprinted to the door to find his wife pulling their 4-year-old from the bath. She was banging the child on the back, water spurting from her tiny nose and mouth. "What the hell…" Jordan stopped dead at the scene before him.

"She was drowning." Angelique screamed. Helena was sitting on the floor in the corner of the bathroom. Jordan looked over and thought he saw the smallest hint of a smile on the older child's mouth but when he looked back, she was sobbing into her hands.

"I'm sorry, Mommy. She got dirty at the tea party. I was giving her a bath," Helena said between sobs.

Heaven sputtered and started to laugh, hugging her mother's neck. "I swallowed my bath, mama," she said. "It tasted soapy. I don't like the bath."

Jordan realized he had not been breathing until that moment. The relief caused both he and Angelique to howl with laughter with tears of joy rolling down their cheeks.

Chapter 6:

Chapel Hill 1996

Heaven woke slowly and stretched her long arms and legs. She hadn't slept that well in quite some time, not since she had last been in the safety of her cabin.

She thought back to the day she bought it. She had walked into a small realty office in Chapel Hill and told the attending realtor what she wanted. "Something small, on a little bit of land, ready to move in to. Not so remote that I feel isolated but a bit off the beaten path."

"I know exactly what you mean," the realtor assured her. "What's your price range?"

"Will $75,000 be enough?" Heaven asked.

"More than enough!"

"Good because that's all the cash I have on me," Heaven responded.

The realtor nearly fell off her chair. Two weeks later, Heaven was moving into a fully furnished cabin that had been used by a writer who moved to New York City to be nearer to her agent. It was decorated in a country style; a sort of rustic chic and Heaven like to think that the writer had created some great works sitting at the big oak table. She didn't need to add much to the place but did purchase a drafting table to work at when designing her clothing line.

During the time she spent waiting to close on her cabin, she had rented a room in a little motel near the downtown area of Chapel Hill. The sparse but clean room didn't have a kitchen to cook in and she really didn't care to cook much anyway so she explored the restaurant and cafes of the town. She discovered a great little French restaurant that made the best salad with a homemade blue cheese dressing and lots of vegetables. There was also a terrific steak house that served their steak with smoked oysters on top; just the way she liked it. But her favorite place was little café called, *The Peace Frog*, that served the best lattes, homemade baked goods, and interesting entrees. She loved the eclectic décor and the homey feel of the place. But most of all she loved the owner Louisa and her teenage son, Lono. Lono's father was a war hero of Hawaiian decent and his mother full blooded Italian. He had thick dark wavy hair and an olive complexion. His eyes were as black as coal and he was stocky strong young man, full of life and always smiling.

"What nationality are you?" Heaven had asked him, once she got to know him a little better. "You have such an interesting look."

"I'm a Hapa," he replied.

"I've never heard of that, is that a small island or something?"

"No silly," Lono answered and giggled. "It's Hawaiian for mixed. My Dad is Hawaiian, and my mom is Italian. How about that for a mutt?"

She would stop in nearly every day to see Lono and his

mom. She never asked where Lono's dad was, but she started to get the message that he was not well in some way and not in the picture much if at all.

Now that she was back in Chapel Hill, she looked forward to her first visit to the café. But for the first several days she planned to hole up and work on designs. She laid out all of her drawing accoutrements and got going. Hours went by, she worked long past lunchtime and into the evening rarely moving from her drawing table. Around 8 pm she realized her stomach was growling and she obliged it by stopping long enough to make a ham sandwich which she washed down with an ice-cold glass of milk. The food in the Carolina's was always so fresh. The local stores she grabbed supplies at on the way in carried fresh fruits and vegetables and wonderful dairy products from the farms in the area. She had even gotten some ice cream made locally.

Around midnight, she felt the tug toward her bed and repeated the night before by falling straight into a deep slumber. Her routine was nearly identical for the next two days that followed. Finally, on her fourth day in her little hideaway, she had exhausted her itch to draw and was ready to take a break. Besides, she was out of pretty much everything and tired of cold sandwiches. She longed for a hot meal, a great cup of coffee, and the company of her little pal Lono. So, she fired up the big gold Caddy and drove the few miles into town.

When she walked through the doors, Lono had his back to her, waiting on a table of four pretty young ladies, no doubt there as much to see Lono as to get coffee and cakes. They were flirting with him and laughing in that high-pitched way girls do when they're excited.

"Okay, ladies," Lono said "Be back in a jiff with your order." He spun around and found himself face to face with Heaven.

"Holy cow! She's back. Woo hoo! Hey mom," he hollered in the direction of the kitchen. "Get out here, look who came back to the nest."

Louisa came out of the kitchen, drying her hands on a towel. She was wearing a full bistro apron and her hair was trying in vain to stay tucked up into the black baseball cap she wore a slight tilt on her head.

"OH! Heaven… I mean, it is Heaven today, right?" Louisa said with a little trepidation and moved toward Heaven to give her a hug.

"Of course," Heaven said a bit confused. "Forget me already?"

Louisa gave Lono a quick look that said they shared a secret thought. "No, no, my friend. We could never forget you. We're just glad you're home."

Heaven sat down at her favorite table and ordered a big plate of beef stew, a vanilla latte, and a piece of Louisa's cherry pie.

Lono brought the dessert to the table and sat down with Heaven. "You sure do love pie, don't you?" he asked.

"Yes, but I particularly love your mother's pies. She's a

genius in the kitchen."

"Don't I know it," Lono said and rubbed his slightly protruding belly. "She's making me fat already and I'm not even old enough to drink. I should not have a beer belly."

"It's a pie belly, and it suits you. Skinny is overrated. Besides, you look to be doing just fine with the ladies," she said under her breath and nodded toward the gaggle of girls in the window booth who were taking turns sneaking glances over at them. "I think your harem is getting the wrong idea. Maybe you'd better not sit with an old lady like me too long."

"Old, I know how old you really are, and don't you forget it. You're barely older than me."

"How do you know how old I am?" Heaven asked, perplexed. "I'm nearly 22, that's a world older than 17," she laughed. "Besides, you're like my kid brother. Those girls have nothing to worry about."

Lono took her statements in stride. He knew how old she was because he had been the one to get his friend, Paul to get her the ID that said, Ura, age 21 a few months earlier. He thought Heaven was one of the most wonderful people alive, but he also thought something was screwy in her head. She'd come in one day saying she'd lost her ID and didn't know what to do. She was confused and when he called her Heaven, she said, "No, my name is Ura." She said she needed her ID to go on a trip. He knew a guy from school who had graduated a year ahead of him and was making fake ID's for all the kids so they could go clubbing.

He charged $50 an ID and did a really good job making them. Paul was making a killing with his little sideline. Lono took "Ura" to see him and he hooked her up with a great looking ID that said she was 21 and from Dayton, Ohio. After she got the ID, she disappeared and now she was back and calling herself Heaven again. As much as her odd behavior worried him, he did have sisterly love for her and made it his mission to be kind to her and watch over her in any way he could. Lono had a good heart and he could see people for who they were deep down inside. He sensed from day one that Heaven had a heart of gold, no matter who she thought she was on any given day.

After she finished her meal, Heaven went back to the cabin. She continued to work feverishly, stopping every few days to go into town, grab a meal, see Lono, and his mom and get supplies.

After nearly a month of this routine, she called her brother-in-law, Ryan. She knew he would be pleased to see what she had for him. He arrived two days after he got her call. "These are astonishing, Heaven. They're more sultry, more alluring then your last designs. Your work is always stunning, but these show a new maturity. Women are going to go crazy for these pieces. I can't wait to get them into production."

"Thank you, Ryan," Heaven responded. "I'm very pleased with them too. I'm glad you think they can sell well. Did you bring me the money I need?"

"Of course, in cash as always. But you have us very worried, Heaven. Won't you come home for a little while?"

"This is home… at least when I'm drawing," she answered. "I appreciate your coming to me and your concern but I'm fine."

"Will you be staying here in Chapel Hill?" he asked.

"I don't know. I feel like I need to be somewhere else soon but wherever I am, I'll be fine, and I'll send for you when I have new work."

"You're designs saved this company, Heaven. We can't thank you enough and I'm glad to help make you a very rich woman. Well deserved."

"We're a team, Ryan. We do this together. Now, if you don't mind, I'd like to rest. My head is starting to hurt a little," she said.

After a quick hug, he turned and walked to the door of the cabin. "Be well, Heaven. Remember we all love you and you have a home anytime you want to come to us."

With that he left and Heaven, feeling the pounding in her head, went to her bed and straight to sleep.

Chapter 7

Waking Up in Tampa 1996

Ura opened the window shades to palm trees and burning sun. She could feel the heat through the cheap glass pane. It was white hot outside the window. After a quick look around, she concluded that she was in a modest motel room. *What the hell is going on? Where am I? For that matter, who am I?* she thought. She tried to focus and clear her head, but no memories came. She sat down hard on the bed and looked across the dresser to see herself in the mirror. She had no recollection of the young woman staring back at her. Try as she might, she had no memory of a family, or stability, or normality. In a way, she enjoyed the odd feeling of "not" knowing. This could be heaven, no tangible problems, no deep concerns for anyone. Trying to conjure them up just brought a sharp pain to her head.

"Maybe this is hell," she said out loud, pressing her hands hard against her temples to ease the pain. Her words fell on the deaf ears of the walls surrounding her. She was utterly alone.

Possible clues to her life or who she was were scattered around the small room as evidence. Four pair of tall, thin spiked, high heeled shoes sat lined up in the corner. Dresses, some looking very sophisticated, some baby dollish, others simple and chic, in varied in styles hung in the tiny closet. Ura walked into the bathroom to see that there was surprisingly little makeup and no jewelry on the counter. A feeling of complete emptiness came over her. *I wonder if my life is a gift or a torture*. Her toes tingled, an odd kind of feeling, almost numbness. *Oh hell, my stomach's churning. I have got to have some food. A steak sounds good, with smoked oysters on top, a beautiful salad, with blue cheese dressing, and a cold Red Killian beer. Yes, that's exactly what I want. That will make me happy and I choose to define happiness as food at this moment.*

She realized she had no idea what time of day it was and searched for a clock finally seeing one on the bed stand, almost completely covered by a dark green, very sheer long scarf. As she pulled the scarf away from the clock, a business card fell to the floor. The writing on the back had the name Ura printed neatly on it. On the front of the card, in brassy looking gold print is said, "Where the Girls Are, Gentlemen's Club." The address and phone number were at the bottom.

She looked at the clock; 4:00 p.m. *I guess there's only one way to find out who Ura is.* She showered quickly and choose a simple black dress, very chic, size 2, which fit like it was custom made for her. After applying just a little bit of makeup, she spied a curling iron, but decided to leave her long blond, still slightly wet, hair straight.

I need food, my stomach is making angry noises, she thought hearing the low growl in her gut.

On the floor beside a pair of casually discarded blue jeans thrown over the motel chair she found a key chain with a large Cadillac emblem and two car keys on it. She slipped her feet into a pair of leather low heeled black dress shoes, looked in the mirror to see someone looking back at her she simply did not know.

Who are you? Who ...are you? The only word that came to mind was heaven. *Maybe I'm dead and this really is the afterlife.* She looked into the mirror once more and the eyes of the woman looking back did not seem at peace. *No this isn't heaven.* The pain in her head said otherwise. She grabbed the room key that was sitting on the dresser and added it to the business card and headed out, not having a clue where she was or how to get where she was going.

As she passed the front lobby, a man behind the desk looked up, "Hi Ura; I have to say, I love your hair when you leave it straight. Bye now gorgeous. Stay cool out there."

"Thanks," she managed a reply and with a smile and a wave, rushed out the door. The cold air from the lobby, mixed with the intense heat of the outside air, and her empty stomach, nearly made her pass out.

Okay, Ura, I must be Ura. But why is my name on the card?

In the parking lot of the motel she saw a stately looking Cadillac. She walked up to it and tried the key, vaguely aware that it was going to fit. She slid in and found a purse on the passenger side floor. In what can be described as a rush of calm, she slowly picked it up and looked inside. Three books, nothing else. She unzipped a small pocket on the side to find a wad of money folded with a rubber band around it. She pulled the cash out and counted it; $800, in fifties and twenties. *Good, I guess Ura can eat. What a name.*

Leaving the parking lot, she had to decide; which way to go. Instinct kicked in and she swung the Caddy out of the motel parking lot and turned right. Before she could find a decent looking restaurant, she saw the bight neon sign for a club with the name, "Where the Girls Are."

"Well, here's one mystery I can try to solve." She said and pulled into the parking lot to the side of the building. There was a vivid yellow Corvette pulling in directly behind her. Ura parked close to the door and hopped out to lean up against the Cadillac.

The man in the Corvette pulled up next to her and jumped out. "Ura you're back," he said clearly very excited. "Thank God. You had us all worried. We were about to hire a detective to search for you. Are you okay?"

"I'm fine. Sorry I had you worried. I had to take care of something," she said winging her answer.

Dennis frowned a little. *How do I handle this?* He thought. *I'm just so glad she's back. Don't scare her off you idiot, just be cool.* "Are you here to come to work tonight?" he asked her, trying to sound casual and not over eager.

Without thinking she replied softly, "No… Dennis. I just stopped by to say hi." *Dennis, his name is Dennis, that's right. At least I think it is.*

"You are the most interesting girl I've ever met and the certainly the best dancer. That's why the customers love you. But you're a mystery. Like two people in one body. To see you onstage, you'd think, that's one wild-child, but they don't know this weirdly quiet person. I don't even think you work for the money. No, I don't think that's why you do it," he mused.

"Maybe not," she replied. "I'm not sure why any of us does this."

He stood a moment staring at her. She was so young and yet, not. In that moment, he was so happy to see her, to be there in that parking lot with her, and all he wanted to do was keep her safe. She wasn't safe. He was sure of that. *What is she running from?* he wondered. Finally, he spoke, "C'mon inside, I'll buy you a glass of wine."

"No, I'm hungry, I thought I would get a steak. I really need food."

"I was beginning to wonder if you actually eat. I love the way you mother all the girls to eat right but you look like you don't eat much yourself." He hesitated for a moment, "Mind if I go with you?"

Ura hesitated for a second. *I must know him. It has to be okay. Maybe, I can get some answers from him.* "No I don't mind, I'd enjoy the company," she agreed.

"Really? So, after three months of trying to get you to go on a simple date with me, and then your little disappearing act, I'm in?"

"Not a date, just a steak. No one likes to eat alone."

"How many guys do you know who would buy a bar just to get a girl to go out with them?" Dennis laughed. "Give me five minutes to open the place up, Lenny should be here any minute. C'mon in for a few minutes. Cool?"

"Cool." She smiled and followed him into the bar. *Who the hell is Lenny?*

Chapter 8

It's Only Dinner

Once inside the club, Dennis excused himself saying he would be right back. Ura took a seat at the bar and watched the redhead who was dancing on the stage. Two other girls were dancing for men at their tables and as the girls start to notice that Ura had walked in, heads turned, and a low almost unperceivable buzz started to happen. There were a few guys sitting at the bar as well. They recognized Ura too and straightened in their bar stools a little. Ura felt a bit nervous at the attention she seemed to be causing. A minute later Dennis came out of the office with Tony in tow.

"Hey, our wandering gypsy has returned," Tony said rushing up to Ura, pulling her off her perch on the bar stool and into his burly arms. "You have no idea how much we've missed you. You scared us half to death leaving unannounced like that. Don't let it happen again or I'll sic the Tampa police on you. Where the hell were you?"

Is he kidding? Ura thought. *I must know this guy, why can't I remember his name?*

"Shut up, Tony! You'll scare her away," Dennis said. "We don't care where you were." He looked Ura dead in the eye. "We're just glad you're home."

Home? Home. It did kind of feel like home.

"Let's go eat," Dennis said and pulled her toward the door.

"Hey, bring her right back," Tony said.

As they walked out the door, the red head on the stage waved at her and smiled broadly.

Maybe this is where I belong, Ura thought.

"Let's take my Vet. It doesn't even make sense to take two cars." Dennis insisted and opened the passenger side door to his corvette. It was a cool older model which said something about his personality. He set Ura into the seat gently holding her elbow and closing the door for her. She instinctively reached over and unlocked the driver's side for him. He seemed to melt with this simple gesture as he slid into his seat and turned over the powerful engine, gliding the car out of the lot and onto the busy street.

"How about the Green Tavern? Great steaks there." Dennis suggested.

"Sounds great," she replied. She had no idea what the Green Tavern was like but if there was steak there, she was in. Her stomach growled at the mention of food.

Dennis heard the grumbling noise. "I guess your stomach agrees with the steak concept," he said laughing.

"Sorry. I'm starving." She suppressed a giggle. She felt comfortable with this man. Safe.

"Well, feeding you is what I live for in this moment. So glad I can do something nice for you. And so glad you're really here," he replied.

It was a stunning summer day and the ride to the restaurant was brief. Dennis's excitement was palpable. He didn't want to say too much and pry into where she'd been, but he was curious as to what made her take off like that.

Maybe I shouldn't have done this. Clearly, I am one of his dancers, but if I'm a dancer, then why should dinner with this charming man scare me? I feel the need to control every moment and I am not in control right now, Ura thought.

When they got to the restaurant, there was a valet standing at the door. The young man in his crisp uniform reached for the door, opened it swiftly, putting his hand out for Ura who gracefully took it as he helped her out of the low flying sports car. Then he sprinted to the other side where Dennis handed him the keys. Dennis came up alongside Ura, gently took her elbow and guided her to the entrance where the doorman stood waiting to open the door. The restaurant had a lush lobby, more elegant than Ura was expecting. The hostess stepped up to greet them and grabbing two menus and a wine list, led them to a softly lit room, and a small intimate table. They no sooner sat down, when a waiter came rushing over.

Dennis was already perusing the extensive wine list. "Should we get a bottle of wine? I'm partial to Italian reds when I eat steak. Tony has me trained," Dennis said.

"I really was in the mood for a Red Killian, and by the way we are going Dutch," Ura replied firmly. "But if you want wine, by all means, don't let me stop you," she replied.

"Beer for the lady, Killian's Red, and I will have a glass of

Chianti," Dennis said to the waiter who was patiently waiting. "Oh, and bring us some nice warm bread, please." The waiter nodded and turned on his heel to go fetch the first of there order. "And we are NOT going Dutch," Dennis said, turning back to Ura. "This is a celebration. You're back and I get to spoil you, young lady. That is an order from your boss. Got it?"

"Got it… boss," Ura replied and smiled shyly. *He is a very likeable man,* she thought. *And not hard on the eyes. This meal might be fun after all.*

The waiter returned with their beverages and bread. "Are you ready to order, sir."

"I am," said Ura.

"Go for it," Dennis replied.

"Please bring me a salad with lots of vegetables, blue cheese dressing, steak, just past medium rare, smoked oysters on top, no potato, and hurry please. I'm starving," she ordered rapidly.

"What she said, but hold the oysters, make my steak rare, and add a baked potato all the way," Dennis added.

When the waiter left, Dennis held his glass of wine up. "To your return and hopefully many more steak dinners," he said.

Ura clinked her beer against his wine glass and smiled more broadly. "Thank you, this is very nice," she said. There was a sudden lull in the conversation. Neither of them knew what to say and each was a little nervous though for very different reasons. Ura finally broke the silence. "So, Dennis, what you got started in the strip club business?"

Ura, you know the story. Are you okay? You're not quite yourself tonight."

"I meant, you're a smart guy, why didn't you become an attorney or something?"

He looked at her "Oh, I see. Truthfully, you're the reason. I'd never seen anything like you on stage or off. It didn't take much to convince me to jump in with both feet after that. But I thought you knew that."

"Um, no. I guess I didn't know that."

The waiter brought out the salads and they ordered another round of drinks then began to eat in relative silence, for which Ura was thankful. She knew she ought to remember all of the things this lovely man was talking about, but it wasn't quite registering with her. *Clearly, I have life I can't remember. Why can't I remember any of it?*

Both the food and the company were wonderful. Ura felt like she was eating for the first time in a long time. They drove back to the club slowly and in the parking lot, Ura started for her car.

"Aren't you gonna come in for a while? I know the gang would kill me if I don't bring you back to see them all. The girls have been worried sick about you. They all missed their little mother hen," Dennis said.

"I'll be back in a while. I just need a couple of things from the drugstore. Girl's stuff, you know."

"Gotcha. I'll see you back here later," He replied, then jogged to the door and headed in. His steps were light, like a man who had just had a great date and was feeling good.

Ura got into the Caddy and drove down the busy road in search of a drugstore. She found one just a few blocks away and pulled into the parking lot. In the store, she picked up a few items, some lipstick, Tylenol, and a pack of spearmint gum. She was sure the food had left her breath less than minty and she had a feeling she would be up close and personal with a few of the people at the bar. Knowing her breath would be fresh made her feel ready for any conversations she might have to have. When she looked in her purse, she realized she was carrying a small, well-worn bible which had no name inside. Some passages were highlighted though.

When she got back to the car, it was starting to get dark outside, so she decided to go back to the strip club and check it out; after all, it appeared that she worked there. When she pulled open the dark wooden door to the club, a pretty blond was near the front practically knocked Ura over with a bear hug and welcome home accolades. She wheeled Ura toward the bar where Tony was sitting holding court with some of the local patrons. They didn't see her at first.

"We're going to do a Girl's Only Night soon guys. Bring in those Chippendale dudes, no guys aloud in," Tony was telling a couple of regulars.

"That sucks. What are we supposed to do?" one of them asked.

"Thank me profusely," Tony replied.

"Why?" the other guy responded.

"Because that show will start at 8 pm and be over by 10 pm at which time we will let you fellows back in the club where about a hundred, tipsy, worked up, horny females will be waiting for you losers. There are just so many Chippendales to go around and I think most of those guys are gay anyway, so you have a shot for once. You're welcome," He finished with a tiny bow.

Ura, overhearing him, couldn't help but laugh and at the sound, one so familiar, Tony and the other guys turned to see her standing there.

Tony blushed a little. He hoped he hadn't offended her in any way. Business is business after all and getting butts in seats was Tony's job.

"Hey! Our star is back. How was dinner?" he asked hoping to change the subject. "Bring Ura a drink," Tony called over to Lenny who had just surfaced behind the bar. "What you in the mood for?" Tony asked her.

Dennis emerged from the office just in time to hear her order.

"I'll have a Long Island Iced Tea please," Ura said and sat down on a stool. Tony and Dennis both looked at Ura, and in unison as if planned exclaimed. "Ura!"

I guess I am not a big drinker, Ura thought. *Oh well, too late now.*

"Bring this lovely lady a Long Island Iced Tea," Tony turned to Lenny and shrugged slightly as if to say, beats me.

Ura tried hard to remember the surroundings she was in. Nothing looked familiar. While she sat quietly scoping out of the place, each of the girls came over to say hi and hug her. They all seemed so pleased that she was back. One of them was a little standoffish, not the prettiest of the bunch, but even she was polite and cordial. Everyone asked if she was planning to dance that night, but she begged off saying she was tired from her trip and that she would wait a day or two to take the stage. *God, I hope I can dance as well as they all seem to think I can,* she considered. *I guess I'll find out soon enough.*

While observing the girls she could see which ones were more anxious than the others. She could tell by their movements and the tense look in their eyes that, for some, the money was very important. She hated to see them distraught. They were an odd mixture of worldly yet innocent, conflicted in many ways. Were they thinking about the groceries they could buy, or possibly drugs? She was concentrating hard. When she went to use the bathroom, on the wall between the ladies and men's rooms, there was a blackboard with a list written on it.

- Viper room $75 each half hour for the bar
- Limo ride $100 to bar for each half hour
- Private dances - $50
- Absolutely NO prostitution

- Absolutely NO drugs
- Any complaints about inappropriate behavior by a customer will mean said customers removal from the club and could mean permanent banning

Well, looks like they're trying to run a clean place, she said to herself. When she went back to pay her bill, there was another drink waiting for her. Just as she sat down, an exotic, dark skinned beauty of a girl with long, luscious jet-black hair came rushing in the front door. She claimed loudly that she was back from a limo drive. Cheyanne looked over to see Ura and nearly burst into tears. She ran over to her and hugged her so hard Ura felt her ribs might crack.

"Oh! Ura, thank god you're back. I missed you so much!" Cheyanne pulled 2 one-hundred-dollar bills from her little suede, fringed purse and showed them to her friend and mentor. "Look! And he was such a gentleman. We stopped at a dance club and danced for an hour and all he wanted was to show me off to his friends and have someone to slow dance with. Best limo customer ever!"

"That's great, Cheyanne," Ura said without thinking. *Cheyanne, yes, this is Cheyanne. She likes me to comb her hair.*

"Ura, please help fix my new outfit. It just doesn't seem to fit right, but it's sooooo pretty," she said and pulled Ura backstage where she showed her the new costume. Ura jumped in, and in a few minutes, tucked the material in a few places and with minor adjustment made it perfect for her friend.

Throughout the rest of the night, Ura helped many of the girls with their costumes, changing this and fixing that. Dennis kept a watchful eye on her but didn't interfere as she helped the girls. He brought her a cup of much needed coffee at one point and gave her a light hug that told her he was very pleased she was there.

She stayed till closing without realizing the time flying by. She sat and talked small talk with some of the men and the girls. At the end of the night, as they all walked out into the velvet Florida night, the girls were yelling, "come to breakfast with us." Ura waved and politely declined as she got into the Cadillac. As she was driving out of the parking lot, Terri, the plain girl who was more standoffish than the others, was getting into a car with one of the patrons. They had both been drinking a bit though Terri was not at all drunk. They had a strict policy about that at the bar and the owners stuck to it.

As she drove away, all she could think about was the mousy brunette and wondering if she was making a bad decision. Was she, for some reason, so lacking in her own self-love that she accepted attention from men as a substitute? After considering whether or not to confront her at some point, Ura had a moment of self-doubt. *Who the hell do I think I am? We only control ourselves. Do I think I have some superior knowledge regarding what Terri should be doing with her life?*

Then, just as quickly, she heard a little voice in her head as if she could hear someone saying, "Don't stop offering your kindness and love, even when others stop. You may be able to help them get on the road to becoming a better, happier, person."

I wonder who told me that?

Chapter 9

Angelique and Heaven 1985 - 1988

As Heaven got older, the bond between her and Angelique grew stronger and stronger. Heaven was clearly artistic in nature and even as a little girl she loved art, music, and dancing. Jordan loved walking in on their little impromptu dancing lessons. Angelique would be in the kitchen cooking, music blaring and while waiting for the water to boil or the cookies to bake, she would dance with Heaven.

"Spin me around again, Mama," Heaven would beg.

"Give me your hands," Angelique would demand grabbing Heaven's chubby little hands in hers. She taught her youngest daughter all the dances she had learned as a child, the twist, and the pony and as she got bigger, she taught her the jitterbug and even the waltz.

Angelique loved to dance. She had been a lonely child whose parents divorced when she was seven years old. Her mother was French, and after the divorce, she took Angelique with her back to her native land. Angelique visited her father in Manhattan for a few unpleasant weeks each summer but when she turned thirteen her mother became very ill. She died of cancer two weeks prior to Angelique's fourteenth birthday, leaving her only child be sent back to America to lead a lonely existence with her strict and unhappy father. He was cruel and abusive, but Angelique was forced to live under his rule until her seventeenth birthday. She saw an ad in a magazine looking for fresh young faces and she went to a job fair where she was picked up by a modelling agency. She didn't tell her father about her modelling work, sneaking off to gigs and saving all the money in a bank account he knew nothing about. Her father forced her to live under his roof until she turned 18 but by then she was making enough money to afford a shared apartment with two other models. She left his home and never looked back; never spoke to him again.

Angelique had always dreamed of being a clothing designer. When she met Jordan, she was so taken with his designs and was in awe of him. She loved to draw but had none of the training or discipline he had. She gave up her dream to go to design school when they married. She had secretly started to draw her own designs again after Helena was born but then Heaven came along, and with two young girls there never seemed to be time to draw or to have that much alone time for that matter. By the time Heaven turned ten, Helena was a teenager and was busy with friends, boys, and school. Jordan and Helena spent a lot of time together talking about business. Helena didn't have an artistic bone in her body, but she loved finance and numbers. Her math skills were off the charts and by the end of her freshman year in high school, she had her heart set on getting into the prestigious Warton Business School. She and Jordan would sit after dinner and on weekends going over business plans and marketing strategies to grow his design business.

That gave Angelique time alone with Heaven. One rainy weekend, while Jordan and Helena were in the studio happily crunching numbers, Heaven and Angelique were left to their own devices to amuse themselves. "Look what I drew in school yesterday, Mama," she said, holding out a drawing for her mother.

"You drew this?" Angelique asked in honest awe. "Where did you get the idea for this drawing, from a magazine?"

"No, Mama, from my own head," she answered. Heaven was not yet eleven years old and the drawing of a woman in a stunning outfit looked like something a first-year design student would turn in at a college.

"This is amazing. Would you like to draw with me sometime?" Angelique asked.

"Yes, Mama. Can that be our rainy-day thing?"

"Yes, and our, whenever we feel like it thing," Angelique answered.

"Let's keep this our secret thing," Heaven said. "I don't want to share you with Helena and Daddy. Just for when we draw. Okay?"

"Cross my heart," Angelique replied.

After that, mother and daughter found every opportunity to draw together they possibly could, but it would be several years until Jordan got to see Heaven's work and by the time he did, things had changed in their lives most dramatically.

Chapter 10

Tampa 1996-97

As time passed, the whole group began changing. Even Terri started to allow herself to get closer to the other girls. She started to believe that the three crazy guys that had bought the bar weren't just in it to exploit the dancers and staff. She wanted to feel closer to them, but her past experiences held her back from fully trusting that things were actually good and that she could be friends with the people she worked with. She wanted to feel safe and well treated but it was hard to let herself believe that her luck had changed a little. Slowly, Terri started to get with Ura's program of trying to add class and sophistication to the shows. She changed her stage name to Candise, at Ura's suggestion.

"Candise?" Terri said a hint of sarcasm in her voice.

"Yes, with an S," Ura pronounced the name again drawing out the S sound. "It's so much classier than Candy," Ura replied putting her spin on the name Terri was originally considering.

"Classy? Me? That's a first," Terri responded. The little hint of a smile told Ura she had hit a nerve but in a good way. She very much wanted to build Terri's confidence. She was the one girl Ura was having trouble reaching. Ura knew that Terri had some deep seated self-abusive tendencies and had let men hurt her a great deal. The girl drank too much and Ura was sure there was some drug use, but worst of all was the men Terri allowed into her life. There was a revolving door of low-lifes that seemed to come and go in Terri's life. Ura promised herself she wouldn't lecture her, but she wanted to shake her at times and tell her she was worth so much more. What she did instead was to slowly build Terri's self-image and confidence by helping her with her make-up, hair, clothing, and even dance moves. While Terri was never going to win a beauty contest, she had strong, almost noble features, good hair, and a great figure. Ura taught her to tone down her make-up and work with her skin tone instead of against it. She created a look for the new "Candise" that was sexy and elegant at the same time. She designed all of her clothes in various tones and shades of blues. Layers of midnight blue to baby blue that worked with Terri's best feature, her deep blue eyes that were in contrast to her wavy dark brown hair. Slowly, Terri began to see her own self-worth and it seemed like the men that she went out with after work started to be of better and better quality.

Over the next few months since Ura had returned, Dennis and Ura became closer and closer. Since their first "date", dinner at the Green Tavern morphed into a weekly outing, so much so that the staff there knew their names and dinner order.

"I think we're regulars," Dennis said one evening when they were seated at their usual table. The waiter, Jaimie, didn't bother to ask what they wanted to drink. He brought a glass of chianti and a Killian's red with the warm bread and butter to the table minutes after they were sat.

"Good Evening! Miss Ura, you're looking particularly lovely this evening," he said as he set her ice-cold beer down in front of her. They had been coming in nearly every Tuesday night for months now and he enjoyed serving the handsome and pleasant couple. "The usual, sir?" He asked Dennis.

"Yes, Jamie, and make sure my steak isn't over done tonight. It was cooked to medium last week. Tell the chef to just cut its horns off and scare it. That should make it rare enough." Dennis chided.

Ura burst out laughing at his suggestion. "You've never heard that expression, I take it," he said smiling at her.

"No, I haven't. But then it seems like there are a lot of firsts where you're concerned," she replied and looked deep into his eyes.

"Good firsts, I hope," he answered matching her gaze as he took her hand in his across the table.

"Always," she answered.

"Well, good because I have another first to propose," he said.

"I hope this isn't the part where you get down on one knee, mister. A few steak dinners and you're using the word propose," she said laughing.

"You're safe," he said, no rings hiding in the oysters, I swear."

"Good. Just two professionals enjoying a weekly steak, right?"

"Right!" He replied. "Except…"

"Except what?" she said teasingly. She knew how he felt. She supposed everyone knew. It was obvious they were far more than friends though not much had happened other than steak dinners, a few movies and a little light kissing in one car or the other. But there was an electricity between them that was palpable. They stole glances at one another every chance they got. He watched her every move when she danced and everyone knew they were dating, even if no one ever declared it aloud.

Tony was happy for his friend. He knew how Dennis felt about Ura, but Lenny didn't share Tony's happiness for their pal. He was a little jealous. He knew that Ura was out of his league, but it bugged him that Dennis and Tony always seemed to live a charmed life. He scowled every time he saw Dennis and Ura sneak away to be together and even said a few less than pleasant things to a couple of the girls. His taunts fell on deaf ears, however, because the girls were all rooting for Dennis and Ura or "Dura" as they good naturedly called them. There was even a small pool going as to when Dennis would ask Ura to marry him. But it was all in good fun and with good intentions.

"Well," Dennis started and took a deep breath. "I know that you live in that tiny little motel room and I was thinking…"

"Thinking can be scary. Yes, I live in that tiny little motel room, but I do have maid service and free cookies in the lobby."

"Yes, but I have a spare bedroom and we can make cookies anytime we want because I also have a kitchen," Dennis said.

"Are you saying what I think you're saying?" She asked.

"I'm saying that I like being around you and I have a big old house with plenty of room to spare and we're always together anyway. So, why not move in?"

"Dennis! We've never even given this a name. We haven't even said we're dating and now you want me to move in with you?"

"Well, yes!" He said resoundingly. "I think it's a damn fine idea and I also think it's about time we say we're dating," he finished firmly, then sinking a little lower in his chair, he spoke again, this time with a lot less bravado. "I mean, we are dating, right?"

In that moment, he looked like a very little boy to her and her heart melted. "I guess we are indeed dating," she said smiling. "But I am not moving in with you. At least not yet."

"Yet!? So, that's a maybe?" Dennis asked brightening visibly.

"That motel is pretty cramped. And your house is pretty big, so, it's a maybe. Can you wait a little while?" Ura asked.

"Ura," he said taking both her hands in his. "Please know that, for you, I will wait forever."

Two months to the day later, Ura moved into Dennis's house lock stock and luggage. She'd never been so happy in her entire life. They had stopped trying to pretend that this was a casual thing and the betting pool on Dennis popping the question tripled. They ate together, went to work together, and shared his king-size bed. At first, she was very shy about intimacy and Dennis kept his cool, letting things progress at her pace, never pushing her.

On their first night together, Dennis made Ura close her eyes as he pulled her into the bedroom. He had snuck home ahead of her, saying he had an errand to run and would meet her there. He had three dozen candles lit and spread out on the dressers and end tables around the bed. The petals of a dozen roses made a path to the king-sized bed and covered the white bedspread with their deep red color. There was a cream-colored silk negligee laying across the pillows. "Open your eyes," he said.

"Oh, Dennis, it's amazing." Ura gasped. Soft jazz music was playing on the stereo and Ura turned to Dennis as he wrapped his arms around her. He released her slowly and reached for the negligee.

"I bought you this. I thought you might like to wear it tonight."

"It's lovely. Give me a few minutes to change into this and freshen up," she said and headed to their bathroom.

Dennis stripped down to his boxers and pulled back the comforter on the bed. He nervously positioned himself on the bed trying to look relaxed and in control, but he was neither. After a few minutes, Ura appeared. She was wearing the lovely nightgown and her hair was down and flowing around her perfect face. The light from the bathroom behind her made her look like she was glowing as she stepped into the candlelit room. To Dennis, it appeared as if she were floating toward him. He caught his breath at the site of her and stretched his hand out to pull her toward him.

Ura slid into the bed and lay next to Dennis side by side facing one another. "Hi," she said shyly.

"Hi," he returned. "I'm glad you're here."

"Me too," she said.

"We can take it slow, okay," Dennis said. "We've got all the time in the world."

"Okay," Ura said. "But it's okay, Dennis. I trust you and I want to make you happy."

Dennis smiled at her and touched her face. "You already have," he said then he kissed her lightly on the mouth. He noted the serious look on her face. "This is supposed to be fun, you know, right?" The open look of joy on his face made Ura smile.

"Yes, I've heard that about sex. The rumors are that it's supposed to be enjoyable," she responded.

Dennis kissed her again, this time with a little more ardor. He began gently stroking her arm and running his open hand along her shoulder and neck. He ran his hand through her hair grabbing a handful in his big fingers. He continued kissing her, gently easing his tongue into her mouth to tease her tongue. He slipped the thin strap of the negligee off her left shoulder with the thumb of his right hand and moved to kiss her shoulder. He moved his mouth to the small hollow where her neck met her shoulder, kissed his way up her neck to her ear. He took her ear lobe in his mouth and sucked gently on it then ran the tip of his tongue over the edges of her ear.

Ura moaned when he began to kiss her ear and positioned herself to be on her back. Dennis slid his right foot up Ura's leg till his leg was between hers to spread them apart slightly. He eased the other strap off her shoulder and began kissing the hollow space of her throat. He ran his hands all over her torso, moving the soft silk material across her skin as he slid his hands up and down. He played with her hardening nipples with his thumbs enjoying the feel of them as they rose under the smooth material. He reached down and ran the index finger of his right hand up the inside of Ura's left thigh, slipping under the silk that covered the tops of her legs and circled his fingers around the inside of her thighs, teasing and playing with her, purposefully holding back from entering her with their long thickness.

Ura's hips began to undulate, moving with him. She began kissing his neck and chest, this time making Dennis moan. Then, surprising him, she pushed Dennis onto his back and rolled over to kiss her way down his belly. Spreading her legs, she straddled him, and he could feel her hot wetness against his belly making his arousal more ardent. She slid herself over his hardness making both of them moan in harmony, then worked her way down to take him in her mouth.

"God, Ura!" Dennis cried out.

Ura used her tongue and mouth to bring Dennis near to climax then lifted up and moved her hips until she was directly over his erect penis. She grabbed both of his hands and slid herself down onto him taking him all the way inside her. They began to rock together like they had been making love this way their entire lives, starting with long, slow strokes, she moved to the music on the stereo increasing the tempo as Dennis followed her dance until, with one final movement they exploded in unison.

Ura rolled onto her side and Dennis pulled her to him, wrapping his muscular arms around her. She lay her head on his chest and he buried his face in her hair.

"Was that what you meant by fun?" She asked.

"Uh, yeah! I think we may need to do a lot more of this though. You can never have enough fun," Dennis replied, making them both laugh. They lay in each other's arms until they both fell into a deep and happy sleep.

Their love making became more and more ardent. Ura moved in bed much in the same way she did on stage, insisting that there always be music and candles. He had never been a romantic man, or at least he didn't think he was, but he loved every minute of it. They gave each other massages with essential oils, took long sensuous baths together. After a month of living together, not a night went by when they didn't make love, often trying something new; a new position, a new technique, a new room or place in the house or yard and in the pool. Dennis took Ura on a little vacation to Saint Augustine where they stayed in a bed and breakfast, missing breakfast each morning to enjoy each other instead. They swam in the ocean and ate at fancy restaurants. Ura loved the quaint old streets and the unusual shops. He bought her little gifts in several of them and she got him a shaving kit and a straw hat. They were in love and there was no denying that fact.

***

Tony called for a special meeting, but he asked the girls to pass the word that Ura was not to be told about it. They all gathered in the dressing room at 6 pm on the designated Tuesday evening.

"Okay, gang, I asked you all to meet me briefly about something very special. Dennis and Ura are on their Tuesday night standing date so this was the only time I could get away with this," Tony laughed.

"This coming Sunday is Ura's birthday and we want to do something special for her. She's done so much for all of us and for the club that we're throwing her a surprise party. So, I gathered you all up to come up with suggestions as to what we can do to make this the party of the century."

For the next twenty minutes, ideas were tossed around, tasks were assigned, and the entire gang was poised to throw Ura one hell of a party.

Sunday evening came quickly, and the plans were in full swing. Dennis was to take Ura to an early movie and Tony, Lenny, and the girls got moving the second they left. They had signs ready that the club was closed for a private party and Terri was put in charge of the door to make sure only invited guests were allowed in. It wasn't really that much different than any other Sunday night because most of the regulars were invited.

Tony had hired a caterer and food was set up buffet style. A jazz combo set up in the corner and a huge birthday cake sat on a table just to the left of the band. The girls decorated the place in pink and yellow streamers, they got silly party hats and a fake birthday tiara for Ura to wear. Everyone was dressed in their nicest clothes and at the designated time they took the private party signs down so as not to tip Ura off, dimmed the lights, and waited for Dennis to escort Ura through the front door. It went like clockwork. The door opened and Dennis gently guided Ura into the room."

"Wow, it's dark in here," was all she could say when a huge SURPRISE erupted from the crowd. She was floored and teared up as everyone crowded around her wishing her happy birthday and hugging her.

The band played happy birthday and then swung into light jazz and classic tunes.

The night went just as planned. Ura opened her gifts, everyone danced to Frank Sinatra and Ella Fitzgerald tunes. Dennis wielded Ura around the dance floor proud as a peacock that this beautiful woman was his. Everything was fine.

Until the cake.

The cake was on a little buffet table on wheels and they rolled it out for Ura to blow out the twenty-three candles, twenty-two for the years she had lived and one to grow on. None of them knew that in reality this was only her twentieth birthday. No one would have guessed that.

As she stood over the cake using her last breath to extinguish each of the little flames, Ura's head started to pound. The room began to turn a bright white. Everyone was cheering and laughing and when she finished, she excused herself, saying she needed to use the rest room. Dennis was concerned that she seemed suddenly out of sorts.

After she had been gone for more than five minutes, he began to worry that she had taken ill. The party was a lot of excitement and he considered that she might be overwhelmed. "Cheyanne," he said pulling the young lady aside. "Would you mind going to the ladies' room to check on Ura? She's been in there for a long time. She may not be feeling well."

"Sure Dennis, happy to."

Cheyanne headed to check on Ura as Dennis stood nervously waiting. Cheyenne returned two minutes later looking a little confused.

"Are you sure she went to the rest room?" she asked.

"Yes, she said that's where she was going."

"Well, she's not in there."

Dennis started to sweat. He didn't want to cause a scene, so he quietly pulled Tony aside and told him what was going on. They searched the bar and backstage dressing rooms, the office and both bathrooms.

"No sign of her," Tony said when they met up back at the bar. "Hang on a minute," he said and headed out the front door. Tony returned a few seconds later looking very glum.

"I hate to tell you this pal. The caddy's gone."

Dennis stuck his hand in his pocket, feeling for the small velvet ring box he had hidden there and sighed deeply.

Chapter 11

Chapel Hill 1997

Heaven drove fast, very fast. The blinding headache was subsiding by the time she reached I 95. The signs for Saint Augustine made a little tugging feeling at her heart. *Why do I suddenly feel sad?* She'd never been there so she wondered why reading the road signs made her eyes tear up a bit. Soon she saw the signs for Jacksonville and felt a little more at ease. She would be at her cabin by early morning if she just kept driving. *What in the world was I doing in Florida? Why can't I remember?*

She drove through the night, windows down on the caddy until she hit the South Carolina border where the night air was a little too cool for her taste. She knew she should stop at a motel and sleep, but she wanted to get home. It felt like she hadn't been there in a very long time. *How long had it been?* She had no idea. She crossed over into North Carolina at about 5 am and when she saw the signs for Fayetteville, she swung the caddy to the northwest, passing Fort Bragg and heading straight for Chapel Hill.

It was 8:30 in the morning when she finally pulled into her little circular drive. She had run on adrenaline and coffee all the way there and as soon as she opened the door, she walked straight to her queen-sized feather bed and face planted without so much as removing her shoes.

Heaven woke up twenty-two hours later, desperate to use the bathroom and equally desperate for coffee and food. Peace Frog and Lono were the first words to pop into her head. She took a fast shower, pulled on a pair of soft, stretchy jeans that showed off her perfect legs, added a light blue sweater to complete the outfit and took off for town.

Heaven entered the café and seeing the back of her young friend's head bent down over a school book, she couldn't resist the urge to give his thick dark locks of hair a light tug. Lono nearly fell off the stool he was sitting on when he turned around to see his lovely friend standing there.

"Holy moly… as I live and breathe. Where have you been?" He asked her then pulled her into his strong arms for a bear hug.

He's a lot taller and he's filled out a great deal, she thought. *How could that have happened? Wasn't I here just a few weeks ago?* "Don't crush me, I'm just a little girl," she laughed and pulled out of his strong grip.

 Heaven sat down at the counter and Lono jumped behind it to grab her a coffee cup which he filled to the brim, remembering that she took it black and strong.

"I can't believe you're back," he said, leaning on the countertop to get eye level with her. "God, we've missed you so much. I thought we might never see you again."

"You act like I've been gone forever. I was just here," she said sipping the heavenly dark brew.

"Just here?" he laughed heartily. You missed my graduation and most of my Freshman year of college. I took an art class and was praying you'd come back and give me some pointers. Not that it matters, as it turns out, I have no talent for drawing but I'm pulling a solid C so it's all good."

What is he talking about? How could I have missed all that? She needed to look at a calendar. She needed to call her brother in law. Her head was spinning but she didn't want to appear crazy, so she played along and apologized for missing Lono's graduation making her best attempt at an excuse while her mind raced trying to piece together her lost time.

After a good breakfast and some catching up with Lono and his mom, Heaven went back to her cabin to survey her situation. She looked into the fridge to find there was nothing there but some very old eggs in a carton and some bread that looked like a science experiment. She tossed them out and made a list of supplies she would go to town to retrieve. First things first. She dialed the number and waited for him to answer.

"Hello, Ryan speaking."

"Hi Ryan."

"Heaven... Heaven is that you?" he said excited to hear her voice.

"It's me."

"Thank God. Where have you been? Never mind. I don't care and Helena won't care either. Just so long as you're okay. You're okay right?"

"I'm fine. I'm in Chapel Hill and I'm ready to get some work done. How are things there?"

"They're great. We've landed two more major stores in the last year and a half. Nordstrom's is carrying our line. The last designs you created put us over the top. We can't supply them fast enough."

They talked for about twenty minutes. Heaven promised she would have some new designs for them in the next few weeks. Ideas were swirling around in her head. She had some wild ideas about mixing American Indian elements with sexy evening wear. She wanted to use some leather and turquoise as accents. And she had an idea to do a whole line of lingerie in nothing but tones of blue. She had no idea where these inspirations were coming from, but she was happy that she was back to work and that her mind was so clear and focused.

For the next two months, Heaven lived a quiet, peaceful existence. She spent her evenings working on new designs and enjoying the time alone. She ate her breakfast and lunch out most days, took long walks in the woods surrounding the cabin and read every afternoon before taking an hour's nap to rejuvenate her senses. She was happy, really happy but there was only one thing that disturbed her simple pleasant existence; she was lonely. She had never felt this kind of loneliness before. It was as if there were a hole in her heart where something used to be that was no longer there. She felt like she had lost something, the way you feel when you go on a trip and halfway there you think, *I forgot something important at home. What could it be?*

She created some amazing designs and set up her usual meeting with Ryan to hand them off to him. She called to let him know she was ready to meet him, and a few days later his BMW pulled into the driveway.

"It's good to see you, Sis," he said as he took off his coat laying it over a chair in her living room.

"Good to see you too."

"You look rested, happy even," he stated.

"I am happy, mostly anyway and I think you'll like these new designs. They're a bit of a diversion from some of my work."

Ryan took the portfolio of designs from her, sat at the table, and studied each one carefully. The mix of American Indian influence and near erotic fantasy was unparalleled. How in the world she was able to make that work was stunning to him. He had never seen anything like them, and he told her so, beaming with pride in this young, strange creature he so admired. "I'm astounded," he said. "And the blues in these designs, the layer of color combinations. I need our seamstresses to match these exactly. They're perfect. We should be able to get these into production in a couple of months. I can't wait to show the buyers these designs. They will lose their minds over them."

He stayed for a quick supper of cold chicken, potato salad, and Iced tea, all of which she had picked up from the Peace Frog. After dinner, Ryan handed Heaven her check. "If you need anything else, more money, help with anything, you'll call us, right?"

"Yes, I promise. But I'm fine. I'm always fine." She answered.

Ryan kissed her lightly on the forehead and soon was driving away. Heaven watched as his taillights disappeared from her driveway and soon after was deep asleep.

A week later something occurred to her. She could not remember the last time she had had her period. *That's odd, I'd better see a doctor*, she thought. *Could just be stress, but what have I got to stress about?*

Chapter 12

Angelique goes to work 1989

"We could use the extra money!" Angelique argued her position with Jordan. He was less than thrilled to have her working, but he knew she was right. His design company was holding its own but living in New York with two girls to care for, one a teenager and the other nearing her teens as well, was costly to say the least. "It's just part time, Jordan," she continued. "Three afternoons a week and a few weekends when Charlotte has a show she needs help with. You know I love the modelling business and now that I'm a little too old to model, helping with the business will be fun for me… and bring in some cash."

"Okay! Uncle! I give. I can never say no to you. Besides, it's pointless to try when your minds made up."

"Good, that's settled," she said.

For the next several months, on Wednesdays, Thursdays, and Fridays, Angelique would leave the house around 10 am and return in the late afternoon, not too long after the girls got home from school. Sometimes she worked on Saturday in the early afternoon and into the evening coming home well after dinner.

Helena was a sophomore in high school and Heaven was in the seventh grade when Angelique started her new job. During their summer vacation she worked a bit less but still kept similar hours. Heaven begged to go with her to her job, but she always said she was too busy and that children were not allowed at the office. She still found lots of time to devote to their drawing sessions and dance lessons. Heaven excelled at both. Helena was at the age where nothing her mother did could possibly be right. She was rebellious and often sharp tongued with both Angelique and Heaven and she displayed no interest in doing anything with her younger sister. Heaven wanted Helena to like her and she admired her sister's abilities with numbers and difficult math problems. She went to her for help with her math homework which Helena reluctantly assisted her with, though secretly loved that she had so much superiority over Heaven in those types of subjects. Heaven was all art. Math, science, anything that required critical thinking seemed to float in and out of Heaven's head. She wanted to draw more than anything and she spent hours each day perfecting her talents in that department. Heaven would not show anyone but Angelique her artwork and designs and made her mother swear she wouldn't show Jordan or Helena her work until she felt ready to do so.

Heaven was excited about entering eighth grade. One more year and she would be in high school, a freshman in her sister's senior year so they would be in the same building again before Helena would go on to college, but that was a year away and this, her final year in middle school, would be a fun one. She had seniority and she and her small but close-knit group of friends would be the older and wiser ones in the building.

Heaven had a crush on a boy named Bobby Lee. He had longish blond hair that he was always brushing out of his beautiful hazel eyes. He was one of the tallest boys in the class which Heaven liked because she had reached her full height and stood over five foot eight inches tall herself. Most of the boys in the class had not had their growth spurts yet and she towered over them; but not Bobby.

When it came time for the Homecoming Dance, she hoped he would ask her, but he didn't. He chose to take Sophia De Angelo, a dark-haired, olive skinned beauty, whose breasts had filled in over the summer making her hour glass figure fully rounded out. Sophia was only five foot two and Bobby had to bend down to slow dance with her, but he looked very pleased with himself out on the dance floor.

Heaven attended anyway, spending a lot of time sitting on the sidelines with her girl pals waiting for the occasional boy to come and ask her to dance which a few of them did. She wasn't very upset about Bobby. She knew Sophia pretty well and felt that she was a very nice girl. Heaven wasn't prone to jealousy even at twelve. She had a sense that there was no use being jealous over something that wasn't hers to begin with. There would be other dances and other boys. When she did get up to dance with her girlfriends, she was shy about dancing the way her mother had taught her. She sensed, even then, that there were some moves Angelique had shared that might not be appropriate at a middle school dance so she moved gracefully, but not in a way that would draw too much attention. Heaven was still a fairly shy girl and wanted to be liked but wasn't quite ready to be in the spotlight around her peers.

With the new school year back in full swing, Angelique added to her work hours, sometimes more sporadically than other times. Some weekend nights, she would leave the house right after dinner and not return till rather late in the evening, long after both the girls had gone to bed. She and Jordan began to fight about the hours she was keeping.

"I don't understand why they need you to work these kinds of hours," Jordan said.

"Because I'm part of the team there, Jordan. If there's work to be done, everyone pitches in."

"And your smoking too much again. I can smell smoke on your clothes. I thought we agreed to stop," he complained.

"It's a nasty habit but I can't seem to quit," she admitted. "Can we just stop arguing about my work? I love it and you have to admit the money helps out around here."

He knew she was right, but Jordan became more and more jealous of her work and he was resentful of the money she brought home. Her paychecks were getting bigger and bigger. Jordan didn't know Charlotte, but he knew of her company and they seemed to be quite successful. He wanted to be proud of his wife for working so hard, but he had a jealous nature and it felt like she was somehow working for the competition. He asked to go to a couple of the fashion shows Angelique was working at, but she begged him not to attend.

"Your being there will make me very nervous and you know you can't come backstage anyway. I'll be behind the scenes the entire time so I wouldn't even see you if you did come."

But there was a far greater reason she didn't want Jordan to attend any of the events.

"Thanks for doing this, Charlotte," Angelique said handing over the fat wad of bills to her old friend.

"You know I would do anything for you, Angelique. I don't mind, but I worry about you. Please be careful, okay?"

"Always!"

"Why do you do it? I mean, I know I couldn't pay you a third of what you're making but I get the feeling it's not just about the money."

"No, it's not. I mean, the money is a plus and I don't give you all of it for these pay checks. I've started a bank account of my own and I put money in every week. I need to know I have a back-up plan and money of my own that Jordan doesn't control."

"If you're afraid of him, honey…"

"No, not so much afraid. I know that he wouldn't hurt me or leave me. It's just that he's older and he has always been very controlling. I had enough of that with my own father. I guess I have daddy issues," Angelique said with a wry laugh. "It's about more than any of that. It's the only time I feel *I'm* the one in control, I have the power. Can you understand that?"

"I sure can. Men have all the power. Even in the fashion industry, men still rule the roost. Ralph Lauren, Calvin Klein, Christian Lacroix, they all make far more money than most of the women in my world. Not that I'm complaining. The company is thriving and I'm grateful," Charlotte said.

"And I am forever grateful to you for covering me on this. There's no way I could explain this to Jordan and if he ever finds out the truth…"

"I'm always here if you need me. I've got you covered. Just stay out of harms way," Charlotte begged her old friend.

"I promise," Angelique said, and made a little cross over her heart with her index finger. "See you in two weeks, okay?"

"Of course."

With that Angelique hustled out the door of Charlotte's office and down the elevator to the parking garage. She would bring Jordan her "paycheck" to deposit in their joint account. What would he think if he knew she had nearly $5,000 stashed away in an account in a small bank in New Jersey? More importantly, what if he found out what she really did to earn that money? She hoped he never would and especially that her girls wouldn't find out, though she somehow thought Heaven might approve. Angelique knew that her youngest was cut from a very special cloth.

I bet she wouldn't mind at all, she thought as she headed for home.

Chapter 13

Chapel Hill

"But why Portland?" Heaven asked Lono.

"My cousin, Kai lives there, and he says it's a hopping place. I figure after college I might go out there and hook up with him. Lots of Hawaiians live there. Our ancestors migrated to Oregon way back in the 1800's."

"Wow, you're up on your history."

"I want to get to know my Hawaiian family. Dad is too disconnected from them, you know. It's a big part of who I am," he said.

"Well, I think that's great, Lono." Heaven squeezed his hand. She sat at the counter drinking coffee and picking at her biscuits and gravy. She felt a little queasy when she woke up and thought it was just hunger but now she was starting to worry it was something else. She'd been sick for the last three mornings in a row, but the feeling passed by lunchtime each day.

"Coffee is a big thing there too and beer. Starbucks opened their first place there about ten years ago and that started a revolution. All kinds of coffee brewers are trying to make their mark there," Lono explained.

"I've heard of Starbucks, but I've never been to one. I bet their coffee isn't as good as the Peace Frogs," she replied.

"I don't know, our is really good, that's true. We use a guy who roasts his beans locally but Kai says we can hook up with some of our family in Hawaii and import Kona beans and make a killing. Best coffee there is. Even better than ours here."

"That's hard to believe," Heaven said taking a big sip of the terrific coffee in front of her. "I'll be happy to be a tester for you though. Quality control."

"You're on. You can be my first customer when I take Peace Frog, Hawaiian Blend to the streets of Portland."

"The streets? What does that mean?" she asked.

"Food trucks and food carts, baby! They are huge out there. Kai says street food is getting to be Portland's big thing. Music, coffee, beer, and food trucks. We'll set up a Peace Frog food truck, bring our special Kona coffee and mom's secret baked treats, and set up outside bars at night. People going to hear music come out for coffee and food before they head home."

"What's the music like there?"

"It's been a great place for Alternative Rock for a few years now. Lots of bands and music venues."

"Does your cousin own a food truck?" Heaven asked.

"No!" Lono laughed. "He bar backs in a couple of strip clubs. There are tons of them in Portland. He works days in one and nights in another. He says he makes a lot of money and he's gonna save all he can till I can get out there and partner up with him."

At the words strip club, Heaven felt an odd sensation, a kind of tingling in her hands and feet. Suddenly she felt a little dizzy. Lono noticed and rushed around the counter in time to catch Heaven in a swoon that would have had her falling off the stool she was sitting on if it were not for his strong arms and quick thinking.

"Hey, you okay there?" Lono asked and helped Heaven to a lower chair at one of the nearby empty tables. "Put your head between your knees," he said and helped Heaven bend her head down toward her lap. After a few seconds, she slowly lifted her head.

"That was an odd sensation," she said.

"I'm going to get you some water," Lono answered. "Stay right there, don't move. I'll be back in a jiffy.

Lono when into the kitchen to get a glass of cold water. He let the water in the sink run a minute to get it to be colder and went to get some ice from the ice machine. He was gone all of two minutes, but when he got back to the dining room, Heaven was gone.

"Damn!" he said. "That girl worries the hell outta me."

***

"Hey, I remember you, you're Lono's friend. I made you an ID before. Weird name, Yoro? No, that wasn't it. Ursula? No, it was shorter than that." Paul remembered when Lono had brought her the first time. She seemed disoriented and Lono was nervous. Paul thought Lono had some sort of crush on the girl, but he wasn't sure. He just remembered the whole thing being a little odd and off putting.

"Look, I think you got me mixed up with somebody else. The name is Selena." She spoke with a thick New York accent.

That's different, Paul thought. *Maybe I do have her mixed up with someone else. Lono's girl sounded midwestern, not much of any accent really and she was a blond not a brunette.*

"I can't find my freakin' ID. Musta lost it someplace. Can ya make me a new one, and pronto? I got a long ride ahead a me."

"Sure... um Selena. What do want it to say?" Paul asked.

"The truth. 23, brown hair, green eyes, 5'8", Brooklyn, New York."

"Okay, you got it. I need about 20 mins. Sit over there and I'll get a quick picture."

Selena sat on the little stool her back to the plain white wall behind her and smiled broadly. Her perfect white teeth and ruby red lips made an excellent image for the ID.

Man, she is a looker, Paul mused. *If she isn't the same girl, she's a dead ringer for her. But if she is, she's a total kook.*

Paul finished up the ID in record time and walked his new customer out to her car. *A Caddy, now that's too much of a coincidence.* As she drove away, Paul hit the side of his head with his palm, "Ura, that's the name. Yeah, same chick. I need to call Lono tomorrow." He said and went back inside to continue with the video game he was playing and the joint he was smoking when she had arrived. Somehow calling Lono got forgotten with a puff of smoke and a joystick.

Several hours later, Selena was driving the big gold Caddy west on Highway I 64, singing along with The Backstreet Boys at the top of her lungs.

"Quit playin' games with my heart, with my heart…."

Chapter 14

Portland 1997

Selena spent ten days on the road to Portland stopping in major cities and small towns along the way. She went clothes shopping in St Louis and saw the arch, had amazing barbeque in Kansas City, and veered off to spend a little time in Denver, Colorado. She found Salt Lake City, Utah to be one of the most interesting places. Utah's terrain was odd to her, like she was on another planet and the influence of the Mormons was everywhere in their gigantic and stark architecture. Nampa and Boise Idaho were a pleasant surprise. Cool little cities with a lot to offer but she had a destination ahead, so she kept her visits short in every place along the way. Finally, I 84 took her through the Mt Hood National Forest and into Portland. It was a lush and bustling city with lots of greenery. Portland saw more rain than any other city in the country most years, but they fought the drab and dreary weather with colorful buildings and equally colorful people.

Selena drove around the city getting a feel for the place. There were bars, strip clubs, restaurants, bakeries, and it seemed like a person would never want for coffee or donuts again by living here. She loved it. After several hours of exploring, she was hungry. She stumbled upon a Mexican bodega that served homemade tamales and the best coffee she'd had since she started on her journey across county. She learned that she was in the Alberta District and decided she had found her spot. After walking around the neighborhood for an hour or so, she found a small motel that had been converted into a boarding house just off Alberta Street. The place offered clean, comfortable rooms for rent at a reasonable price. The owner, Mrs. Haverty, was happy to tell Selena all about the Alberta District. She'd lived there most of her life and was pleased to see its progress.

The area had once been dilapidated, but by the mid 1990's it was turning into a hot spot drawing in artists, craftsman, and foodies. Selena loved good food. She didn't drink alcohol or smoke cigarettes. Her one vice, if you could call it that, was trying out different cuisines and eating out constantly. She couldn't fry an egg herself but admired people who knew how to cook and do it well. Something about this neighborhood appealed to her more than Downtown or the Pearl District which was rapidly growing more and more upscale. Alberta Street and its surroundings felt like home to Selena. It's bohemian style and, still rough around the edges, ambiance made the artist in her find it a little easier to breath.

Selena spent the next few days resting, exploring, and eating her way around Portland. One afternoon, she was walking down a busy street just at the edge of her neighborhood and she saw a bright neon sign that caught her attention. It read, Bare Beauties, Adult Exotic Entertainment. She pulled open the heavy red wooden door and entered the club. It was 5 pm, happy hour was under way, and Selena was surprised to see nearly as many women in the bar as men.

Portland sure is a different kind of place, she thought, and sidled up to the bar. A woman who looked to be in her mid-thirties was behind the old wooden counter, pouring a pitcher of beer. She had dirty blond hair, buzzed short on the sides and spiked up into sharp little frosted tufts on the top of her head. She had angular features and a firm jawline, and her expression said, "Don't mess with me." Selena liked her instantly. *This is a woman you don't get into a fight with unless you plan to get the shit kicked outta ya,* she thought.

"What can I get you?" the tough bartender asked Selena.

"Ginger ale with a splash of bitters," Selena replied.

"Stomachache?"

"Yeah, you guessed it. Too many donuts and way too much coffee today," Selena said a little surprised at the bartender's response.

"Well, you're in Portland," the bartender cracked an unexpected little smile and went to fetch the mixture for Selena.

"So, you're a real bartender," Selena said sipping the concoction placed in front of her. "Only the real ones know this trick."

"Bartender, bar owner, beverage master, chief cook and bottle washer. Christine... but my friends call me Chris. And you are?"

"Selena." She put her hand out and they exchanged a firm handshake.

"Welcome, Selena. This is your first time in here, isn't it? I don't think I've seen you in here before."

"Yup. Only been in town a couple a days."

"Well, glad you stopped in. New Yorker?"

"What gave it away?" Selena laughed. She knew her accent was pretty thick.

"Just a hunch," Chris said sarcastically and with that glided off to survey the bar, checking on other customers, refilling drinks, and chatting briefly with the servers as they came up to get more cocktails for the patrons at the tables. She moved smoothly and swiftly, much like a dancer herself but her stage was behind three feet of polished mahogany and brass railings.

Selena watched her for a moment then turned on her stool so she could get a good view of the dancers who were performing. There were two women on the stage. One looked to be about twenty and the other a fair bit older. Their dancing was good but nothing special. The bar was classier looking than the name implied but the bare part was accurate. They didn't leave a lot to the imagination with their attire, or lack of it. *I've never danced completely naked,* she thought. *How freeing would that be?*

Finally, Chris came back around to Selena. "How's the belly ache?"

"Oh, way better, thanks," Selena replied. "Say, Chris, are you hirin' any more dancers?"

"We're always looking for new talent. Are you any good?"

"I've been told I am."

"Do you have a problem with nudity? We don't require our girls to go nude but topless is a given and well... the rest is up to the girls but most of them go full nudity at some point in their shift."

"I don't have a problem with it but I'm into putting on more of a show."

"So, more burlesque and less prancing around randomly?"

"That's pretty accurate," Selena said.

"We're working our way in that direction, so your timing might be perfect. During the day and right through happy hour, we mostly get guys and of course the lesbian crowd in to grab a beer, a burger for lunch or the free wings we put out at 5 pm. All they want to see is a naked chick strutting her stuff and getting up close and personal for them. But we're trying to build a better nighttime clientele, especially on the weekends. My girlfriend has been working with some of the girls to make it more Flash Dance and less tits and ass."

"When can I audition?" Selena asked. "I'd love to show you my style. I design and make all my own costumes and I think I might fit in with what you're shootin' for."

"How's tomorrow at 10:30 am?" Chris asked. "We open doors at 11 am so that will give you time to show off a couple of numbers."

"Perfect. I'll be here."

"Bring a couple of your outfits and any music you want to work with."

"Will do!" Selena said enthusiastically. "See ya in the mornin'," she said and headed back out into the uncommonly bright and warm evening air.

Selena was up bright and early the next day. She was excited about her audition. Something about the place felt right to her. The inside of the bar had almost a cozy feeling. Maybe because the building itself was so old. The walls were rough brick and the décor mostly deep reds and velvets which reminded her of bars she'd been at in New York and New Jersey. It felt lush and warm to her. Selena was also a good judge of character and had a sixth sense about people. There was an energy about Chris that had goodness in it. Selena knew instinctively that Chris was a decent person and could be trusted. She didn't know how she knew; she just knew.

She was five minutes early for her audition, but the door was locked when she got there. She knocked hard and after a minute, the door swung open. The younger of the girls who had been on stage the evening before was standing there in tight, jean short shorts and a baby tee with the Bare Beauties logo stretched tight across her ample chest. "Hey, c'mon in," she said roughly. She seemed less than thrilled to extend the invitation and turned away from Selena quickly leaving her to follow her into the main seating area.

"Hiya!" Selena said to the back of the young dancer as she scurried off. "Nice to meet ya," she said to no one. "Nice to meet you too," she answered herself jokingly, in a mock conversation with the buxom girl who'd left without a word. She put her outfits down and went over to see if anyone was in the DJ booth, but no one was there, so she sat at a table and waited. A few minutes later, she heard loud voices coming from the backstage area. She couldn't make out what they were saying, but it sounded like a pretty good fight was underway and one of the voices sounded like Chris, the owner.

Selena looked at her watch, 10:40 am. She tapped her foot nervously and waited. The yelling ceased and a second afterward, both Chris and the young dancer came out from the backstage.

"Sorry," Chris said, coming over to greet Selena, her steps quick and purposeful. "This is Denny, she's a dancer too but she DJ's sometimes. She'll take care of your music."

Selena handed Denny the cassette she had made with her two songs she was planning to perform. "Thanks, Denny. Good to meet ya, "Denny grunted a vague affirmation and headed to the sound booth.

"I just need to change. Okay if I go backstage? Is there a dressing room?" Selena asked Chris.

"Sure, we have a very nice dressing room. Just come out when you're ready. I'm going to grab some coffee."

Selena went back behind the stage area and indeed the dressing room was clean and had nice furniture and mirrors with little dressing tables. She hung her second outfit and donned her first one, a skimpy top and a sarong like skirt cut on an angle so that her right leg was mostly exposed while her left was mostly covered. The material was a bright green and had a sheen to it that glistened under lighting making her look almost like a mermaid. She took a deep breath and stepped out onto the stage. Her first song was "Cream" by Prince. Selena took the stage and replicated many of the moves from the video of the 1991 hit song.

Chris moved closer to the stage and could not take her eyes off the creature moving to the sexy rhythmic song. As the song progressed, Selena slowly and seductively disrobed. First one strap of her top, then the other letting them slip off her shoulders, then she turned her back to Chris and removed the top using it as a prop before turning around to reveal her full and perfect breasts. She did the same with the sarong inching it off her in a way that was near to agonizing until she was wearing the tiniest G string. By the time the last cord of the song had ended, she had removed even that and was on her knees, on the stage, sitting back slightly on her haunches, fully nude.

"You're hired," was all that Chris said. From the DJ booth, a commotion erupted, and a beer glass went flying to hit the nearby wall.

Chapter 15

Rain, Rain, and Scooters

Selena fell in love with Oregon. It was as if any worries or questions she had disappeared into the quiet, nearly constant, rain. On days when the sun snuck its big yellow head out to dry the damp streets and rich earth, Selena would go exploring. She discovered she liked hiking and spent some time on the trails of Forest Park and on particularly nice days, Mt Hood.

She became a coffee snob and worked her way around the city trying out various roasts as well as some of the baked goods that were also sold at the coffee houses. But donuts became her arch enemy. For some reason, she constantly wanted a jelly donut and Portland had all manners and types of the best of those a donut aficionado could ask for. One day, she saw a little cream colored vespa on the lawn of a lovely old house. It had a for sale sign on it so she marched right up to the front door and knocked.

"Can I help you?" A young woman answered from behind the closed screen door. She was very, very pregnant.

"I saw the sign," Selena responded, captivated by the enormity of the woman's belly.

"What sign?"

"On the scooter," Selena said, her eyes still glued to the woman's stomach.

"Oh, yes," she answered. "I almost forgot. We're selling my Vespa."

"Why? It looks like it would be blast to ride on." Selena said.

"Um…" The young woman looked down and Selena realized how silly a question it was. "It's twins. No more scooters for me at least for a long, long time."

"Well, that makes sense, Whata ya askin' for it?"

"Five hundred dollars. It's pristine, only two years old and all I ever did was use it for going back and forth to work when it wasn't pouring out, that is."

"I'll take it," Selena said.

"Just like that, no haggling?"

"I don't haggle, especially with women who are havin' twins. Bad idea." She pulled her wallet from the pocket of her jeans and took five crisp one hundred dollar bills out and handed them one by one to the pregnant woman.

"Okay!" she said a little in shock as she took each bill from this strange and exotic creature standing on her stoop. "I'll go get you the keys. Be right back."

A minute later she was back with a cream-colored helmet that matched the Vespa perfectly. She signed the title over to Selena, handed her the keys, and wished her luck.

"Cool! Thanks," said Selena. She turned, jogged back down the walkway and hopped on the scooter. It started right away and purred like a kitten. She was in love. For the next two weeks she tooled everywhere she went around town on the Vespa. It made travel in the city easier though she had to be careful of the slick streets and sidewalks on rainy days. She didn't mind it when the rain was light, but on really rainy days, she stayed indoors in her tiny but lovely little studio apartment. On those days, she drank herbal tea with locally sourced honey. She tried all different blends and loved the aroma of the teas as they steeped.

She decided to take up cooking as a hobby. Starting with simple omelets adding different cheeses and veggies like spinach and red onion and working her way up to pasta dishes, fish, and chicken. But the meal she most enjoyed was one she only ate at her favorite little local eatery, Joey's Steaks and Chops.

"Let me guess, a salad with lots of vegetables, blue cheese dressing, a NY strip, medium rare topped with smoked oysters, baked potato and a nice fresh roll and butter," Joey said, leaning over the wooden bar smiling at his new best customer.

"How dya guess?" Selena replied.

"I'm smart like that. Plus, you're in here every Tuesday night and you never order anything else. Killian's red to wash it down?" The place was tiny, but the food was upscale and awesome, and Joey always worked behind the counter on weeknights. He liked to talk to his customers and this one was exceptionally beautiful and interesting. He looked forward to seeing her on Tuesday nights.

"You betcha, Joey."

Christine put Selena on the schedule for every Friday and Saturday nights and she had her in for lunch through happy hour on Mondays, Wednesdays and Thursdays. Chris started to notice a big up tick in business on the days Selena worked. She would have her in every day and night if she could, but she took her business seriously and was smart enough to know that overworking people came with diminishing returns. She was grateful for the extra business Selena brought in and would never push her like some bar owners might. Maybe it was because she was a lesbian and had more concern for women or maybe because Chris had come up through the ranks. She started dancing at seventeen with a fake ID and had worked in half the bars in Portland. She was the lead dancer at Bare Beauties for nearly ten years and when the owner said she was selling, Chris didn't hesitate to buy the place. She'd been saving up for it for a long time. Once she was the owner, she hung up her dancing shoes and took to business like a Harvard Grad. She was smart and serious as a heart attack about making the place a clean, decent environment. In the two years since she took over, she had fully remodeled and had moved away from strip bar and towards exotic dance club. Her girls weren't quite there yet, but they were starting to work up more of a burlesque show rather than just topless and nude dancing.

And the clientele got better and better. The local lesbians started coming in more and more and classier groups would come in to see the shows on the weekends. Lunch and happy hour had been pretty much stripping until Selena showed up. She brought Friday night energy and class to the stage every time she danced no matter what time of day or who was in the audience. She was a showgirl, not a stripper. Chris couldn't take her eyes off Selena when she danced, and it was causing a little issue with her very jealous young girlfriend.

Denny watched Chris watching Selena and seethed. Denny was the top dancer at Bare Beauties, not just because she was sleeping with the boss but because she was damn good. Denny had wavy chestnut brown hair that cascaded down her back and her eyes were brown with flecks of gold. She was slender and tall. In fact, she was at least two inches taller than Chris and more than ten years her junior. Chris was thirty-seven but youthful and full of energy. To watch her behind her bar, hustling drinks and lugging heavy cases of beer or tubs of ice you would think she was in her early twenties. Denny at twenty-six was far more feminine with a willowy stature. She was more the type to have things carried for her than to be the one doing the carrying. She was very overprotective of her relationship with Chris. Denny had never had a serious relationship with a woman before. She'd dabbled in sex with other girls but had dated men, if you could call them that, mostly tattooed, uneducated, loud mouths who treated her badly, drank too much or worse, did drugs. They loved dating Denny, the stripper who made lots of money every day and could be intimidated into handing over her cash with a simple back handed swipe. When Denny met Chris, it was as if her whole world turned upside down. She had never been treated like a lady before. She was scared to death of it at first, but after two years together, she couldn't imagine being with anyone else. For Denny, this was it. This was the rest of her life and she watched over their relationship like a mother hawk watching the nest. Selena scared the hell out of her, and she didn't care for the feeling.

What was worse was that Selena, for all her tough sounding talk, was really sweet. She was nice to everyone and despite her rise to fame at the bar, the girls all liked her. She was always bringing in lattes or donuts for everyone. And Selena had the best costumes which she made herself. One of the girls asked her for help with an outfit that was falling apart, and she jumped right in and fixed it. That started the avalanche. The word got out that Selena was a seamstress and could make costumes, so they all started bugging her to fix something or sew something.

Selena was big, New York friendly, open, easy going, funny albeit a little sarcastic, which if Denny was being honest, was engaging.

"What did that guy say to you?" asked Honey, one of the other dancers at Bare Beauties. She had seen Selena bend down to hear something one of the customers was saying while she was dancing. The guy had been pretty persistent, standing right at the edge of the stage, motioning Selena to come talk to him.

"He said, 'how much for you to come home with me?'"

"Classic. What did you tell him?"

"Oh, I just told him, $10,000," Selena said offhandedly.

"Selena!" Honey gasped, "You didn't. What did he say?"

"He said, 'Shit, that's a lot of money. How many times are we gonna have sex for that much money?' I said, oh we're never gonna have sex, but for ten grand I'll come home and meet your mother, so she stops askin' you when you're gonna meet a nice boy."

Honey nearly spit out the mouthful of coffee she was sipping. Denny, having overheard the exchange, stifled a laugh but had to turn away to hide her grin.

"Selena, you are a horse of a different color," Honey said.

Selena had been in Portland for a little over a month, when one day, she noticed her tummy was starting to distend a bit. When she first arrived, she was still having that morning nausea that she experienced on the road trip across country, but it had subsided after a while. She remembered that she hadn't had her period for some time, and she became a little concerned. She hadn't had sex anytime in the recent months. At least she couldn't remember having been with anyone. Then again, she was a little foggy on where she'd been before coming to Portland. She must have been somewhere on the east coast but for the life of her, she couldn't remember where. All she remembered was her epic trip across country and all the amazing places she'd seen along the way. She'd fallen in love with her new home and all the people and places she was experiencing so she put the fact that she had all the signs of being pregnant out of her head. It didn't seem possible, so maybe she was sick.

"Chris," Selena sat at the bar drinking her usual ginger ale this time without the bitters. "Listen, I'm a little worried, I may be having some female issues. Do you have a gynecologist you could recommend?"

"Geez, I don't. I'm healthy as a horse. Not much for doctors anyway but ask Denny. She has one she's used a bunch of times. I can't remember her name, but Denny seems to like her."

"Okay, will do."

"Hey, whatever it is, don't let it wait. And look, we're here for you. I know you don't know many people here yet, but in Portland, we take care of our friends."

"Thanks, Chris. It's nice to have friends."

Selena found Denny in the dressing room, cleaning up a little and getting things organized for the Saturday night crowd. There were a few parties booked and the girls had some great entertainment planned. A bunch of women were coming in with a bride to be and there was a group of lesbians having a send-off party for one of their pals who was going into the Navy. There would be more women than men in the place that night, so they had some fun things planned and some great music chosen for the show. Denny would be dancing the first set and closing out the night behind the DJ booth. She was slowly transitioning away from dancing and moving more toward management. Chris wanted it that way and whatever Chris wanted, Denny was down for.

"Hey, Denny. Got a sec?" Selena asked.

"What's up?" Denny responded without looking up from her task of organizing her makeup.

Selena got the sense that Denny wasn't thrilled with her, but she thought it was a little dancer jealousy. She knew dancers sometimes felt like the new talent was there to rival the existing talent. Selena had no interest in being better than anyone or taking away from anyone's income. She just loved to dance. It made her feel alive and powerful and free. She figured Denny would get more comfortable around her in time. Maybe a little bonding over her health issue would help. "Well, I think I may be having some health issues, women stuff. I need to see a gynecologist and Chris said you know are good one, a female doc."

"You asked Chris?"

"Well, yeah. She's lived here her whole life I just figured…"

"Well, you figured wrong," Denny said sharply looking straight at Selena, her eyes locking with Selena's. "If you need something, ask me. Chris is busy."

"Gotcha. Will do" Selena paused a moment waiting. "So, uh, the doc?"

"Oh, yeah. Doctor Lu. She's Chinese. Into a lot of Eastern medicine. She's great." Denny said and turned back to her sorting.

"Do you have her contact info?"

"She's on Overton Street in the Pearl District. Only Doctor Lu there." She said never looking up.

Selena got the message and with a quick thanks, left Denny to her devices.

I guess I better see what's going on with me, Selena thought. *Doctor Lu it is.*

Chapter 16

1990 Angelique Gets Caught

"This is getting to be too much, Angelique. This is the third weekend in a row you've had to be away for work. No job is worth this. We need you at home."

"Why exactly, Jordan? Helena will be in college in a year and Heaven is starting high school in the fall. They're not babies. How long before no one needs me? I have a career and I like it. What's so wrong with that?"

"I need you too, not just the girls. And Heaven is just thirteen, she needs her mother more than ever. She's starting to like boys and she's going to have questions I would rather not answer."

"Well, deal with it because I like what I do and I'm not quitting."

The fights happened more and more often. Heaven would hide in her room when they got going. It bothered her to see her parents at each other's throats. A few of the kids in her school came from broken families and while they said it was cool to have two of everything, two Christmases, birthday's, two parents fighting for their attention and outdoing each other, they also seemed pretty sad a lot of the time. Heaven was a sensitive teenager. Turning thirteen meant a lot to her. She wasn't a little kid anymore, but she wasn't ready to be from a fractured family and the way her parents were constantly going at it, she feared the worst.

"What will we do if mom and dad split up?" Heaven asked Helena during one of their parent's brawls. They had retreated to Helena's bedroom where they were further from the brawl. Helena couldn't wait to get to college and get out of the house. She knew she would have to share a dorm room with a stranger, but she preferred that to her having to deal with her little sister barging into her room constantly. Heaven annoyed Helena. She knew Heaven was Angelique's favorite and always would be. Even though Helena was much closer to their father than Heaven was, she wanted her mother to see her the way she saw Heaven. She wanted to be special, artistic, ethereal, and beautiful. Helena was a pretty girl. She had very nice features and a decent figure, but she would never look like Heaven. Even at the awkward age Heaven was, it was obvious she was going to be a raving beauty. Her skin was perfect, her green eyes and flaxen hair made her stand out in any crowd and now her figure was starting to take shape. Heaven's breasts were beginning to form, her waist narrowing to show off full hips above her long, colt like legs. She was reaching her full height and stood three inches taller than Helena.

The worst part of it was that Heaven was completely oblivious to her looks. She was awkward around boys and was never asked to any of the school dances. She assumed that it was because she was simply not attractive to boys or that they found her uninteresting. The truth was, they were in awe of her and none of them had the courage to approach her to ask her on a date or to escort her to a dance. She grew more beautiful every day and every day she seemed more untouchable to the young men who were just becoming teenagers themselves.

"Mom and dad will never split up," Helena answered annoyed at the question. "Dad worships mom. He will never let her go. She'll win this fight and every other one and I bet she won't be quitting her job anytime soon." She turned over on her bed putting her back to Heaven and buried her nose in the book she was reading. "Now stop bugging me," she said over her shoulder.

But Heaven wasn't convinced. She continued to worry that her parents would wind up divorced. She thought about what she would do if they asked her to choose between them. Where would they all live? Would she go with her mother and have to live someplace new? Would they leave New York? It upset her to think about and yet she couldn't stop thinking about it. It often consumed her and gave her nightmares.

As the school year came near to an end, Heaven's school arranged for some fun activities for the graduating eighth graders. There were picnics and parties and even a Ho Down where everyone got to dress like cowboys and cowgirls and square dance.

One afternoon, the whole class got to go on a field trip to the Bronx Zoo as a graduation gift. Everyone piled onto busses at around 10 am and headed to the zoo for a fun day of animals and adventures. The zoo had gotten a new acquisition. Just a couple of days before Heaven's class made the trek, the zoo had received a female Sumatran rhinoceros named Rapunzel. At the time, the zoo was one of only three in North America to hold the critically endangered species. Heaven was taken with the name Rapunzel and with the massive beast.

Maybe I'll name my first daughter Rapunzel," she mused to her best friend Heather.

"And have her named after a big, fat Rhino? You might want to think that one over," Heather said laughing.

"Well, that ruins that idea," Heaven gave her friend a fake punch on the arm as they followed the class to see the snake house.

On the way home, the bus went through a neighborhood that was on the slightly seedy side. There were lots of bars and pawn shops and a couple of places with signs that advertised topless dancing. The boys were trying to act cool and were calling out the names of some of the places.

"Jack's Pawn shop, we buy gold! Bare Bottoms Up! I wonder what they sell in there." The guys were laughing and whooping it up.

"That's enough fellas," said Coach Williams. "There are ladies present. Enough, we can all read the signs without the commentary from the peanut gallery." After that, the boys whispered and giggled quietly among themselves.

Just at the edge of the neighborhood, as it started to become somewhat nicer, there was a bar called, "The Palace". The bright blue neon sign flashed, Girls, Girls, Girls. The bus stopped on the corner at a red light right in front of The Palace and, out of the corner of Heaven's eye, she noticed a familiar figure. She turned, and there in the parking lot was her mother. Angelique was leaning on a big gold Cadillac. She was wearing a very skimpy, gold skirt and a cropped black top held up by thin spaghetti strap strings of gold to match her skirt.

What the heck is my mother doing there? Heaven thought. She stared at her hard and blinked. Maybe the woman was just a dead ringer for her mother. Heaven's mind raced. She hoped no one saw her mom or at least no one on the bus recognized her from school functions or parent's nights. Before the bus moved again, Heaven noted the street signs; Fifth and Broadway, and burned that and the name of the place into her mind. She thought long and hard about what to do. She didn't want to confront her mom only to find out it was all a big mistake and besides, if it had been her and Heaven asked her, why would she tell the truth? How would Heaven know what was actually going on? No, she had to follow her or at least go back to The Palace and wait to see if she showed up there again. School was out for summer in the next few days. She would wait for the right moment and make a plan.

It was a week before Heaven could execute her plan to follow her mother. It was the first Friday of summer vacation and, now that school was out, Angelique had been home all week. Helena had a summer job at a neighborhood pizza parlor taking orders and handing over slices. She was saving for college and worked as many hours as they would give her, but Heaven was too young to even baby sit or do odd jobs for people. Angelique had come up with some fun activities and even signed Heaven up for swim classes and a sculpture class at the local community center. On Friday, Heaven had her sculpture class which was supposed to go from 1 pm to 4 pm. Angelique told her that she would be running errands and Heaven was to go straight back home and check in with Jordan by 4:15.

"I should be home by seven and then the four of us will go out for a nice dinner someplace. Helena is off at six. Tell her to shower and change and be ready to go out. I'd rather she didn't smell like meatballs at dinner. I'm thinking Chinese Food at The Ming Garden," Angelique said.

"Sounds great, Mom."

Then she dropped Heaven off and drove away. Heaven went into the building, stood in the lobby, and counted to ten. She stepped back out onto the hot Brooklyn sidewalk and walked to the corner. She'd mapped out the busses that would take her within a few blocks of The Palace. It would take an hour to get there even though it was no more than a twenty-minute ride by car. She got lucky and caught the first bus within minutes of getting to the bus stop, and a little more than an hour and two more bus rides later, she stood in front of the strip club where she had seen the woman who resembled her mother. She was frozen in her tracks, the hot June sun beating down on her head. *What now?* She thought. *Well, she was driving her car. Wouldn't that be here somewhere if she is here?* The parking lot next to the bar had several cars in it but none were her mother's little Honda. Heaven walked through the lot and discovered it curved around behind the building. There was a grey metal door near the back of building and as she turned to go behind the bar, she saw several more cars. There, under a small oak tree, was her mom's silver Civic.

Heaven felt the blood rush to her face. She was a little woozy. *She's really here. I was right. What should I do?*

She knew she couldn't just waltz in through the front door of an establishment like this. She was thirteen years old and she was savvy enough to know that even if she looked a little older, she was clearly not old enough to get into a bar without ID. Running on adrenalin and instinct, she walked over to the grey door and gave it a gentle pull. She was a little surprised when it opened.

Heaven stepped gingerly through the door into a dark hallway. She could see a few doors to her left and straight ahead there was a curtain with colored light leaking out from beneath it. She could hear loud music coming from the main part of the building, but no one was back in the hallway at the moment, so she slowly crept toward the curtain. *I need to know what's behind that,* she said to herself. Somehow, she knew whatever she saw on the other side, would give her the answer to this riddle.

She grabbed the black velvet material and inched it to the right just enough to be able to see out beyond it. The lights were very bright; white, blue, red, and green and flashing from color to color. She could smell the cigarette and cigar smoke that was making the haze the lights illuminated. The back wall of what looked like a stage was running along to her right and she could see two floor-to-ceiling poles anchored vertically on the stage. There didn't appear to be anyone on the stage, but she heard whispers and whistles coming from the left where the crowd must have been sitting. She was about to turn away when a flash of gold swung onto one of the poles. The woman grabbed the metal bar and hoisted herself into the air, legs over her head in one swift, acrobatic move, then shimmied down onto her back, legs splayed. She wore nothing but a tiny gold mini skirt, and when she moved, the skirt rode up to reveal a thin, black, G-string that left nothing to the imagination. As the woman swung around again, Heaven got a full view of her face.

"Mom!" she said aloud without realizing it.

Angelique heard her daughter's voice and looked over to see Heaven, curtain now pulled back, standing in the hallway stage left. Calmly, she slid off the pole, waved at the crowd and walked off stage to meet her daughter.

The boos and cat whistles were deafening as Angelique made her exit. She grabbed Heaven by the hand and walked her down the hall. She knocked on one of the doors, opened it and said, "Donita, cover for me quick. I have a little emergency."

"Sure thing, Angel," said the dark-haired beauty that emerged from the dressing room. She hustled up onto the stage, looking quizzically at the teenager in Angelique's grasp as she passed.

"Let's take a drive," Angelique said. She pushed open another door to reveal a little room with a dressing table and a rack of costumes. She grabbed her purse and a light wrap, then pushing the metal door open, pulled Heaven into the bright sunlight. Heaven's eyes needed a minute to adjust from the darkness of the bar. "I can explain everything," Angelique said as they walked to the Civic.

Heaven got in and sat in the passenger seat, eyes straight ahead, her stomach churning with nerves.

What the hell was going on?

Chapter 17

Portland 1997

Selena walked back to her scooter in a daze. The good news was, she wasn't sick; quite the contrary. Doctor Lu had said she'd never seen a healthier pregnant woman. Ah, there it was though.

Pregnant! What?

Selena couldn't remember the last time she'd had sex with a man, and she was pretty sure she wasn't birthing the second coming of the Christ child, so how had this happened? Well, she knew how it happened. She was aware of how babies were made, but when, and with whom? She had been in Portland for nearly two months and she hadn't had her period that entire time. She remembered driving here across country and the couple of weeks on the road but everything before it was a blur.

"I dance for a living, Doctor Lu. Will I be able to continue that at least until I start to show?"

"I don't see why not, but I don't think you have long in that department. You're very thin and sometimes thin women don't see the effects of the baby immediately, but you should start to see pretty serious changes in your body in the coming weeks," the doctor answered.

"Weeks! Wow."

"I know it can be tough if finances are an issue. I work on a sliding scale here if you need financial assistance. Do you mind if I ask if the baby's father is in the picture?" Doctor Lu asked gently.

"No, I... no he's not. Money isn't the issue as much as working is. I like to work. I like to dance. It makes me happy, keeps me sane I guess you would say," Selena replied.

She had money. She always had money. She had to admit she wasn't always sure where it came from, but she had credit cards that never came with a bill and when she went to check the balance on her checking account, there was more than fifty thousand dollars in the account. She could afford to have a baby, but she didn't want to have one. She didn't want to raise a child on her own.

What now?

She went back to the bar to talk to Chris. Chris was so level-headed. She would know what to do. Besides, Selena couldn't keep this a secret for long. She wasn't going to be able to work, at least not as a dancer for much longer. She had just gotten comfortable at the bar. She liked the other girls and she knew most of them liked her too. They liked the way she helped them with their costumes and a few of them had come to her to ask her advice on song choice, costumes, and even dance moves. Two of the girls that danced at Bare Beauties were lesbians, and one of them, Charlie, had been mooning over Selena for a few weeks now. Selena didn't return the feelings, but she wasn't upset by the attention. She felt that love is love and she was flattered even though she wasn't interested in having a relationship with a woman; at least not with Charlie. She didn't honestly know if she liked women that way. It had never occurred to her, or at least she didn't remember having any interest along those lines, but then again, she was pregnant and had no idea who she'd been with. Had she been in a relationship with someone and if so, why did she leave and why didn't she remember him?

Charlie was like a puppy dog following Selena around, asking her out for coffee and drinks, but always with some of the other girls. She hadn't worked up the nerve to ask Selena out on a date and Selena hoped she wouldn't. It would be too awkward, and she had no intentions of leading Charlie on. The dancers were a mixed bag of sexuality; a couple of straight girls, a couple of espoused bisexuals, and Charlie and Amelie who were both declared lesbians. Selena also knew that Amelie really like Charlie, but she was only nineteen years-old and Charlie was twenty-five. Not a big age difference in the long run but at their ages, it may have seemed a huge difference.

I need to get those two together, Selena thought. *The last thing I need is a relationship, but I do love to matchmake.* Selena parked the scooter at the house. The skies were getting dark and it was going to rain hard in a bit. She pulled the little vespa around to the backyard and covered it with the thick plastic cover it had come with. She pulled it as far under the eaves as she could and scurried into the house to change and grab the keys to her caddy. She wanted to get to the bar before the skies opened completely.

She tossed on a pair of worn jeans and as soft gray sweater, pulled her thick mop of chestnut hair into a ponytail, and headed down to her car. She arrived at the bar just as the first raindrop fell, and by the time she got safely inside the building, the skies had opened. Chris was behind the bar. It was early afternoon, the lunch crowd was gone, and just a few folks were scattered around at tables near the stage watching Charlie do her thing. Denny was sitting at the bar, paperwork spread out in front of her as well as a tall glass filled with a dark beer and a half-eaten cheeseburger. She was bent down making notes on the pages, scribbling then erasing what she wrote.

"Hey, Selena," Chris waved Selena over to sit at the bar. Denny, upon hearing Selena's name, lifted her head and turned her attention to toward Chris. She watched her girlfriend like a hawk, searching for any sign that she was more interested in Selena than she should be. "Wanna drink?"

"Yeah, ginger ale please."

"Do you ever drink?" Denny asked an edge of exasperation in her voice.

"Actually, no. Now I guess I can't even if I wanted to," Selena answered. She sat in the bar stool next to Denny and placing her elbows on the bar, she dropped her head into her hands.

"What do you mean?" Chris asked placing a ginger ale in front of Selena's bowed head.

"Well guys, Doctor Lu had some news for me. She's great by the way," Selena said turning to Denny.

"Thanks for turnin' me on to her."

"Not bad news, I hope," Chris said.

"Well, it depends on how ya look at it," Selena replied. "Seems like I'm pregnant."

"What?" Both Denny and Chris spoke in unison.

"You had no idea?" Chris asked. "I mean, there has to be a guy in this picture somewhere. How far along are you?"

"Almost three months."

"Well, you must have had a clue. Who's the father?" Denny asked sharply.

"Denny!" Chris barked. "It's none of our business."

"No, it's fine," Selena said and touched Denny's arm gently. "You can ask, Denny, but I can't tell you."

"As in it's a secret or you don't know?" Denny asked her tone softening a bit.

"As in, I don't remember the last time I had sex with anyone. I guess I must have, but it's foggy. A lot of things are."

"Maybe you have some sort of amnesia or short-term memory loss," Chris suggested.

"I guess. Doesn't matter anyway. Thing is, this is what is. I'm havin' someone's baby and I have no idea what to do. I won't be able to dance for much longer guys. I'm sorry. I don't think the clientele will want to see my soon to be protruding belly."

"Well, you can still work here, if you want." Chris said.

"Doing what? You have enough cocktail waitresses. I have no idea what to do behind a bar and the last thing you want is me in the kitchen. I burn toast," Selena declared.

"Why don't you help Denny with the paperwork, scheduling, and business stuff and then maybe the two of you can put your heads together and start working on taking our shows up a notch. Denny has been trying to get the girls to organize some event nights. We want to do a queer night where we get the GLBTQ community to feel more welcome."

"That would be great," Selena answered. "Denny, you would be perfect to headline a burlesque night. With your height and those gorgeous long legs. Man, I could make costumes that would make you and the gang look like Vegas show girls."

"Yeah?" Denny perked up and was practically grinning. "I do have great legs, right babe?" she asked Chris.

"The greatest," Chris answered. "And I know you're not nuts about doing the books and schedules. If you two team up, the place will run smoother and I can focus on marketing and advertising, not to mention doing all the orders and making sure the place keeps running. What do you say, Selena? I mean the pay won't be a ton, but we can keep you in diapers and formula."

"You won't need to pay me much and I won't be needing diapers. I don't know how this happened, but I do know I'm not ready to be a mom. I can't see myself getting an abortion. I'll have the baby but when I do, I'll do what's right for the kid. There are plenty of people who are desperate to have a baby and can't."

"Okay. Well. Your body, your kid, your life. We're here for you though, whatever you need," Chris said.

"Thanks, guys. Both of you," Selena said. "Well, let's look at all that paperwork, Denny. No time like the present to get started."

Selena slid a little closer to Denny and the two of them dug into the week's schedule.

Chris shook her head and laughed. *It's a crazy world*, she thought.

***

As the weeks rolled by, Selena's pregnancy became more and more apparent. She told the other girls and they were very supportive. Denny warmed up to Selena a great deal more. Selena confided in her about Charlie's crush and Denny felt more comfortable thinking of Selena as a straight and quite pregnant woman, not one that was interested in stealing her girlfriend. For the next couple of months, they worked on putting together some great shows. They got Amelie and Charlie to work with them on the GLBTQ nights, deciding that every Thursday would be dedicated to focusing on entertainment that would bring in a crowd.

They agreed to have the bar sponsor the youth group at the gay community center and each Thursday a portion of the proceeds went to the fund that helped troubled GLBTQ kids who needed counseling, places to live, or financial assistance. Bare Beauties was packed every Thursday night. They offered a buffet dinner, drink specials, and a show that Charlie and Amelie headlined. Sometimes they would bring in a drag queen to host and Charlie would perform as a drag king stripping down to a tight cut off tank top and a special "jock strap" that had the ladies screaming and rushing the stage to hand over their cash.

The Saturday night burlesque show was Selena's favorite. She made the girls all kinds of costumes and incorporated feather boas, hats, long sleeved gloves, and sexy lingerie she designed and sewed for them. Denny was the star every Saturday night and she loved it. Her confidence was so greatly boosted by it that it made Selena proud to watch her blossom. She'd come to really like Denny and hadn't realized there was any serious jealousy over Chris. Selena had never thought of Chris that way, so it wasn't an issue in her mind. On Saturdays, Denny would host the show, announcing each girl as they came up to do their special numbers. They even hired a couple of comedians to round out the shows and Denny would have three prime numbers each performance where she would wow the crowd with her sultry dance moves and killer body, especially those long, luxurious legs. Selena worked with her to step up her dancing and she took to it like duck to water. It felt oddly familiar to Selena to teach this young woman to dance; like something she'd seen in a movie somewhere or something from a past life. *Déjà vu I think they call it,* she thought as

Denny moved around the stage following Selena's instructions.

Everything was going smoothly. Selena's belly was getting bigger by the day. She was about six months pregnant when things took a turn she could not have foreseen. It was a Sunday afternoon, she really didn't need to go to the bar, but she was bored and thought she would rather be there than sitting home. She didn't feel like driving and she'd lent the scooter to one of the girls, Nelly, who needed something to get around. It wasn't like Selena would be driving it in her present condition.

"Borrow it as long as you need," Selena had told her when Nelly said she was bussing and walking several miles a day to get to work. "I'll borrow it back once I get this kid outta me," she had joked.

So, not able to scooter and not feeling like stuffing her belly into the Caddy, she called a cab and headed to the bar. When she got there, Chris was alone and just getting the place open.

"Hey, how's our little mama?" Chris asked when she saw Selena walk through the door.

"I'm great. Well my feet are swollen, and I constantly want a jelly donut but hey, can't complain," Selena said situating herself on a bar stool.

"Your wish is my command," said Chris.

"What?"

Chris reached behind the bar and pulled up a box of jelly donuts. "Donut?" She said laughing.

"Wow! I didn't say I was coming in," Selena said surprised. "Do you just walk around with jelly donuts?"

"Well, yeah. I kind of do. They're your number one craving, right?" Chris walked around the bar and sat next to Selena placing the donut box on the bar in front of them.

"Yeah, but how did you know I was coming in?"

"I didn't, I just hoped you might," Chris said locking eyes with Selena. "I like to make you happy."

And suddenly Selena saw something she had missed. The look in Chris's eyes was unmistakable. How could she have not realized the way this woman felt about her?

"Chris, I..."

"It's okay, I know you don't feel the same way I do," Chris confessed. "And I know you want to give the baby away. I just wish things were different. I would offer you and your child the moon if you wanted it, but I know you don't," she finished.

Selena turned and took both of Chris's hand's in hers. "Oh, Chris, I am so flattered, but..."

The door to the bar swung open and in walked Denny just in time to see Chris and Selena sitting close, hand in hand. "Am I breaking something up," she asked angrily. "I didn't see your car, is this a secret meeting?

Selena dropped Chris's hands quickly.

"Don't be ridiculous, Denny," Chris said as she jumped from her stool and walked back around the bar.

"You're not breaking up a thing. Chris was trying to make me feel better about giving the baby away." Selena said as convincingly as she could. "I'm just feeling a little bad about it."

"Oh!" Denny recovered a bit. "Well, I guess that would suck. Sorry if I got the wrong idea."

"Nothing to be sorry about. I'm sorry to bend Chris's ear. I just needed to vent a little."

"It's fine. You can vent to me too if you want, you know," Denny said sheepishly.

"I do know, and I'm grateful to you both. You've been great friends to me, and I appreciate it. I'll never forget it," Selena said.

"Anytime," Chris said. But the tone in Selena's voice said that Chris's confession had caused a riff and things were likely to change.

Chapter 18

1990 Changing Tides

Angelique wielded her little Honda Civic down the city streets while Heaven sat in the passenger seat waiting for her mother to speak. They finally came to a stop near the base of the Whitestone Bridge that led into Queens. Angelique parked the car near a little park that looked over the bridge.

"Let's take a little walk," she suggested. They got out of the car and walked a little way towards a bench with a great view of the bridge. It was a warm, early summer day and there was a little breeze off the river making the trees sway a little. Angelique sat on the empty bench and motioned Heaven to sit beside her. "How much did you see?" she asked when she finally spoke.

"I saw you dancing on that pole bar in the middle of... was that a stage?"

"Yes, that was a stage," Angelique replied. "I dance on stages like that all the time."

"Does dad know?" Heaven asked.

"No, and I don't want him to know. Do you think you can keep it a secret if I explain why?"

"I can try. It's a big secret," Heaven answered as honestly as she could. "Why do you do it? Do we need the money? Are we in trouble or is Dad?"

"Not exactly, no. I mean, we can always use money. Dad's business is fine, but we need more income and he thinks I work for a friend of mine helping with her modeling agency. And I did help her. In fact, once in a while, I really do help her, so she takes my cash and gives me checks. She's a very good friend and she's known me almost all of my life. She understands why I dance."

"What do you mean, she takes your cash?" Heaven didn't understand.

"Well, I dance and people, mostly men, give me cash. Sometimes they sort of throw it at me. Sometimes they, well let's say they hand it to me while I'm dancing."

"And you like doing this?"

"I more than like doing it, I need to do it," Angelique explained. "When I was about your age, some bad things happened to me. I kind of let myself forget about those things. I met your father and we had you girls and I thought I was fine but over the last couple of years, I felt like I needed to do something. I needed to express myself. One day, I was driving down a street in Queens looking for an art supply store I'd' heard about and I saw this place, this... bar I guess you would say. Something about it made me want to go inside."

"And you did," Heaven said.

"And I did. And there were women dancing and men were watching them, and the men knew that watching was all they were allowed to do. Do you understand?"

"I think so. Were the women on a stage too?"

"Yes, and there was a big man to the side who protected the women. If a man got too close or did something the women didn't like, the big man would go over and tell the guy he had to sit down and behave or get out. I liked that. I sat and watched for several hours. I watched the girls and how they danced, and I thought, well, I can do that. I **want** to do that. So, I asked the bartender if they were hiring dancers and he said, always. He said to come back in a few days and audition. So, I did. And I've been dancing ever since."

Heaven sat in silence for several minutes. She loved her mother more than anyone on earth. She was her best friend, her teacher, her protector. If dancing made her mother happy, *who did it hurt*, she thought. "Okay, so, you leave the house and Dad thinks you're going to work at the modeling agency but you're really going to bars to dance. Even in the middle of the day?"

"Yes, I started working day shifts, but it's better at night and on weekends especially Friday and Saturday nights." Angelique got a faraway look in her eye. "The noise, and the lights are all flashing different colors and the music feels like it covers me, gets inside me, and surrounds me. I know there are people watching me; some women come but it's mostly men. I don't see them as much as I feel them, their eyes burning my skin a little. Everyone is having fun and when I go on stage, they cheer. They pay attention to me and I know I'm in control. It's my time, my stage, and no one can take it away from me."

Heaven watched her mother intently as she described a life she had no concept of until today. She knew her mother was not going to stop this duel life and she wanted to help her, protect her. She would not tell her father. She would keep the secret, and in that moment, she knew she would have to. As young as she was, she had the realization that this is what kept her mother alive and without it, she would die.

"I want to see you dance," Heaven said suddenly.

"What?" Angelique realized what Heaven was asking. "You mean you want to come to one of the clubs and watch?"

"Yes, can I, please?"

"I don't know Heaven. These are very adult places. And you wouldn't be allowed in. I suppose I could sneak you in the back sometimes."

"I got in all on my own today. How hard could it be. I would hide in the back. Sneak looks at you from some hidden spot. Please Mom, let me come with you."

Angelique took Heaven's hand in hers and sat looking at the bridge high above them and the river below. They sat like that for a long time until Angelique looked at Heaven and nodded, yes.

***

"Are you sure she won't be in the way," Jordan asked.

"Of course not, Charlotte said she could help keep the dresses straightened. We'll be back in two days. Helena is working a lot and she'll eat at work, so I left you a half a meat loaf and some cold cuts. Don't get so bogged down in your work you forget to eat."

"I won't," Jordan replied but he was already nose deep in creating a new pattern for one of his newest creations. He was working on his fall and winter lines so that he could have things ready for the next season. His summer line was doing well but he was having trouble coming up with ideas for the show he would have in early September. He was happy to have all the women in the house out of the way for a few days, though he didn't tell them that. He was feeling feisty though and was in the mood to argue because of his work struggles.

"I don't know. Maybe she needs to stay here. I'm not sure I like her hanging around with models. She'll get ideas to become one of them." Jordan said.

"Well, she's certainly pretty enough," Angelique mused.

"Yeah, that's it. She's not going," Jordan said in a harsh tone.

Angelique knew this game. Jordan was in a bad mood and there was only one way to change it. She knew sex would loosen him up and help his creative juices flowing. She moved to stand behind him and began kneading his shoulders.

"If you really don't want her to go, I'll tell her. She'll be very disappointed though. You need to relax though, baby." Angelique moved her hands down his back working the strong muscles that were tight with tension. "You're a bundle of nerves, Jordan."

"Yeah, well, these designs aren't going to jump onto the paper by themselves," he said.

Despite his rhetoric, Angelique could feel the tension releasing as she moved her subtle hand expertly over his back and down to his hips. He sighed a little as she rubbed his lower back. Jordan leaned back into her. Angelique knew it was time to make her move. She stepped away from him and quickly closed and locked the door to his studio. She grabbed his hand and pulled him from his chair over to the sofa bed that sat under the window in the studio. Jordan often slept there when he worked late into the night. She pushed him down on the sofa and began to unzip his jeans. He was barefoot, and he let her pull his jeans from his legs exposing his burgeoning arousal pushing at the soft cotton of his black boxer briefs. Though Jordan was no longer a young man, he was still very handsome and quite virile. He had a full head of hair though now it was more salt than pepper in color. Despite the fact that they had started to grow apart over the years, Angelique still found him very attractive. In moments like this, even though she had ulterior motives, she was surprised by her own ardor and wanting of him.

"Stop," he said.

"Why," Angelique asked moving back from him.

"I want to see you dance," Jordan asked. "You never dance for me anymore."

Angelique was taken aback but realized he was serious. Slowly she began to move her hips. She had not danced for Jordan in a very long time. They never went out dancing anymore. They had lost that connection and it was hard to regain it. The dancing she did now was for strangers, for men she didn't know, and that dancing made her feel powerful and in charge, something she didn't feel often with Jordan. His age and attitude often kept her feeling like a little girl around him.

As Jordan leaned back to watch her, Angelique began to hear music in her head. She began moving as if she was hearing the thumping of drums. She swung her hips and torso in a way she never would have so many years ago when she danced a far more innocent dance for her brand-new lover in her tiny apartment that was less than a mile away from where she stood now. Her movements were sultry, more sensual than he had ever seen from her.

They were the movements of someone who danced for money.

Jordan was taken aback. He didn't recognize this Angelique. Suddenly, his wife of so many years looked unfamiliar to him. He was surprised and repulsed by her.

Angelique became more and more lost in her own momentum. She could see the men in the bars, sitting front and center, throwing folding money onto the stage at her feet. She could nearly smell the smoke and hear the tinkling of glass and the light laughter of the audience. She was transported as her moves deepened.

Suddenly, she had the oddest image flash before her eyes. A little girl, dancing for an older man. The man was silver haired and naked and touching himself as the little girl moved in front of him.

"Lift your skirt for me, Angel," she heard the man say, and just as suddenly, the image disappeared. She stopped dancing and looked at Jordan who was sitting upright, staring at her as if he had never seen her before.

Jordan reached for his jeans and pulled them on. "Take Heaven with you. I have work to do. She'll just be in my way," he said as he zipped his pants. He returned to his work and didn't look up again as Angelique slowly unlocked the door and slipped out of the studio.

Heaven and Angelique grabbed their travel bags and headed out to the Civic. They drove out of the city and soon were on the New Jersey turnpike headed south.

"Atlantic City, here we come," Angelique said. There was a club just outside of Atlantic city where she often performed. She was booked to dance there Friday, and Saturday night and she got along with the girls there very well. She knew she could sneak Heaven in, and they would help keep her out of sight backstage. The stage had wings left and right of it and she could sit Heaven off to the side where she could see her dance and not be seen herself. Plus, the club was not a nude or topless club. It was more of a show bar so Heaven would see her at her best, not like some of the places she performed. She wanted her daughter to be proud of her but more importantly, she wanted Heaven to understand her and not judge her someday for this. She wanted her love and approval more than anyone in the world. She loved Jordan and Helena, but the bond with Heaven was stronger than with them. She hated to admit it, but Heaven was her soulmate like she was somehow bound to her younger daughter in a near mystical way.

Two hours later, they pulled off the Garden State Parkway onto the White Horse Pike. They drove to a little motel just a few miles outside of Atlantic City and Angelique went into the office to pay for their room. It was a cute little place, with a small swimming pool in front and clean, neat little rooms. They each had a queen-sized bed and there was a TV and a mini fridge as well.

"Okay, we have time to go get an early dinner before we go to the club. I have to work until 1 am tonight so after we eat, we're taking a nap, okay?"

"Okay," Heaven agreed. She was so happy and excited to be with her mom. She didn't think she would be able to sleep, or even eat for that matter.

"Tomorrow we'll go into Atlantic City and see the boardwalk and go to the beach. You'll love the shops and we'll get some saltwater taffy. It's the best candy in the world," Angelique said.

"I can't wait. Thank you," Heaven said.

"No, thank you. I'm so happy you're here."

They got sub sandwiches and ice-cold Cokes and brought them back to the motel room. Then they lay down and rested a bit. Neither of them could sleep so they watched an old movie on TV until it was time to go to the club. When they arrived, Angelique instructed Heaven to wait by the car out of site until she opened the back door of the club and waved to her to come in.

"When you see me come out, run like hell to the door. We don't want anyone to see you. I need to make sure the coast is clear so I can get you in and to the dressing room with the other girls."

Heaven waited patiently. She was ducked down behind the front of the passenger side of the car, watching for her mother and staying in the darkness so she wasn't seen by anyone. A couple of cars pulled in nearby, but the passengers headed straight to the front of the building and didn't see her hiding there. About ten minutes later, the back door of the club opened and there was Angelique waving wildly. Heaven popped up and sprinted for the door. In a flash, she was inside in the dark back of the club behind the stage area. Her mother whispered to be very quiet and slowly they threaded their way to a well-lit room off to the right of the stage.

"Girls, this is Heaven. Heaven, the girls," Angelique said.

"Oh, my. Isn't she beautiful," a buxom red head said.

The other women chimed in with words of praise for Heaven.

"Those eyes. Man, are they green."

"Better lock her up, Ang. You're gonna need a baseball bat to keep them away from her."

Heaven had never felt so beautiful. All these women, with their big hair, all made up and wearing skimpy, sexy clothes and they were going on and on about how pretty she was. It made her blush.

As the night wore on, the music seemed to get louder and louder. Angelique sat Heaven on a low stool backstage behind a black set of curtains where she could peek between the folds and get a good view of the stage. She sat in the darkness and watched as her mother danced in the way that only Angelique could. Heaven had seen her mother dance around the house, and she loved when her mother would teach her some of her steps, but this was different. This was all out wild abandon. At thirteen, Heaven knew what sexy was but didn't have a full understanding of the power sex wielded. Sitting there in dark, watching her mother move about the stage, using every inch of space and every part of her body to express herself, for the first time, she began to understand why men were so attracted to women. She began to recognize why her mother needed to do this, and she saw her mother in a completely different way, a more adult way.

Heaven spent some time in the dressing room, watching the women put on makeup and change their hair, clothes, and shoes as they prepared for their turn on stage. She listened to their idle chatter about boyfriends, girlfriends, husbands, even kids. They seemed rather normal to her, like anyone at any job, not exotic dancers heading off to show off their bodies and dance for strangers. It was surreal but she liked it. She felt bizarrely at home. At the end of the night, Angelique hustled Heaven out to the car, putting her big raincoat over Heaven's head and making a mad dash for the Civic. Once they got in the car, they burst out laughing at the fact that they had gotten away with it.

The next day was spent at the beach, eating hot dogs and taffy, and walking the boardwalk looking at shops and stores. They went into the lobbies of some of the hotels. Heaven liked the older hotels better than the newer ones but most of the older hotels were gone and all of the hotels had casinos now. Heaven was too young to go into any of them and she didn't mind. The noise and flashing lights were like an assault on the senses and it didn't look like anyone was having fun. People had their heads down pulling handles on slot machines, wearing grim faces, and some were even cursing at the machines when nothing fell into the tin pans below.

"Hey, I'm hungry," Angelique said. "I think we need a real meal. What do you say?"

"Sure," Heaven replied.

They hailed a man pushing a little wicker cart on wheels and hopped in to be pushed several blocks down the boardwalk. Angelique told the "driver" where to stop.

They entered another hotel lobby, this one more modern and took the elevator up a couple of floors to a restaurant looking out over the ocean. The tables were covered in white linens and had shiny silverware and crystal water glasses at every place setting. The napkins were pink and black and folded into little fans on the tables. It was only five o'clock in the evening and the place was mostly empty.

"Two please, near a window," Angelique requested.

"Of course," the hostess said and showed them to a table overlooking the Atlantic Ocean.

When the waiter came, Angelique ordered for the both of them. "We'll each have a salad with lots of vegetables, blue cheese dressing on the side. Then for the main course, we'll have your small New York strip steak with the smoked oysters on top, medium rare, and baked potatoes, lots of butter and sour cream."

"Yes, ma'am."

"And I will have a Killian's red and the young lady will have a ginger ale."

The meal was perfect, and as Heaven watched the waves washing up to the shore, the people swimming in the deep blue grey water with its white foam caps, she thought she was the luckiest girl in the world.

Chapter 19

Leaving Portland

Selena knew she couldn't continue to work at Bare Beauties, at least for now. She didn't want to hurt Chris nor did she want to be any part of anything that would break Chris and Denny up. Denny was young, but she was devoted to Chris and she was good for her. Selena knew that if she removed herself, things would go back to normal with them. This was infatuation, not real love. What Chris had with Denny was real. The fact that Selena was pregnant had brought out a parental instinct in Chris.

I think she wants kids but is afraid of what that means. Maybe once I'm gone, those two will figure that out and have one of their own. Artificial insemination has become a lot easier and more commonplace. I hope they figure it out, Selena thought. But now what?

For the next couple of days, Selena considered what to do. She didn't want to keep the baby. She didn't know who or where the father was and didn't feel that she would be able to take care of a child alone. It wasn't fair to do so, in her mind. She told her landlord that she would be leaving and hoped that if she ever came back, there might still be a vacancy with her. She packed her things and loaded up the Caddy, swinging the nose of the big gold car eastward.

Selena stopped for the night in a quaint little motel just outside of Denver Colorado. She was bored so she turned on the TV to take her mind off things. She already missed Portland, and the friends she had made there but she knew leaving was the best thing. They were running a marathon of reruns of the TV show Dallas and she decided that would be fun and engaging. The local pizzeria placed menus in the room saying they would deliver to the motel room, so she ordered a pizza, some bread sticks and a bottle of coke and set out to relax. She fell asleep with the TV on and when she woke, Dallas was still on. She took a shower, repacked her suitcase, got back into the caddy and swung southward.

Around Amarillo, she saw a sign for Tilly's homemade jams and preserves, next exit. She turned off. A mile down the road, just off Highway 27, was Tilly's. It was an old house that had been turned into a souvenir shop. When she entered the front door, it made a tinkling sound to let the proprietor know that someone had come in. A busty woman in her mid-forties with a mop of untamable red hair came out from behind the counter. She was wearing tight fitting jeans and a white shirt adorned with pink fringe.

"Hi there. Let me know if you need any help," she said, her accent thick and sweet like honey.

"Okay," Selena said. "Are you the actual, Tilly?"

"You know it," She responded cheerfully. "I am the chief jam and jelly maker and owner of this fine establishment."

She reminded Selena of a red headed version of Dolly Parton, only with that bigger than life Texan flair. She liked her immediately. *This is a person I could be friends with,* she thought. "What is there to do around here," Selena asked.

"Are you visiting, Honey?"

"Passing through but might stay a little while. I'm doing some travelling."

Tilly noticed the bulge in Selena's belly. *I wonder if this young woman is in some kind of trouble*, she thought. "All by yourself?" Tilly asked.

"Yup, just me."

"Well, there's not much to do right around here. Amarillo has a few nice nature preserves and the botanical gardens are pretty. There's a couple of museums too. I'd suggest some great bars for country music and dancing but, if I ain't bein' too forward, looks like you're in the family way."

"You think I'm pregnant? Shit, no, I'm just fat," Selena said.

"OH! oh my God, I am so sorry. I... I" Tilly's face went beet red with embarrassment.

Selena looked at her sternly for about ten seconds then burst into laughter. "I'm just messin' with ya," she said in her thick New York accent. "I'm totally knocked up."

For just a moment, Tilly was silent. Then she to burst into laughter and that was all it took. "How far along are ya, you crazy thing?"

"Almost five months."

"Is there a Mr. Crazy thing?"

"No, there is no mister anything."

"Did he leave you? Men today suck, don't they?" Tilly asked.

"I don't exactly know."

"You don't know if he left you?"

"It's a little more complicated than that. Mind if I sit down? My feet are killing me."

There were a couple of comfortable chairs in the corner of the store. Selena sat down and three hours later, she was still sitting there, working on her second cup of tea and plate of Texas barbeque Tilly had heated up for her and a biscuit with the best strawberry jam Selena had ever tasted in her life. She told Tilly all about Portland and the girls there. How she didn't remember who she had been with and whose child this was. She even told her about her last conversation with Chris and how bad she felt about leaving, even though it was the right thing to do.

"Where are you plannin' to stay tonight?" Tilly asked as Selena wound down the conversation.

"I guess I'll look for a motel. It's getting late." Selena answered. She looked outside to realize the sun was coming down fast. "Any recommendations?"

"I know this great little place. They have a lovely four poster bed with white linens and when the sun comes up, a nice big window for it to shine right on in. The breakfast is excellent too."

"Wow, sounds perfect. How do I get there?"

"Well, if you go out the front door here and look to your left, you can see the place. It's the peach colored house with the porch swing. Great place to relax and regroup."

"You mean there's a bed and breakfast on this property?"

"Well, there's a bed and no one's using it since my daughter went off to college. I eat breakfast around 8 am if that works for you and I have plenty of bacon, eggs, and a course, jam," Tilly said laughing. "And the price is right too."

"Are you inviting me to stay with you?"

"Why not? I reckon you're about my Caroline's age. It'll be fun. Kinda like havin' an exchange student. New York might as well be a foreign country around here," Tilly said with a smile. "Whatdya say? Hang out a night or two with a lonely old lady who misses having a young person in the house?

"You are not old, and I would love to."

***

The door to the shop opened and a couple of blue haired women walked in.

"Hi, Mrs. Sutton, Mrs. Sweetwater. What can I help you ladies with today," Selena asked.

"We're here to pick up the jam for the church breakfast. Did Tilly leave a box for us?" asked Mrs. Sutton.

"She sure did. It's just under the counter here," Selena tried to bend over but her belly was fighting her every step of the way. She was eight months pregnant and bending was not the easiest task.

"Oh, no, Selena. I'll get that, git on out of the way, child," said Mrs. Sweetwater rushing behind the counter to get the box and stop the very pregnant Selena from hurting herself. "Not much longer now, I guess, huh?"

"No, Ma'am. Doc says about three weeks."

"Have you picked out a name yet?"

"Charity. After all Tilly's done for me, it seemed like the perfect name."

"Well, I think she feels the same way about you. Before you came, she was chained to this place. You helpin' out has given her a little free time. And she would never have gone on that first date with Mr. Ganley if you hadn't encouraged her. Now they're out dancin' and havin' dinner a couple nights a week. You've been real good for her, Selena," said Mrs. Sutton.

"Even if you are a New Yorker," Mrs. Sweetwater chimed in making all three of them laugh.

Two weeks later, to the day, Selena was looking up at the vast Texas sky. Tilly had packed her a picnic lunch and told her to get outside for some fresh air.

"You been cooped up in this store for days. That baby of yours ain't never gonna come if she thinks the whole world looks like the inside of a jam and trinket store," Tilly said. "Go show her the great outdoors of Texas."

Selena went to a nearby park, pulled her car next to a picnic area, and plopped down on one of the old wooden benches that sat amidst the sweet-smelling grass. The sky was clear and blue with just a few wispy clouds drifting by. *This is a beautiful place*, she thought. *In some ways, I wish I could stay here forever.* Suddenly her heart began beating fast and she had a fleeting feeling of extreme joy. Selena felt the first shock of the pain that comes with a contraction. She waited for the next contraction then gathered her picnic items struggled to her feet and prepared herself for the next step. As she did, her water broke. She managed to drive herself the mile or so back to the shop. When she got there, she honked the horn loudly several times.

"What the hell is goin' on out here," Tilly said as she came out the door of the shop. One look at Selena's face and she raced back in, grabbed the little bag they had ready for this event and headed back out locking the store door as she went. "Move over, I'm driving," Tilly said.

Selena slid her big bellied self over to the passenger seat and they headed straight to the hospital. Six hours later, Charity was born. They put her in Selena's arms for a few minutes. She kissed her on the head and held her close, tears rolling down her eyes. ';

"Are you sure about this, Selena? You can both stay with me for as long as you like, honey," Tilly said.

"You are the kindest woman I have ever met, and I am so grateful for that offer, but this is the right thing to do for this little one."

A few minutes later, the woman from the adoption agency in Dallas, walked into the room and gently took Charity from Selena's arms.

"Hey," Tilly said. "I don't know what the rules are, but that little girls name is Charity. Can you see to it she gets to keep her birth given name?"

"I don't know, ma'am. But I can suggest it and try my best," said the young social worker. She turned and walked out of the hospital room as Tilly and Selena sat holding hands and silently weeping.

Three days later, Selena woke at 6 am. She left a letter on the kitchen table, and without a sound, slipped out of the house, down the porch steps of Tilly's house, and into the Caddy where she tossed the bag full of her belongings which now included a few western shirts and brown cowboy hat.

She swung the car out of the driveway, past the shop, and toward the highway that would take her east. Once again, felt the sting of hot tears on her cheeks.

"Goodbye, Tilly," she said. "I will never forget you, or what real Charity is."

Chapter 20

An Unexpected Detour - 1998

The rain pelted the roof of the gold Caddy as Heaven drove through the center of Nashville. She had seen the signs on the highway and was intrigued. She had never been to Nashville, but it looked exciting and unique. She was looking for a motel for the night and planned to spend a night or two experiencing the much-touted music scene there. The rain was making visibility poor, but she saw a sign for a Holiday Inn just off route 40 and she took the exit.

The area looked safe enough with some restaurants, bars, and shops. Heaven pulled in under the overhang in front and went inside. The motel lobby was clean, and a young, attractive, African American girl was at the counter.

"Can I help you, Ma'am?" she said with a thick Southern drawl.

"Do you have a room for a couple of nights?" Heaven asked.

"Yes, ma'am. How many people?"

"Just me."

"King bed or two doubles?"

"One bed is all I need. King would be nice. Just a clean room and hot water for a shower."

"King bed it is," she said smiling. "That'll be $47.00 a night. Room 145."

Heaven took the plastic room key from her and handed over the cash for the room. "Let's do two nights," she said.

Once she settled in her room, she realized she was starving. She took a fast shower just to refresh herself and went back out to the car. The rain had slowed to a light drizzle and Heaven decided to explore a little. She pulled the map from her glovebox and found directions to the center of town. Broadway was lit up with bars and restaurants and as the rain subsided she was able to roll down her windows and hear music coming from every open venue. She pulled into a space on a side street and walked from there. She loved the vibe of the place and soon found herself sitting at a table in a bar that served big cheeseburgers and cold beer and had a tiny stage where a young man sat playing guitar and singing. She had never heard any of the songs he was playing and assumed they were most likely his own originals.

She ordered a cheeseburger medium rare with fried onions and cheddar cheese. She was midway through the enormous meal in front of her when the musician announced that he was taking a short break and would be back in 20 minutes. She was so focused on her food that she didn't realize he was standing in front of her until she heard him speak.

"May I join you?" he asked. He was taller than he had looked sitting hunched over his guitar. His hair was jet black and his eyes steel blue. Seeing him up close, she realized he was probably no more than 22- years-old.

"Um, yeah, sure," she managed, her mouth still half full.

"Thank you," he answered. "I'm usually not this forward but I saw you sittin' here alone and thought, now there's a woman I'd like to meet. You've never been in here before, have you?"

"No, I'm just passing through. I've heard so much about Nashville, I thought I might like to stay a night or two and see what it's like."

"Are you a country music fan?"

"I'm a music fan. Can't say I know much about country music, but I like what you were playing. What's your name anyway?" she asked.

"Oh, sorry. Where are my manners. Most everybody in here knows me. I forgot to introduce myself. My name is Trent Marlboro, and you are?"

"Heaven," she said and put her hand out to shake his.

"For real? Your name is Heaven?"

"Yup, for real."

Well, I'll be. Your mama sure picked the right name for you. You look like you dropped right outta the sky."

"I bet you say that to all the girls," she said laughing.

"Nope, just the ones that look like angels with the good sense to be named Heaven. Listen I have one more set. Would it be too forward of me to ask you to stick around till I'm done? I'd love to show you around a little. There's a lot of music to hear in this town any given night. I've got friends that are playing in different bars and clubs up and down the strip. Care to get a country music education?"

"That sounds delightful," Heaven said.

"Great! Now don't go changin' your mind and up leave on me; no matter how bad my last set is. Promise?"

"I'll be right here," she said and crossed her fingers over her heart.

After Trent finished his set, they headed out of the bar, and for the rest of the night, Heaven got a real tour of the music scene of Nashville. Some of the entertainers she saw were raw and still learning their craft, some were polished and professional. The venues ranged from tiny little holes in the wall where they were holding "open mics," which she came to learn meant anyone that signed up got to play a little, to famous places like Tootsie's Orchid Lounge where so many country stars had at one time or another performed. Some of the people they heard play were very good, some not as much, but all of them were there hoping to learn and grow and become country super stars. All of them shared that dream. The music varied in style. At a place called, The Station, they even heard bluegrass music and on the walls were pictures of Dolly Parton, Gillian Welch, and Randy Travis all of whom had guest starred there at one time.

At around 1 am Heaven told Trent she needed to call it a night. She was beat and needed to sleep.

"Did you have fun?" he asked.

"I most certainly did," she answered honestly.

"Well, how about I take you to lunch tomorrow and show you Nashville by day?"

"I'd like that," Heaven answered.

They arranged to meet at the same bar she had met him at 12:30 pm and the next day she was there to pick him up. They went down to sit by the river and Trent had packed a light picnic lunch of sandwiches and ice-cold Cokes in a little cooler. He spread a blanket out on the soft grass and assisted Heaven to sit beside him.

"Trent, this is so lovely," Heaven said.

"I do try, ma'am," he answered with a wide grin.

They sat and talked like old friends for about an hour and then Trent suggested they take a ride. They went to see the Grand Old Opry and took a backstage tour. They visited the Hermitage, the home of Andrew Jackson, and the Belle Meade Plantation. By early evening they were both very hungry and Trent suggested that she had to see the opulent Opryland Hotel.

"We used to have a theme park called, Opryland right next to the hotel property but it closed last year. It was fun, pretty touristy but it brought families to town. The hotel is like nothing you've ever seen, and it just keeps getting bigger," Trent offered. "I think you'll be pretty impressed."

And she was. She had never seen anything like the inside of this hotel. The hotel's *Delta Atrium* was Cajun themed with enormous pathways that wound around though flora and fauna and there was a quarter mile-long indoor river running through it with little flatboats that carried guests along it and past a water feature that included jets which were choreographed to music. They walked along hand in hand and arrived at, The Old Hickory Steak House, which was built to resemble an antebellum-style mansion. The smell of the steak broiling was intoxicating to them both and Trent pulled Heaven inside.

"We'll never get in Trent," Heaven said. "You surely would need a reservation for a place like this."

"Do you have a reservation, sir?" the hostess asked.

"Told you so," Heaven said and poked him in the ribs jokingly.

"Yes, Trent Marlboro for two at 7:30," Trent responded.

"What?" Heaven was confused.

"Yes, sir," the hostess said, looking at her seating chart. "Follow me." She grabbed two menus and a wine list and headed toward the dining room. Trent guided a confused Heaven to follow the hostess.

"How did... what the.."

"Let's just say I was hopeful," Trent replied to her stammering. "And I pulled a few strings. I know the maître d'. He's my cousin."

Dinner was amazing. They each had a steak, Heaven had hers with smoked oysters on top, Trent choosing an enormous rib eye with a creamy horseradish sauce. They had baked potatoes and big salads and shared a peach cobbler with a Jack Daniels sauce for dessert.

"I can't move," Heaven said. "You may have to carry me to the car."

"Gladly, but who'll carry me," he responded.

"This was a simply wonderful day, Trent," Heaven said.

"What now?" Trent asked.

"Now I think I will go back to my motel and collapse. You're not playing anywhere tonight?"

"No, I have the night off. It's still early. We can go catch some music or grab a drink or…" he drifted off but smiled hopefully.

They paid the bill and headed to the car. Heaven handed the keys to Trent to drive and told him where was staying. He wielded the big machine through the streets of Nashville and pulled into the space in front of her motel room. They sat in awkward silence for a minute.

"Well, here we are," Heaven said finally. She opened her car door and stepped up to her room pulling the keys from her purse. Trent opened the driver's door and got out but stood next to the car, unsure of what to do. "Well," she said. "Are you going to stand there or come in?" she said smiling.

Trent was beside her in a flash. They entered the neat little room and Heaven dropped her purse on the dresser. Trent handed her the car keys and she place them in her purse.

"I have cold Cokes in the mini fridge. Want one?" she asked.

"Yes, please," he responded.

They were both very obviously nervous. Trent sat gingerly on the edge of the king-sized bed as Heaven handed him a Coke. She stood for a moment then sat down next to him. Trent took one long sip of his soda then moved to place it on the beside table. He tenderly reached for Heaven and pulled her into his arms. "You are so unbelievably beautiful," he said and slowly kissed her waiting lips.

They kissed for what seemed like an hour, kicking off their boots and giggling like children, enjoying the taste of one another's lips. They moved toward the center of the bed. Heaven leaned back against the headboard and took Trent' middle finger into her mouth, sliding it in and out, making him moan with lust. Trent moved to kiss the small hollows where her neck met her shoulders and slipping the material of her loose-fitting blouse away to reach her creamy skin, he slid his tongue to the space between her breasts. And as she closed her eyes and sighed, he worked his way back up her neck and kissed each of her eye lids then moved back to her mouth, easing her lips open to tease her tongue with his own.

"I could do this forever," Heaven said softly.

"Good," He said. "Because we have all the time in the world."

Trent lifted her blouse, nearly painfully slowly, over her head, making her gasp.

"You're so beautiful," Trent said locking eyes with her as she unbuttoned the pearl buttons of his tailored western shirt one by one. She leaned into him and kissed his neck then moved to kiss his chest flicking her tongue across one of the nipples.

Trent slowly lowered her onto the bed and began to remove her ruby red, lace bra taking her full breasts into his mouth teasing each of her nipples with his tongue. "Fair's fair," he said as she moaned with longing and arched her back with desire. Trent reached down to undo the top button of her jeans, slowly lowering the zipper, and then reached to undo the buttons of his own jeans. He slid her jeans to her knees as she writhed beneath him, then pulled them off revealing the red lace thong that barely covered her. He ran a finger around the edge of the lace and inside the triangular patch of silk to touch the wet throbbing space between her legs.

"Oh, God,' she cried out as he moved his fingers in and out of her.

After a few minutes, Heaven was lost in wanting, arching her back to meet his rhythmic musician's fingers.

Trent was overwhelmed with his own desire. He stood and quickly removed his jeans and underwear. Heaven sighed at the site of him, standing over her, clearly aroused. He lowered himself to cover her with his body and spread her legs wide open. He was about to enter her when Heaven placed her hands on his chest.

"I can't," she said opening her eyes.

Trent stopped and looked at her. She was crying a little, gentle tears welling up in her eyes. "What is it?" he asked softly.

"I don't know. You're wonderful and I want you. I want you inside me, but it's wrong."

"What's wrong, Heaven? I want you too. I have never met anyone like you. This is not some one-night stand. I want more than that."

"I know. You're a good man, Trent. I could fall in love with a man like you, but I think I already have."

"So, there's a guy in your life," Trent said sitting up slowly. "Of course, there would be. I was hoping there wasn't but how could there not be?" he said dejected.

"Yes, I guess so," she answered.

"Are you unsure? Is he a good guy?"

"I think he is. I can't quite remember but I think so," she answered in a half daze.

"You can't remember?" Now Trent was starting to be concerned. She seemed to be in a fog. "What do you mean you can't remember? I'm confused. Are you married or in some sort of committed relationship? Was he mean to you or did he hurt you? Why are you alone in Nashville?"

Heaven's head began to hurt from his rapid questions and the lights in the room seemed to be getting brighter. "Trent, I am so sorry. I shouldn't have brought you here. I was having such a wonderful day, and you're handsome, and funny, and so kind. I just can't have sex with you even though I know it would be amazing. I can't remember all of it, but I know if I sleep with you, I'd be hurting someone that loves me more than anything in the world and I would break something, something very important. Can you ever forgive me?"

Trent pulled her into his arms and hugged her tightly. They stayed that way for a minute then he pulled back and put one hand on each of her shoulders. Looking deeply into her eyes he said, "There's nothing to forgive. Meeting you, spending time with you, will be one of my favorite memories. If you ever decide this guy, whoever he is, is not the one, will you come look me up?"

"I'll do you one better," she said. "When you become famous, I'll be in the front row center at your biggest concert. Just watch for me."

Trent stood, saying he would hail a cab from a bar nearby. "I could use a beer anyway," he said, then gave her one last hug, slipped out the door into the cool night air, and out of her life.

Heaven slept until 8 am. She packed her things and left Nashville behind heading east.

Chapter 21

Designs, Designs, Designs 98 - 99

Chapel Hill

Heaven was on fire. She'd been home in Chapel Hill in her little cottage for a month and had not stopped drawing new designs for anything but the occasional meal, supply runs, and sleep, which she did better in the big feather bed there than anywhere else. She had stopped in on Lono for coffee and catching up, but she bolted out quickly and back to her drawing board. She was working on three entirely different clothing lines and though she had no idea where her inspiration was coming from, she was excited that the floodgates had opened so widely.

Her first series of designs were a classic, chic take on western wear, like high-end New York fashion meets cowboy/cowgirl clothing. She designed skirts made of suede with leather accents, in deep rust, cocoa brown, and even a midnight blue. Accents of reds and golds rounded out the colors and lace tied the themes together. Blouses for women were to be made of soft silk with thin wisps of fringe hanging from the sleeves, big cuffs and wide collars. She was designing boots, shoes, hats, and even handbags, something she had not previously done, but the designs she was creating needed to be head to toe.

She had an inspiration that she needed to create a clothing line for the gay, lesbian, and transgendered community.

She designed button down shirts that were tailored like a man's shirt, but form fitted for women's bodies and a line of cute boxers and stylish jeans. She created clothes that would fit a bigger body and be sexy and feminine all at the same time; dresses and evening wear with broader shoulders and ways to taper and accentuate straighter hips into sexier lines.

And shoes! She designed all kinds of shoes from boots to spiked heels.

Finally, she worked on a line of maternity clothes. She created outfits that would stretch in the belly as the women wearing them needed, but with style and elegance. She worked on some casual wear and some evening wear and a series of work suits for women professionals to wear right through their pregnancy. They were bringing new life into the world.

What could be more important. Don't they deserve great clothes, designs that are carefully considered and that will move with their growing bellies and changing bodies? She certainly thought they did.

When she finished a particularly nice design she would realize she'd been crying. *What's going on with me?* she would ask herself. But she would continue to draw and draw, ideas popping into her head rapid fire.

After three months of non-stop working, she called her brother-in-law and asked him to come and see the work. She was excited but much of this was a departure from her earlier styles and she was nervous to show off her work.

What if it wasn't up to par? She had no way to gauge if it was genius or crap. Ryan would be straight with her. He would know if she had drifted off course or had hit the mark. She called him and he was so excited to hear from her that he promised to be there as soon as possible. Thirty-six hours later, he was ringing her doorbell.

"Ryan, good to see you," Heaven said as she opened the door to let him into her cottage.

"It's always good to see you, Heaven. Helena and I worry constantly when you disappear."

I don't disappear Ryan. I just sometimes seem to lose time. It's confusing and I don't mean to worry you. I know you depend on me for these designs and money is always there when I need it. My bills are always paid. I know that's you, Ryan."

"Your bills are paid because your designs sell, Heaven. You're a genius. I can sell and market and, lord knows, your sister is a business maven, but without your designs, there would be no Angel Wear. We're grateful for you and we don't want to interfere in your life, but can't you tell me where you go? I worry for your safety."

"I don't know where I go. I just know that I always come back here. I always contact you. My mind drifts but I know how to come home, and when my brain is filled with designs, I have to get them out or my head will explode. It literally feels like the designs are objects inside my head and they're pushing from the inside to get out."

"That must be difficult for you."

"It can be, but once we get to where I am now, it's worth it. Let me show you all three of the new lines. Each line will need its own name, its own branding within Angel Wear." She took him over to her drawing board and spread each new line of designs out on the worktable adjacent to it. "I call this is Tex-Chic, a line inspired by the elegant women of Texas, but I want to see women all over the world embrace the style. Texas women are bold and brash, but they are still classy. Lots of leather, some lace accents, suede for winter wear and boots, always boots. I've designed boots that could walk the runway at New York Fashion week or go two stepping on a Friday night."

"Heaven, these are unbelievable. The way you managed to mashup the styles of a high-powered New York City look with something you'd expect to see in Dallas or Houston is like nothing I've ever seen."

They looked over dozens of designs and made decisions about materials, colors, and sizes. Next, Heaven switched gears to show off her GLBT designs.

"I think the gay community, particularly the lesbians and transgendered people are underserved when it comes to design. I've created a line for lesbians I call, *Tommi-wear*. There are lots of lesbians who dress in more traditional feminine clothing, but they can walk into any store and buy women's clothes and feel comfortable. Some of the ladies identify as more masculine and they stuff themselves into men's shirts and pants that aren't tailored for them or snazzy shoes that don't quite fit their feet. *Tommi-wear* addresses that with clothes that fit both the body and the mindset. Conversely, some of the men transitioning to female or prefer to dress in more traditionally feminine manners are still built like men, and it's hard for them to find clothes that hang right, create soft lines in the hips and buttocks, and of course shoes that look and feel good. I want to call this line, *Gurl-Wear*."

"So, both of these lines can be under the Angel Wear label, like sub labels?" Ryan asked.

"Yes, exactly!" Heaven answered her excitement mounting. "I have one more line to show you. I call this one *Expecting Angels*. Double entendre; the women who are expecting are angels to us and they are expecting little angels."

Heaven showed Ryan the elegant and lovely clothes she had designed for pregnant woman and he was moved by how beautiful the clothes were. By the time she flipped to the last drawing, they were both crying.

"Ryan, why are you so upset?" Heaven asked wiping tears from her own eyes.

"These are wonderful, Heaven. We will make so many women happy with these clothes. I'm moved by what you've done here."

"What about you, Ryan? Have you and Helena talked about having kids someday?"

"We have, and she is dead set against it."

"And you're in favor, I take it," Heaven stated.

"Very much so. Maybe your designs will spark something in her. She is a powerful and brilliant woman and I love her more than I could ever imagine loving anyone, but there's something I can't get past to get to her. It's like she has a wall up. I manage to get over the wall, and there's a door, and I manage to break down the door, and there's another wall. I want children, yes, but I want Helena more. If she never wants them, I'll be okay with that."

"I'm sorry," Heaven said touching his arm gently. "We have skeletons, my sister and me. I must have buried mine a long time ago. I can't remember where though. I think Helena keeps hers hanging in the closet next to her best suits and looks at them every day."

"Yes, I think so," he agreed. "I can't wait for her to see these. She's been focused on your father's designs this year. She's doing her best to keep him relevant and current, but he's stuck in his ways. His designs are adequate, and we sell some of his work but not in the way your designs sell."

At the mention of her father, Heaven's body stiffened. "Father will always be father," she said.

"Yes, I suppose he will. He'll do things his way till he dies, and Helena will do what she can to help him and keep him as happy as possible. But you, my dear, you are a rich woman. And these new designs are going to make us all very wealthy. I'll take good care of them and I transferred money into your account, of course, a hundred thousand dollars. Just keep using the corporate credit card I gave you for any expenses you have as well. The accountant will always pay it, and all you need to do is call and I'll make sure you have all the money you ever need," he said. "We love you, Heaven. Helena and I will never force you to come home or invade your privacy, but know that wherever you are, we have you in our hearts and are praying to hear from you."

"I love you both, Ryan, even if Helena can't believe that, it's true. She's my sister and I miss her, but it's best for both of us this way, at least for now. Thanks for being there for both of us."

"Anytime, Sis. Someday, it will all work itself out. It always does."

"Always?" Heaven asked.

"Always. Have a little faith."

Ryan stayed the night, sleeping in the spare bedroom. Early the next morning, Heaven made him as strong cup of coffee and some scrambled eggs and cheese. He ate quickly, thanked her, and left with copies of her new designs.

Heaven went back to bed with a terrible migraine.

***

Tillie was on I40 heading to Dallas, her white Stetson sitting next to her on the seat of the gold caddy. She had her brand-new ID that Paul made for her. She could not for the life of her remember how she'd lost hers, but she remembered that Paul was someone who could fix that for her.

She wasn't sure why, but she needed to be in Dallas. She felt like she'd left something behind there, and her heart told her it was where she needed to be.

Chapter 22

1991 The Year Everything Changed

"Where is she?" Jordan asked Heaven. "I know you know the truth. I've put up with her disappearing act for the last time. I trusted her but I realize I am an idiot. She's been gone nearly a week, no calls, no messages, so I called the agency looking for her. The receptionist had never heard of her. Where is she really, Heaven?"

"I don't know, father. She could be a lot of places."

"Well, give me one of them," he shouted, his anger rising.

Heaven looked down at her shoes. She had a pretty good idea where Angelique was. For the past several months she had been going with her on away trips and often went to the local clubs with her on weekend nights or after school. Jordan knew that Heaven had been with her mom and he thought she was learning about fashion design and modelling. Heaven was certainly pretty enough to model. The fact that she had been going with her mother made the lie more plausible. But Heaven knew something else she didn't want to know. She'd seen her mother lean over a thin line of white powder on the table in her dressing room. She sucked it up into her nostril with a rolled-up bill. She didn't see Heaven standing in the doorway. She was busy laughing with another one of the dancers who took her turn next. Heaven knew those were drugs and her mother's behavior had begun to change. She knew she needed to tell her father, but if she did, she would break her mother's trust.

"Heaven!" Her father shouted. "Tell me the truth or so help me God!" He lifted his hand as if he were going to slap her.

"Don't!" Helena walked into the room. "Don't hit her. Let me talk to her."

Jordan backed down at the site of his older daughter. He respected Helena and trusted that she could get Heaven to talk to her more easily.

"All right. I am going to the studio. I will give you both ten minute and then I want answers." He stormed off leaving the girls alone.

"Tell me where she is Heaven. He's losing his mind and he will beat the living hell out of you. Trust me, I will let him," Helena said.

"I can't tell you, Helena. Mother will hate me."

"Mother may be dead for all we know. She's been gone for six days now. She was supposed to be gone over night to work with the agency which she apparently never worked for. This is a giant mess. You're not helping her by trying to protect her. Where is she!?"

"I don't know for sure," Heaven said with a deep sigh. "But I know a few places she could be."

Heaven told Helena everything. She explained Angelique's reason for wanting to dance and she listed the places she had been with her that were possibilities for where she had gone this time. She knew the name of three of the clubs. Helena wrote them down and told her to go to her room and lock the door.

"He's going to lose it when he hears this, and we are going to have to look these places up and see if she is at any of them. Your best bet is to stay out of sight and out of his way."

"Helena!" Heaven said stopping her sister before she could leave. "There's one other thing you need to know but please don't tell Father just yet."

"What is it?"

"I'm afraid Mom may be doing some drugs. I saw her doing something and I looked it up. I think she is doing a drug called Cocaine. It's very bad for you."

"Jesus! Go to your room! I'll handle Dad."

After several phone calls, they got someone on the phone at the Club in Atlantic City where Angelique had taken Heaven on their first trip together.

"If you mean Angel, yeah, she's performing here. But she's not due in till 9 pm," the man on the phone told Jordan.

It was only 4 pm and Atlantic City was less than a 3-hour ride away. Jordan got the address of the club and told Helena to watch Heaven.

"Don't leave here for anything," he said.

"Are you sure you don't want me to come with you?" Helena asked.

"I doubt it's the kind of place I would want you to see, Helena. I'm going to get your mother and put an end to whatever insanity this is."

She did not tell him about the drugs. She gave him a hug and told him to drive safe and went to her room. She had final exams coming up and she wanted to get to college and put all of this behind her. She'd been accepted to Warton as she had always wanted, and Philadelphia was far enough away to live there but close enough to come home on weekends and holidays when her father needed her to work on the business. She planned to major in economics then get her Master's in Business Administration and help Jordan grow his design company when she graduated. She had big plans and she just wished her mother would not foul things up.

Why can't she be normal, she asked herself. *If she's into drugs, she can ruin our entire lives. Maybe we'd all be better off if she has died.* Helena realized what a terrible thought that was to have but she was sick of her mother's behavior. She had been disappearing more and more over the last two years. She rarely cooked, and there was never enough food in the house anyway. She spent all of her time at home locked in her own office with Heaven working on whatever they were up to. She didn't want her mother to die. Guilt washed over her for her previous thought, but she knew things had to change. *Dancing? What the hell was she doing dancing,* she thought. *This can't end well.*

Jordan parked on the far side of the building and walked into the night club. It was 8:15 pm. He had killed some time sitting in a nearby diner drinking coffee and pushing a piece of apple pie around on a plate. He wanted to be there when she arrived. He wanted to see for himself the mess his wife had become. He had a plan of action and waiting at a table near enough to witness all of this but dark enough to not be noticed was the first part of his mission.

He ordered a gin and tonic, then another. He watched the girls on the stage, strutting around, sliding up and down the pole, gyrating for the men that handed them dollar bills. The bar started to slowly fill up. Men and some women were drifting in, and soon there wasn't an empty table to be had. At exactly 9 pm, a man stepped out on the stage with a microphone in hand.

"Good evening, good evening!" He said jovially. "Are you ready for the show?" The crowd cheered and whistled in response. "That's the spirit. We have some awesome and very sexy ladies here for you tonight. Make them feel welcome and remember, nothing says we love you more than big bills. First up, Ginger!"

A woman came out on stage wearing a green costume that contrasted her flaming red hair. She danced with a chair, her movements mimicking sexual positions. She removed her satin tee shirt to reveal a flimsy lace bra underneath and then slowly stripped down to nothing but a tiny green G string. By the time she finished, the crowd was throwing money at her and rushing the stage to place twenty-dollar bills in the little triangle of material that was all that covered her private parts. As the song ended, she scooped up all the bills and ran off stage to the calls of more, more!

The announcer came back on and picked up a few bills she had missed. "How about that Ginger. Are you ready for more?" he asked. Loud cries of yeah, and you bet came from the crowd. "Get off the stage. We want Angel!" came a cry from the crowd. At that, a chant started. "Angel, Angel, Angel."

"You asked for it, you got it. Here she is folks. Our one and only, Angel."

The music started and out strutted Angelique aka Angel. It was a song called Darling Nikki by Prince from a few years back off his Purple Rain album and the lyrics gave Angel plenty to work with.

I knew a girl named Nikki
I guess you could say she was a sex fiend
I met her in a motel lobby
Masturbating with a magazine
She said how'd you like to waste some time
And I could not resist when I saw little Nikki grind

Angel moved to every word of the song, grinding and lifting herself up and off the ground, floating and spinning around the vertical metal poles planted on the left and right sides of the stage. Jordan couldn't help but be mesmerized for a few minutes. She was amazing. He flashed back to the way she danced when they were first dating, and he froze unable to move a muscle. But as the song became raunchier, and built up to a fevered pitch, his wife began removing more and more of her costume until, like Ginger, she was in nothing but a tiny strip of bright white lace. Men were approaching her and tossing money at her like mad, reaching for her on the chance to grope her or just touch her.

Jordan saw red. He stood up kicking the chair out from beneath him and stormed the stage. In one easy leap, he landed next to his wife and grabbing her by the hair, dragged her off into the crowd.

The bouncers were on him so fast he didn't know what hit him. They tossed him to the ground, then one huge man with long greasy hair lifted him up and used him like a battering ram to push through the crowd. Jordan's head hit the door as the man shoved him outside, tossing him into the air and onto the asphalt driveway. For a moment, he passed out. He came to a second later to hear shouting.

"… And stay out or I'll call the cops. Get outta here, you old, creep." The big guy kicked Jordan in the ribs for good measure and stood waiting for him to get up and go. Slowly, Jordan managed to crawl to his knees and shakily rise to his feet. There were three bouncers out there now, one bigger than the other, towering over him.

"She's my wife," he said turning to meet the gaze of the greasy haired man.

"I don't care if she's your sainted mother from Ireland. I'll give you to the counta three to get the hell off this property." He stood arms crossed, flanked by his two buddies, all of them dressed in tight black tee shirts, black chinos and heavy black boots.

"Please tell her to come home," Jordan managed, tears stinging his eyes as he slumped away towards his car, defeated.

"Yeah, we'll do that," another of the guys said and all three of them started laughing.

Jordan climbed into his car and sat for a moment. He wanted to go back into the bar and get his wife, but how? Those bouncers would be waiting for him and this time they would not go as easy on him. He couldn't afford to have the police involved. He had a reputation to consider and if the word got out about Angelique dancing and him being arrested trying to stop her, it could severely hurt his position in the fashion world.

He stopped at a convenience store and bought some Tylenol and a large can of beer to wash down the pills in hopes of stopping the throbbing in his head. He slowly drove back to Brooklyn unsure what to do.

He could not un-see what he had seen.

Chapter 23:

Tillie 1999

Beau Roland was standing outside the Palace Adult Entertainment Club looking up at the sky. Beau was the owner of that fine establishment and he was stressing the weather because the forecast called for a terrible storm, chock full of the possibility of tornadoes.

His son 8-year-old son, Andy tugged at the sleeve of his bright red Western shirt. "Pa, are we gonna have to go down in the storm cellar?"

"I don't know. Quit buggin' me. Cain't you see I got a lot on my mind right about now? We cain't afford no freaking tornado ripping up the club."

"I know, Pa. I'll help if'n we have to though. I can get some canned goods and water together. You want I should do that?"

"Yeah, yeah, go do that. Keep you outta my hair for a bit anyway."

With that, Andy ran back into the club. He hustled off to the little kitchen in back and found a couple of old potato sacks. He started loading them up with bottled waters, some cans of beans and soup, a church key, and anything he could find that would be easy to carry, eat or drink.

Outside, Beau was still pacing and looking up when a big gold Caddy swung into the parking lot. His attention switched from storm watching to girl watching as a long, perfectly shaped pair of legs emerged from the driver's side of the Cadillac. The legs in question wore calf high white leather boots with pink fringe, and as she emerged, a pair of pink and white striped short shorts appeared followed by a gorgeous red head with a figure a man would go to war for.

"I'll be damned," he said aloud then whistled a low whistle shaking his head at this raving beauty walking toward him.

"Howdy," she drawled. "You know where I might find the owner of this here club?"

"You're lookin' at him. How can I help you, gorgeous?"

"And you are?" she said.

"Oh! Beau, Beau Roland. What's yer name darlin'?"

"Well, it ain't Darlin', it's Tillie, spelled like Millie with an ie. You can help me by giving me a job here."

"You a dancer?" He asked. "Or are you looking to cocktail waitress?"

"Oh, I'm a dancer. Just got into town and lookin' fer the right place. You think this might be it?" She was brazen but she wore a big smile and the twinkle in her eyes said she was almost never serious.

"Where you comin' from?" Beau asked.

"Amarillo," she answered.

"You do realize we have a storm comin'?"

"I heard the news a few minutes ago on the car radio. You closin' the club for the night?"

"Gonna have to. I sent all the girls home. My boy and I are fixen to go down in the storm cellar as soon as the rain starts. You got someplace safe to go, Ms. Tillie?"

"Not yet. Just got here. I was thinkin' I'd get a job first then look for a room someplace."

"Well, ain't you the ambitious one. You want to come in and see the place? Maybe have a beer or two? We got an hour, tops but hell, anyone as pretty as you can have my last hour on earth if it comes to that."

They went inside and Beau gave Tillie the nickel tour. The bar was a bit worn but it had good bones. The stage was a good size and there were two poles planted left and right. The dressing rooms were pretty dismal with old wooden chairs and a wooded counter that had mirrors on the wall behind it every three feet. They were set up to have at least six women in there at one time doing makeup and changing. There were no lockers or cubbies for the girl's belongings though. Tillie was making mental notes as they moved back to the front of the house and then into the kitchen where Andy was still hunting down supplies. He had stopped to help himself to a Yoo Hoo and was sitting on the metal counter, legs dangling, potato sacks by his side, when they walked in.

"Git down off a there!" Beau barked at him. "Ain't you supposed to be loadin' us up supplies?"

"Yes, Pa," Andy said jumping down off the counter. "I'll got a bunch a stuff already."

"Say hello to Tillie. Tillie, this here's my boy, Andy. He's a pain in the ass."

"Hello, Andy," Tillie said extending her hand to shake the little boy's. "I bet you aren't that much of a pain, are you?" she said laughing.

"No, Ma'am. I really am. Ask Pa."

With that, Tillie burst out laughing. "Well, if you say so." Just then, a loud clap of thunder shook the building. Tillie practically jumped into Beau's arms.

"Well, I guess that's our cue. C'mon, you two. We need to head to the storm cellar, now," Beau commanded. They headed back into the main room, and as they passed the bar, Beau asked them to wait a second. He grabbed two flashlights, a 6-pack of beer, a half empty bottle of tequila, and two plastic cups. "Ammunition," he said, and they rushed out the front door into the area behind the parking lot where two grey metal doors jutted up from the ground. Beau pulled a set of keys from his pocket and unlocked the bolt lock then pulled the handles up and hurried his son and Tillie down into the dark room below.

Once they got down there, he flipped on both of the flashlights and handed one to Tilly. Then he located the little battery-operated lights that hung on hooks on either side of the walls.

It was actually pretty cozy in the little cellar. There was a card table with four chairs and a couple of folding camp chairs as well. The walls were carved out of dirt, but cement bricks were stacked up against each wall to make the room feel solid.

Andy dumped the contents of his sacks onto the card table and grabbed a bottle of water. The wind rattled the doors and the rain was coming down harder hitting the metal with loud thumping sounds. They were deep enough underground that the muffled sound of thunder was hardly even noticeable.

"Beer?" Beau said, cracking one for himself and holding another out for Tillie. She took the ice-cold Heineken from him and they clinked bottles in a wordless toast.

"Well, not much to do but wait, I guess," Tillie said. "I appreciate you including me in this little claustrophobic adventure. Not sure where I would have gone."

"We can play cards," Andy said hopefully. He pulled a deck of cards from the back pocket of his jeans.

"No one wants to play a silly card game," Beau barked.

"Oh, I don't know," Tillie said nervously. "Might take my mind off the fact that my precious car is out in your parking lot waitin' to see if the wicked witch of he north is coming to drive it to Oz!"

"There might be witches out there?" Andy asked her wide-eyed.

"You never seen The Wizard of Oz movie?" Tillie asked.

"We don't see no movies, miss. Pa and me's got to run the bar."

"You sound like a very responsible young fella, Andy. You like helpin' your Pa run the bar?"

"He don't run much other than his mouth," Beau said sucking back the last of his beer and starting to crack a second. He reached for the tequila bottle and poured a hefty shot into each of the plastic cups holding one out for Tillie.

"I'm good for now. I still got this beer," she responded. "Maybe a little later, especially if a little later, turns into hours down here."

"Suit yourself," Beau responded and proceeded to drink both shots, one right after the other.

Tillie opted to play cards with Andy. A few minutes later, they heard what sounded like a freight train in the distance. Growing more worried, she acquiesced and took one small shot of tequila and one more beer which she nursed for the remaining hour they were in the root cellar. She also ate a Snickers bar and a bag of potato chips that Andy offered her, but she was still feeling a little tipsy as she sipped her second beer.

"Hey, winds died down a lot. Rains let up too," Beau said. "I'm gonna sneak my head out and see what's what." He climbed up the steps, pulled back the bolt that locked in the doors, and slowly pushed open one of the heavy metal hatches to peer outside. "Well, I'll be damned."

"What is it Pa?"

"It's the most beautiful day I've seen in months. Storms passed. We're good."

"Thank God!" Tillie said. "My car still there?"

"Oh no. That's been swept away but the club is intact."

"What?" she said and pushed past him up the steps and out into the sunlight. She ran to the parking lot and saw that her car was exactly as she'd left it, in perfect shape. Andy and Beau were right on her heels and she turned to face Beau. "Ha! Very funny."

"Sorry, I had to," Beau said chuckling. "Now, let's go inside and see if you can actually dance."

Tillie danced for Beau, and in his entire life, he had never seen a dancer like her. Her moves were sultry and yet, almost innocent. He fell like a ton of bricks and hired her on the spot. The other girls were immediately jealous.

Bobbie, who had been dancing at the club since Andy was born, was beside herself. "Who the hell is this woman, Beau? Where did she come from, what bars has she danced in? You just up and hired a total stranger on accounta she's pretty?" Bobbie asked.

"She's more than pretty and you know it. None a ya'll can dance like that."

"Screw you, Beau. I quit," she said.

"No, ya don't. You don't quit, cause you know this is the best place to dance around."

"Oh really, you think so," Bonnie said smartly. "This place is a dump compared to half the clubs in Dallas. I'll give you it ain't the worst but it sure ain't the best."

"Now, Bonnie," Beau said sweetly. "You know your still by best girl. It's just that Tillie, well, she's got a little extra something. Okay, a lotta extra something. Give her a chance. You might come to like her, and I got a feeling once we let her loose on this place, we're gonna get a lot more customers and a better class of people. She's got something special. Why not cash in on it?"

What he said was true and it hit home with Bonnie. One good dancer could bring in a bigger and even better crowd and that meant more drinking, more spending, more tips. The bartenders would be happier, and Beau would likely feel more generous if he was making more money. She stood there, toe to toe with him for a few seconds more then dropped her attitude a little.

"Well… Okay, I'll stay. But you better be right. This better bring in a better class of cowboys and a lot more money," she said. "I ain't stayin' for your good looks."

It took a little while but in a couple of months, even Bonnie came around to liking Tillie. She was friendly and boisterous and treated the other dancers like sisters. Tillie could hold her liquor and loved a good steak dinner more than anything. She ate her steak well-done and when she could get them, smoked oysters on top, with a loaded baked potato and a big salad on the side.

She started a tradition of getting as many of the girls as could to do Sunday dinner together. The bar was closed on Sundays until 6 pm. The church going crowd wasn't about to go to a bar until services and Sunday supper were well over, so Tillie got everyone to bring a potluck dish to the bar and they all ate together every Sunday afternoon.

The drug of choice was liquor amongst these girls, and thankfully, nearly none of them were into heavy drugs. They were mostly single moms and girls who hadn't finished high school, from broken homes and poverty. They needed the money, and this was the best way to get it.

Tillie soon realized Beau had a serious drinking problem, and by the third or fourth month she was dancing there, Beau's son, Andy had gotten very attached to her. His mama had passed away when he was five and he barely remembered her. Andy followed Tillie around like a puppy dog and she did what she could to help the boy.

Beau had an obvious thing for Tillie. He asked her out nearly every week, and every week, she turned him down.

"Why won't you give me a chance?" Beau asked. "I'm a nice guy. I ain't altogether ugly. I run a good business, make good money. We could be good together. And the boy likes you."

"That's all true, Beau, but I am not looking to date anyone and the last thing I want is an instant family. Besides, you drink too damn much."

"You drink too."

"I do drink some, but I know when to stop. Can you say the same? You get so drunk you can't stand up most weekends. You've got a young son. You need to think about his future. You need to be a role model for him. I'll tell you what, I ain't never gonna date you, but I'll help you. I'll quit drinkin' if you will."

"If I do, will you go out with me?"

"NO, you stubborn thing. But I'll be your friend and I'll help raise that boy of yours some. I'll make sure he gets his homework done, and that he has clean clothes to wear to school, and that he eats better. You can't just give the kid happy meals and pizza. I'll cook for both of you twice a week and make sure your kitchen is stocked with healthy snacks and food for him to take to school for his lunches. Deal?"

Beau looked down at his shoes. "Deal, I guess. I'm not gonna give up on you though, but I guess I could use some help with the boy. He's gettin' bigger and he needs more attention than I know how to give him. His mother knew how to do all that. I haven't done so great with it since…"

"I know and it's gonna be okay. You got a lot of people in this bar that'll help you, Beau. I know Bonnie and the rest of the girls would pitch in more if you asked for the help, especially Bonnie. I think she's sweet on you, Beau. She's a real nice woman."

"She ain't you."

"Well, ya cain't have me," Tillie laughed. "Not as a girlfriend, but you have me as a friend."

Chapter 24

2003

"Happy birthday, dear Andy. Happy birthday to you," the girls sang at the top of their lungs. It was hard for Tillie to believe Andy was turning 11. Harder to believe she'd been dancing at the bar and helping raise him for the last three years. In that time, the Palace Adult Entertainment Club, now just called The Palace, had changed as much as Andy had. Beau fought it at nearly every turn, but slowly, with the help of the women who danced there, they turned what was not much better than a strip club, into a real entertainment club. The place was clean, the dressing rooms were kept neat and organized, and the girls had more self-respect than they had ever had before. They thought about their song choices and costumes and worked on real dance moves. They took some pride of ownership in the place and several of them moved on to go back to school or take other jobs, some working part-time at the bar to supplement their income until they didn't need to anymore.

Bonnie quit dancing altogether and got her license to sell real estate. She sold Mary Kay on the side and came in every week with new products for the girls to try and make-up tips and samples for them. Tillie knew that she also came in to see Beau.

Why is that man so stubborn, she thought. *Bonnie is a catch and she's crazy about him, God knows why.*

Beau tried to quit drinking, even attending AA meetings, but he fell off the wagon after a few months each time. He had more one-month sober chips than any other attendee. But each time he fell, Tillie pushed him back up for Andy's sake. Andy was turning into a fine young man. He did very well in school, particularly in mathematics, and he was starting to help Beau with the books at the bar.

Tillie still cooked for them twice a week as promised and rarely drank herself. She'd kept to her promise and stuck to her guns, fending off Beau's continued efforts for her to change her mind and be with him romantically.

"Never gonna happen, Beau. Why can't you get that through your head?"

"Because there's no woman on earth like you, Tillie. I'm just askin' for a chance."

"Beau, this is becoming difficult. I love Andy and I care about you. You're a good man. You're just a little misguided. You're not good when you drink. You've got a mean streak in ya, Beau, and it comes out when you're drinking. You need to get some help."

"You mean like a shrink or something? I ain't crazy."

"No, you're not but I think something broke in ya when Andy's mom died. You never talk about her or how she died. Maybe you need to talk to someone about it."

"You remind me of her," Beau said sadly. "She was a red head too. Fiery and crazy. But she died, and that's that. I've moved on. I don't think about it anymore."

"That's a crock and you know it. I bet you think about her every day. And I'm not her, Beau. Being with me, isn't gonna bring her back."

"That's enough about her," Beau said, raising his voice. "I don't need to talk about her to you, or some fancy head shrinker, or anyone else. She's dead, I'm not, next subject."

"Alright, Beau. I won't bring it up again."

Bonnie stopped in to bring some new Mary Kay samples for the girls and drop off her orders for those that had purchased from her. She was about to leave when Tillie asked her if she had a moment to talk.

"Any chance you and I could slip out for a cup of coffee," Tillie said quietly. "I want to ask you something but not here and I don't want Beau to know. Can you meet me at the diner down the street in about 10 minutes?

"Sure, Tillie," she said.

"I'll slip out in a couple of minutes and meet you," Tillie said.

A few minutes later, Tillie told Beau that she needed to go to the drug store for some "female stuff," and headed down to the diner. Bonnie was sitting in a booth near the back of the place and motioned Tillie over when she saw her walk in.

"Why all the secrecy?" Bonnie asked once Tillie was seated and had ordered a coffee.

"We've known each other a couple of years now and I'd like to think we've come to be friends," Tillie offered.

"Yes, we might have had a rocky start, but to be honest, that was just my jealousy getting in the way. I admire you Tillie, and I do consider you a friend."

"Thanks, I feel the same way. It's pretty impressive the way you've changed your life, become a businessperson, and are doin' so well. I'm so happy for you."

"You had a lot to do with that."

"Me? How so?" Tillie asked.

"Your commitment to the bar, to Andy, to the other girls, me included, the way you helped shape the place, made it more upscale and respectable gave me the courage to try something for myself. I know Beau is in love with you, and I admit, that hurt at first, but I can't say I blame him."

"There is nothing between Beau and me. Never has been, never will be, but I do love Andy and I've loved every minute of watching him grow up."

"So, I don't think you wanted to talk to me about Andy. What's on your mind?" Bonnie asked.

"It's about Andy's mom. Beau keeps trying to get sober, but he can't sustain it. He falls off the wagon more than he's on it. I've tried to talk to him about his wife's death a few times, but he clams up. I think that might be the reason he drinks so much. Do you know anything about her or how she died?"

"Oh, yes I do. I knew Cecelia very well. She was a wild red head, younger than Beau by about five or six years. She walked in one day and said she was a dancer. She wasn't!" Bonnie laughed. "But she was willing, and she was fun."

"So, she worked at the club?"

"Yup, I taught her how to dance myself, taught her how to work the pole, and the men in the audience. She was so damned pretty that frankly, she could have just stood there in a G string and smiled and the guys would still have tossed their last dollar at her."

"How did she die?" Tilly asked.

"That is not a pretty story," Bonnie said.

"I would like to help Beau. And I want Andy to have a sober father, but I don't know if that's possible. Maybe if I understood what made Beau drink, I could help him stop."

"I doubt that even you could stop him, but I'll tell you the story. Beau was a happy guy. He drank then too, but for fun, and he could hold his liquor. He loved Cecilia more than any man I have ever seen love a woman. When she got pregnant, he stood on the bar and announced, *open bar*, to the entire club. He bought everyone drinks all night and he even went up on stage and did a little pole dance of his own. It was pretty cute."

"So, was it, cancer or an accident?"

"Something like that. There's more than one kind of cancer, friend. There was this guy who came into the club all the time. Rudy," Bonnie said his name with obvious disgust. "He went nuts for Cecelia. Cecelia didn't give Rudy the time of day, but he kept coming around, kept givin' her twenties and fifties. Beau didn't think anything of it. He figured he and Cecelia were good. He didn't think she'd give this guy Rudy a look and he was just some dumb rube givin' his wife big tips like a fool. What he didn't know was that Rudy was meeting Cecelia outside the bar. Turned out he was a drug dealer and a stupid one because he used as well. She took off with him one afternoon and didn't come back. Two weeks later, she and Rudy turned up dead in a motel room in Alabama. Overdosed. Beau went crazy when she went missing. He had the police and even the FBI out looking for her. It was the worst two weeks of any of our lives trying to keep him calm and keeping Andy from wondering where his mama was. But when she turned up dead with Rudy, Beau never said another word about her. Andy had just turned five. He never talked to the child about her either. When Andy asked, he would just say, your mama went to be with the angels, but I think he wanted to say, with the devil. I tried to get him to talk about her that first year, but he shut me down so fast, I just gave up."

"My God, no wonder he drinks. That explains a lot."

"Yeah. He was a good man, once. And he's still a decent man, he's just hurting and broken. I think it's lucky that Andy was so young. He'll probably never have to know the truth. Why tell him?"

"I agree. But Beau is never gonna get sober and I've seen him lose his temper way too many times. I think he needs help."

"Good luck with that, girl. I gotta go. I'm showin' a house to a nice young couple this afternoon."

"Good luck and thanks for tellin' me all of that."

Tillie went back to the club and slipped in the back door. She was in the dressing room getting ready for her stage time when Beau stuck his head in.

"You doin' alright?" He asked her.

"I'm fine, why?"

"Just checkin'. We still on for dinner tomorrow night at your house?"

"Yup, I'm makin' Andy's favorite, Tillie's nearly famous Mac and Cheese."

"I'm sure he'll love that."

The next night, at 6:30 pm, Tillie's doorbell rang. Beau was standing there with a bouquet of fresh wildflowers, but Andy was not in tow.

"Where is Andy?"

"I left him with his babysitter," Beau said. He was slurring his words and had clearly been drinking.

"Beau, I think you need to leave. You're drunk and..."

Before she could say another word, Beau had pushed himself into her apartment and shut the door behind him.

Tillie backed up, suddenly frightened. Beau was more intoxicated than she had realized at first.

"NO! I need to talk to you," Beau said and pushed past her to the living room.

"What is it Beau? What's going on?"

"It's six years to the day. This very day, six years ago."

"What is Beau? What was six years ago?"

"You wanted to know about my wife, about Cecilia and what happened to her. Well, I'm gonna tell you what happened to her."

For the next ten minutes, Beau described his wife, how their lives had been before Rudy showed up, her disappearance, and finally how he had gotten the call that she was dead in a flea bag motel, overdosed and in bed naked, with Rudy. Beau got angrier and angrier with every detail. When he was done telling the story, he went to Tilly, who was sitting across from him in an old easy chair. At first, he lay his head in her lap and cried. She ran her fingers through his hair, feeling terribly sorry for him. But after he stopped sobbing, he started rubbing her calves, and then, as he rose up a little, he moved to run his hands up her thighs and pushed himself toward her, pinning her into the chair. He began trying to kiss her neck and mouth, but she put her hands on his chest and did her best to push him away.

"Beau, get off me," she cried out, but the weight of him was greater than her strength and he kept pushing toward her. In one swift move, he yanked her from the chair and pulled her down onto the floor. He pushed up her skirt and was grabbing at her breast with one hand, while trying to undo the zipper of his jeans.

"Cecilia, why?" he cried out.

"Stop it Beau, I'm not Cecilia. You don't want to do this," she screamed. She felt around the floor for something to hit him with. In the second she had, while he was wrestling with his zipper, she felt something solid and grabbed it. It was one of her boots. She grabbed hold of it and began hitting him in the head with the hard heel. He lifted up trying to cover his head from the blows just long enough for her to wriggle free. On the coffee table, there was a thick silver candlestick. With one swift swing, Tillie hit Beau in his right temple. He toppled over onto his side, blood streaming from his head.

Tillie heard sirens down the street. She grabbed her purse, her boots, and her car keys and ran out of the apartment.

***

Ura saw the signs for Lake City, Florida as she sped down I 75. Two more hours tops, and she'd be there.

Chapter 25

Ura Returns 2003

Ura pulled into the parking lot of the, Where the Girls Are, bar. A flood of memories washed over her. Steak dinners with Dennis, working with the girls on their dance routines, Tony and his good-natured joking. She remembered Ura. She remembered these people, this place, home and family.

She stepped out of the Caddy and walked to the front door. Will he have met someone else? Was he even still here? She knew she had been gone for some time, but she had no idea where she'd been; only that she hadn't been here, here where her heart lived.

She started to grab the handle of the door to pull it open, but it flew open nearly knocking her down. Dennis was on the other side of the door pushing his way out to the street.

"Woah!" he said then stopped in his tracks. "Ura?"

"Yup, it's me," she replied, sheep faced.

"Ura! Holy… URA!" he cried out grabbing her and lifting her right off the ground in a bear hug.

Ura hugged his neck tightly, tears streaming down her face. She breathed in his scent, familiar and soothing. She felt safe, and happy, and loved. Just as quickly as those feelings came, they dissipated. Was he just being nice, caught up in the moment? Was she going to walk into the bar and be introduced to his new girlfriend? Wife? Had she lost him when she lost herself?

"Baby! Where have you been? God, I can't believe you're here." He slowly released her and stood holding both her hands in his. He looked her up and down as if he weren't sure she was real.

"I'm sorry, Dennis. I'm sorry. I don't know where I've been. I just knew I had to come back here, back... back home," she said.

"I'm so glad you're home," he said.

Home, she repeated the word in her head as he yanked the door open and pulled her into the bar.

"HEY!!! Hey everyone," he yelled. "Look who's here!"

Everything stopped. The music, the dancing, every head turned to see why Dennis was yelling like a banshee. Then once they realized what was happening, people started rushing up to hug Ura and gush over her. She was completely overwhelmed and began crying openly. Such warmth and love; why were these people so wonderful to her? She had clearly not been here for some time and yet it felt like she had never left them or him. There he was, as handsome as ever, beaming with joy that she was by his side. She hugged every person in the room and yet she was nervous. Was one of them going to come up to her and be introduced as Dennis's significant other?

After all the hoopla was over, Ura and Dennis went to sit at a high-top table in the corner of the bar area. The dancers and the rest of the staff knew that they needed some time to themselves and slowly drifted back to what they had been doing. The music started again, drinks were being mixed and served, dancers were performing, and to Ura, everything was as it always had been. She sat across from Dennis in silence for a moment, waiting to hear what he had to say, what questions he might ask that she probably had no way to answer.

For several minutes he just sat looking at her, holding both her hands in his across the table the way he had done what seemed like a million times before. Finally, he spoke.

"God, how I've missed you. I thought I might never see you again. There are a so many questions I want to ask you, but frankly, I'm afraid to ask them," he said.

"You can ask me anything and I'll do my best to tell you what I know," Ura replied.

"Where have you been?" he asked.

"I don't know," she answered. "I don't know for sure how long I've been gone to be truthful."

"Quite a while, years in fact. I was worried sick that you were dead or something horrible had happened to you. You never called or wrote." Dennis looked at her sadly. "Did you forget me, forget all of us?"

"I think in a way I did and yet I never have. I never could or will. I seem to forget a lot. I forget who I am. Maybe I'm not sure who I am at all."

"You're Ura. You're my Ura, my girl, my love. That's who you are," he said.

"Am I? Am I still? Or is there a new girl? A new love? I wouldn't blame you if there is, I just need to know."

"There have been girls," he replied honestly. "My friends and the girls here have tried a few times to get me to move on. They've brought women around to meet me and made me go on dates, but it never got past that," he said.

"Why?"

"Because none of them were you," he answered. "None of them could ever be you and I saw no reason to settle for second best. Besides, I knew you'd be back."

"How could you know that? I had no idea I'd be back. I don't even know where I've been," she said.

"I kept hope in my heart. I don't know, I just never stopped hoping you would come back to me. And here you are."

"Here I am," she said finally relaxing a bit. He hadn't found someone else. She was happy to hear it, happy to know there was a chance to get back to where they were.

***

For the next two years, life was bliss. Ura settled back into her life as if she had never left. She and Dennis were the happiest couple anyone had ever seen. In the summer of 2005, Dennis surprised Ura with a vacation.

"Pack light and don't ask questions," he said jovially.

"Where are we going?" she asked.

"Didn't I just say, don't ask. Just bring a bikini, some casual clothes and your sandals," he answered.

"So, even more tropical than Tampa?" she said laughing.

"Uh, maybe?"

Ura packed, and soon a cab arrived to whisk them away. Twenty minutes later they were at the port and boarding a cruise ship. Dennis had booked them on a week's long vacation to the Bahamas and Cozumel, Mexico. Ura had never been on a cruise ship and she was delighted at the prospect. She was so excited and happy.

"I love you so much," she said to Dennis as they boarded the ship. "I feel like a princess."

"You're more than a princess, you're a queen, my queen," he told her and pulled her into his arms for a long kiss.

For the next few days, they lounged and ate and had many, many, cocktails. They went to some of the shows, did a little light gambling, and went dancing each night before bed. They made love in their stateroom laughing at how the rocking of the ship added to the experience.

"Dennis, hold still," Ura said.

"I am holding still, the bed is rocking," Dennis said.

They were trying to find a comfortable place on the twin bed they had in their stateroom.

"It's not the bed, it's the whole ship." Ura laughed. They were tipsy on champagne and their cabin was nearer the top of the ship therefore they felt every sway the waves caused.

Dennis was perched over Ura, naked and hard as a rock. He was trying to time his thrusts with the pitching and yawing of the big ship.

"Roll over," Ura said and Dennis obliged her, rolling onto his right side. Ura moved into a position that allowed them to be in sink with the side to side of the boat so they could continue their lovemaking.

"Yes!" Ura said as she wrapped her hips around Dennis allowing him to enter her again. She arched her back as they found their rhythm. Suddenly the movement of the ship began to work in their favor. Ura writhed, her hips undulating as Dennis's thrusts matched hers. Her throaty moans made Dennis even more excited, but he kept time with the boat, his long, slow stokes in and out of her making their enjoyment last, his strong hands pulling her hips back and forth to him as he moved them toward climax.

"God, Ura," Dennis called out, every hair on his body standing up, his body fully aligned with her. He kept them in this heightened state for several minutes and as if the cruise ship were working with them. The boat rocked hard to starboard then port just as Ura and Dennis exploded in the exact same moment.

As they lay spent in one another arms, Ura suddenly started to laugh. "I think we have this figured out."

"We beat the system," Dennis said and burst into laughter as well. "Wanna try it again?"

"If the boat is willing, so am I," Ura said and pushing Dennis gently onto his back, rolled over to straddle him, her legs spread wide over his thighs. She began to stroke him slowly as he closed his eyes enjoying the motion of her hand bringing him back to rock hard status. Once he was ready for round two, she guided him into her and this time, took control.

They made love until they were both exhausted and fell asleep, arms and legs wrapped around one another, until the sun poured in through the little port hole waking them for a new day.

The fourth night at sea, they were strolling along the deck under the moonlight. As they rounded a corner, a man with a guitar suddenly appeared. He was strumming a familiar song. Ura recognized the melody.

"Oh, how lovely. He's playing "As Time Goes By," she said. They had watched Casablanca together a few months earlier and she was so taken with the film and the story of never-ending love and loss.

"I know," Dennis said. "I asked him to play it."

"What? Do you know him?" she asked.

"Well, I hired him." Dennis said and turned to face her. He suddenly reached into his pocket and dropped to one knee. Looking up at her he opened a small velvet box that he was holding. In it was a platinum engagement ring with a big bright diamond surrounded by a series of smaller diamonds.

"Ura, love of my life, the only woman I have ever loved, or will ever love, will you do me the honor of becoming my wife?" he asked.

She was stunned. He had caught her completely off guard, and yet she could think of nothing that would make her happier.

"Yes," she said. "Yes, yes, yes!"

He stood up, placed the ring on the fourth finger of her left hand, and kissed her, holding on to her for dear life as the ship gently rocked.

Eight weeks after the cruise, Ura realized she had missed her period. She went to see her gynecologist and he confirmed what she already knew in her heart. She was pregnant. She and Dennis had planned a small wedding and they were to get married in just a few weeks. She went straight to the bar after her doctor's appointment.

Dennis was behind the bar, covering the afternoon shift while it was slow. He was pouring a pitcher of beer when Ura walked up alongside him.

"Hi baby!" he said.

"You might want to look down when you say that," she said smiling.

"Look down? Where?"

"At my belly," she replied.

A quizzical look came over Dennis's face. He wasn't tracking. Ura wore a wry and knowing smile.

"Wait for it…" she said.

"Are you saying…? Are you… Are we?"

"Think you're ready to be a dad?" she asked.

"For real?" he said.

"For real, honey," Ura answered tenderly.

With that, Dennis slammed the pitcher down and jumped up on the bar top.

"Attention everyone!" he yelled. "Can I have your attention please?"

The DJ cut the music, the girls on stage stopped in their tracks and the couple of dozen afternoon clients turned to face him.

"Drinks are on the house! My baby is having… MY BABY! I'm gonna be a dad!!!"

People came rushing to the bar, most of them to congratulate the happy couple, a few to get their free cocktails.

"We're so happy for you guys!"

"When are you due?"

Tony had been doing the books and came running out of the office when he heard Dennis yelling. "You better name that kid Tony if it's a boy. I can live with Antoinette if it's a girl so we can still call her Toni."

"I tell you what pal, if it's a boy, we'll name him after you. But if it's a girl, we're going to call her Hope." Dennis looked at Ura, his eyes glowing with joy and love. "I never gave up hope that we would have this life that we are having, that I would marry the woman I love and make a family together. My hope sure paid off."

Their wedding was small and simple with a pleasant reception at the bar. Tony was the best man and Chayanne, who was now lead dancer, was the Maid of Honor. Hope Antoinette Brooks was born March 1, 2006 and came into the world surrounded by love and extended family. She had her father's dark hair that grew in wild and curly and her mother's startling green eyes. Ura didn't work after Hope was born, instead choosing to spend her time being a wife and mother. She learned to be an excellent cook and even got great at baking. Dennis was the happiest man alive. His business was thriving. He and Tony were considering opening another place and were actively looking at locations to build a sports bar with great food and no dancing. Now that he was a dad, he wasn't sure he wanted his daughter to grow up in the world that he and Ura were accustomed to. He wasn't ashamed of what they did, but he was considering what it would mean to Hope's future.

A month before Hope's third birthday, Dennis got a call that a big group of New York businessmen wanted to buy out the bar for a party. Some of them were bringing their wives, and there were some women executives coming as well. They had heard that, Where the Girls Are, was more of a show bar and nightclub, not just another strip club. They wanted to do something different and were willing to pay a lot of money to have a great evening of entertainment. Dennis needed extra staff and more dancers to cover the bar, and for the first time in years, Ura declared that she wanted to dance.

"Honey, I thought you'd put dancing behind you," Dennis said.

"I love being Hope's mom and your wife," she declared. "But I miss the fun of dancing. You need the best talent you have up there. This could be a turning point for our place, Dennis. If one big company does this and loves it, they might spread the word and we can book parties like this more often. I want to help," she said.

"Okay, baby. I can't argue that if they see you up there, they'll tell the whole world about it," Dennis said.

"I need to practice," Ura said excitedly. "Oh! And I'll need to work on my costumes."

She was so excited, and Dennis was happy to see her having such a good time. For the next two weeks, Ura worked on her dance routine as well as helping the other girls put together a terrific show that was a combination of Burlesque and Flash Dance. She helped them choose music, clothes, props, and dance moves. She was enjoying every minute of being back to work.

The night of the event, they left Hope with their babysitter and went to the club to get ready. Ura was backstage peeking out at the crowd as they piled in. They were all very well-dressed and she recognized some of the clothing as being high-end fashion wear. Dennis came backstage to check on her and the girls just before the show was to start.

"Honey, what kind of business are these people in?" Ura asked.

"They're all from the New York Fashion industry. I think they're considering doing some very big fashion show down here in Tampa," he answered.

Something in Ura's stomach did a turn and she felt a little lightheaded for some reason. She snuck to the edge of the stage once more to look out at the group that was settling in their seats to watch the performance. In the front row of tables, a very familiar man was being seated by the hostess. His hair was much grayer than she remembered, but she remembered him. She remembered that face, those eyes and she started to shiver.

How did he find me? She wondered. *Now what?*

As Jordan sat staring at the stage, an uncomfortable look on his face, Ura remembered much more. She remembered who she was. She turned on her heel, grabbed her purse, and thanked God that she had driven to the bar in her own car.

Heaven walked out the back door and drove off into the night.

Chapter 26

1991

When Jordan returned home, his daughters were sitting up at the kitchen table. It was after midnight and they looked tired and frightened. He was still in a daze. He wasn't sure how he had made it home. He had barely paid attention to the road, driving on automatic, his mind's eye replaying the scene of his wife grinding like a whore in front of all those hungry male eyes. He hated her. He loved her. He never wanted to see her again. He wanted to go find her and drag her home. Nothing made sense. Nothing would or could make things right again. This was his new reality and he was stuck in it.

At fourteen, Heaven was still a little girl, but she wouldn't be for long. She needed a mother at this crucial time in her life and she was tainted by all of this. She knew about it. She too had seen this, seen her mother acting this way. How damaged was she?

She looks just like her, he thought. *She has her genetics. Will she be like her?*

He wasn't worried about Helena, she was almost an adult, heading for college in the fall. She was never close to Angelique the way Heaven was. If he divorced his wife, and who would blame him if he did, Helena would be fine. Helena was more like him.

But the thing was, he didn't want a divorce. He wanted his wife back, the girl he had fell in love with. She was ruined now, and he didn't know her or how to go forward from here.

"Heaven, go to bed," Helena said softly.

"I don't want to," she said to Helena. "Did you find her?" she asked her dad, her eyes pleading.

"Go to bed, as your sister said. We'll talk about it tomorrow."

"Where's mom? Is she coming home?" Heaven asked.

"Not tonight," Jordan said.

"But she is coming home, right?" Heaven said.

"GO TO BED!" Jordan barked at her.

Hot tears stung Heaven's eyes. She hated when her father became angry. She wanted her mother. Why hadn't Angelique taken her along this time? She wished she were there hiding in the wings at the club watching her mother perform. She stood quietly and went to her room without another word.

As soon as she left, Helena began peppering her father with questions about what he'd seen, what was going on, and what they were going to do.

"I don't know, Helena. Stop!" he pleaded. "I've had a terrible night."

He proceeded to give her the watered-down version of the night's events, leaving out many of the worst, most sordid, details and playing down the part where the bouncers tossed him around. He cherished his relationship with his older daughter and wanted her to still see him as a strong, capable man, not someone who couldn't handle the situation he was in. The truth was that he couldn't. He felt weak, emasculated, and old. He had lost control of things; his family, his wife, even his business. He felt helpless and small.

"Let's just go to bed, alright?" he said finally. Maybe things will look better in the morning. At some point, your mother will have to come home, and I will deal with her when she does."

"Dad," Helena said hesitantly. "There's something else you need to know, something Heaven saw that's important to know but I hate to say it out loud."

"Spit it out. What else don't I know about my wife?" he asked sharply.

"Heaven saw her doing something she wasn't entirely sure about."

"What?" he asked.

"Drugs. Maybe cocaine. She said it was a white powder. She saw mom sniffing it up into her nose and she looked up different kinds of drugs in a book at the library and said it sounded like cocaine. We learned about it in health class when Mrs. James talked about the danger of drug use," Helena said.

Jordan's face dropped. He sat down at the kitchen table and placed his head in his hands. "Go to bed, Helena."

"But dad…"

"Just go to bed," he said sadly.

Helena stood and put a hand on his shoulder and squeezed gently then left him sitting there.

Riiinnng! Riinnng!

The phone was ringing at 3 pm. Jordan was asleep on his bed. He had tossed all night worried and restless. He had gotten up around 7 am after a fitful couple of hours of sleep. The girls had slept in, and after a poor attempt at breakfast, they had both retreated to their respective rooms. Around noon, Helena declared that she was going to the library and Heaven begged her to tag along. She acquiesced, and they went off, seeking solace in books and to allow their father some space.

The sound of the phone interrupted Jordan's nightmare. He had been deep asleep, reliving a ghoulish version of the previous night's events. In his dream he heard ringing, thinking it was church chimes, but as he lifted away from the dream and into consciousness, he realized it was the phone in his own home and that he was in his own bed, not in a chair at a dingy bar watching his wife strip for a group of naked horny men who were grabbing her and tearing her clothes from her body. He reached over to the nightstand and pulled the receiver from its cradle.

"Hello," he said in a gruff sleepy voice.

"Is this Mr. Kenny?" a man's voice on the line asked.

"Yes, this is he," Jordan answered.

"This is Detective Bronstein of the Atlantic City Police Department, Mr. Kenny."

Jordan was fully awake now. He sat up and swung his legs off the bed. "What is this about?"

"Mr. Kenny, we have reason to believe that a woman found in one of the local motels in our district may be related to you," the officer said.

"Found? Found how?" Jordan asked, fear rising in his belly.

"Can you come down to Atlantic City, Mr. Jordan? We need to speak with you in person."

The officer gave Jordan the address and hung up. Jordan was still in the pants and shirt he had been wearing the night before and checked to see if his wallet was still in the pants pocket. Without further hesitation, he grabbed his car keys and left.

The Saturday afternoon traffic was lighter than usual, and in less than two hours, he was walking into the Atlantic City police headquarters. He was shaking and frightened. Why hadn't the officer explained what he meant by "found?"

"Hi, I'm here to see a Detective Bronstein," Jordan told the female officer at the big desk at the entrance. She picked up a phone and told him to take a seat. A few minutes later, a large ruddy faced man in a crumpled gray suit walked though the doors and over to Jordan.

"Mr. Kenny?" he asked.

"Yes."

"Follow me sir," he said.

Jordan followed him into a small office space. The detective nodded towards a wooden chair next to what Jordan assumed was his desk indicating that Jordan should take a seat. He obliged and sat on the edge of the chair, nervously. "What's all this about, detective?" Jordan asked. "Please tell me what's going on."

"Mr. Kenny, we had a call at 4 am this morning from a motel manager at the Sleep Inn on the White Horse Pike. His cleaning staff went into a room this morning around 11:30 to clean a room that should have been vacated by the guests, but they discovered two people, a man and a woman who were unconscious and lying across one of the beds. We have reason to believe the woman was your wife," he said.

"Was?" Jordan asked softly.

"Yes, sir. It appeared to be an overdose."

"Are you saying my wife is dead?" Jordan asked.

"We need you to identify the body sir, but yes, the ID that was with her was for one Angelique Kenny. The picture on the drivers license appeared to be the same as the deceased," the detective said.

Jordan felt as if all the blood in his body had rushed to his head. The room spun wildly and the next thing he knew, he was sitting on the floor with the detective holding his head. A uniformed policewoman rushed in with a cold compress and placed it on Jordan's head.

"What happened?" Jordan asked.

"You passed out," the detective answered.

"Is my wife really dead?"

"Most likely, sir," he replied. "We're going to need you to come with us to the morgue."

At the word morgue, Jordan felt bile rise up in his throat. How would he live though this? If this woman lying on a cold slab in the Atlantic City morgue was his Angelique, how would he survive this? How would he tell the girls?

"Okay," was all he said.

The morgue was in the basement of the Atlantic City General Hospital. The detective escorted Jordan to the room where an attendant took them in the back where new arrivals were placed. Two bodies were laying on metal tables with sheets covering them. The attendant pulled back the sheet covering the smaller body. It was indeed Angelique. Jordan stood looking down at her. She seemed to be sleeping, her beautiful face still. He started to weep openly. The attendant covered her back up and the detective grabbed Jordan by his elbow and began to lead him gently from the room.

"Wait," Jordan said. "Can I see the man she was with?"

"It's fine," the detective said to the attendant. "Show him. He has a right to know."

The attendant pulled the sheet back from the other much larger body. The man under the sheet had a familiar face. Jordan recognized him as the big bouncer with long greasy hair that had pushed him violently from the club the night before.

"Good riddance," Jordan said and spit on the dead man's face.

"Sir, what do you want to do about your wife," the detective asked.

"Nothing. She's not my wife. I've never seen that woman before."

Several hours later, Jordan was walking slowly up the steps to their Brooklyn home. His legs felt like lead as he climbed the stairs. When he opened the door to the flat, Heaven rushed up to him. Helena hung back, arms folded, waiting to hear any news her father might have.

"Dad, where were you? Did you go to see mom? Is she coming home?"

"No," he answered and walked past her.

"Dad?" Helena said. "Dad!" But he ignored her and kept walking. "Dad! Did you find mom?"

"Yes," he turned to face his daughters.

"Where is she?" Helena asked.

"Atlantic City," he said.

"When is she coming home?" Heaven asked.

"Never."

"Why? Is she mad at us?" Heaven asked.

"No, she's not mad," he said and locked eyes with his youngest daughter. "She's dead," he said, then turned on his heel, went into his bedroom, and locked himself in where he stayed for the next three days.

When he finally opened his door, he went straight to his studio and began to work. He never spoke about Angelique again.

Chapter 27

2009 - 2011

The cabin had a musty odor and a layer of dust covered every surface. Heaven arrived in the middle of the day. It was nearing the end of February, and it was chilly and damp out. She was happy to see there was still firewood in the bin outside the door. She gathered up some kindling and a few logs and started a fire. The cabin began to warm up quickly and Heaven rolled up her sleeves to make the place spic and span again.

After a few hours, she had things in order enough to take a break and make a hot cup of tea. She had stopped on the way and bought a few supplies; coffee, milk, bread, crackers, fruit, and cheese. Realizing she was hungry, she made herself a snack of sliced apple, cheddar cheese, and crackers. She sat near the fire and let out a long deep breath. It occurred to her that she had not taken a deep breath since driving away from Tampa.

What was she even doing there? How did her father find her? She had no idea what she was doing at that club. All she remembered was what felt like waking from a dream to look out into the crowd and seeing her father sitting glumly at a table. She had just reacted. She didn't waste a minute trying to piece together the events that had led her to be standing backstage at that moment in that place. She just turned on her heel, grabbed her purse, walked out the nearest door which led to the parking lot, and jumped into the Caddy. Somehow, she always knew her car would be there just like she always knew her pretty little cabin would be waiting for her return. But where was she returning from? When she peeled out of the parking lot of the bar, she was disoriented. She had driven to the nearest gas station and went inside where she had been embarrassed to ask where exactly she was.

"You're on the Dale Mabry," the attendant told her.

"Okay, but what town is this?" she asked.

"Umm, Tampa," he answered.

"Can you tell me how to get on I95 toward North Carolina?" she asked.

The attendant gave her directions and soon she was on I 4 heading toward Orlando. In a few hours she had reached I95 and began to get her bearings. She drove until she felt herself becoming drowsy. She pulled off and stopped a chain motel, checking in without so much as a change of clothes or a toothbrush and fell asleep in her clothes the minute her head hit the pillow. Early the next morning, she checked out and found a 24-hour big box store where bought a few necessities and some clothes. She changed and brushed her teeth in the bathroom at a fast food restaurant and bought a breakfast sandwich and a cup of hot coffee to go so she could get right back on the road. By midday, she was stopping near the cabin to get the things she would need for a few days and was soon at the place Heaven considered home. Despite the trauma of seeing her father and the confusion that surrounded that occurrence, she felt safe and happy to be back to little corner of the world.

After a few days, Heaven felt as if she was fully back in her own body. She went into town to see Lono only to find that his mother had sold the coffee shop to new people.

"Do you know where the previous owners went?" she asked the young man behind the counter.

"Lono moved out west somewhere. I think either Oregon or California. His mom retired and moved to somewhere in Florida. I think she has a sister there," he told her.

She was sad to have missed her friends. She stayed and had a cup of coffee, and while it was good, the experience lacked the same pleasant feeling she got when Lono sat with her and chatted idly about his life and latest love interest. She missed him, and hoped she would see him again somehow, someday.

Once she got fully reacclimated, Heaven began to get the itch to work. She sat at her drawing table and had an odd inspiration. She began to work on a line of very fashionable clothes for brides; working to create unique wedding gowns and accessories. As always, she worked feverishly at first, trying to get all of her ideas out. But this time she worked in fits and starts. She had ideas that at first she thought were great, but she later revisited and scratched.

This is important work, she thought. *This will be one of the most special days in most of these women's lives. I have to be concise, careful, and create something no one has ever done before.*

The work made her sad at times, making her cry, though she wasn't sure why. She would look at a design and think about the women that would wear the final results of her ideas. She wanted to create looks that were classic and beautiful, but still allow a woman to be sexy, even glamorous. Women deserved to look amazing on their wedding day, and Heaven was determined to make this line of clothing something phenomenal.

Heaven spent months and months on the designs before she felt they were ready. She was at peace doing this work. She took breaks from the designing. She took long walks in the woods as spring and then summer came to Chapel Hill. In mid-summer, she drove the Caddy out to the beach. She explored the area around Wrightsville beach. She swam in the ocean and took a sunset boat ride. She moved from there onto Carolina Beach on Pleasure Island in Cape Fear. She tried her hand at kayaking and loved to sit on the beach in the late afternoon watching the surfers tackling the waves. She spent time on the boardwalk visiting the various boutiques and shops. She got up early in the mornings to do some hiking at Carolina Beach Lake Park. She was lonely at times, but she felt like she was finding some peace and safety even being alone.

When she returned from her vacation, she had a letter. It was from her sister, Helena.

Dear Heaven,

I hope this letter finds you. I know you like your privacy, but I need to see you. If you are indeed in Chapel Hill, please reach out and let me know if it would be okay to come there and talk in person.

~ Helena

Heaven read and reread the short message several times then put it in her desk drawer. She had never been terribly close to Helena, though she often wished she could have been. Memories began to flood in, and Heaven wanted to keep them at bay. For the next several days, she took longer walks than usual trying to clear her mind. She was sleeping fitfully and having vague dreams that woke her with a start in the middle of the night.

After a week of contemplation, she reached for her cell phone and dialed her brother-in-law's number.

"Tell Helena it's okay to come," was all she said.

Three days later, a car pulled up to the cabin. Heaven heard the crunch of the tires on her gravel driveway and pulled back a curtain to see who was arriving. The driver's door swung open and a pair of woman's legs swung out. Helena was dressed in a smart summer suit and sling back heels. She looked rich, and of course, thanks to Heaven's designs and her marketing skills, she was rich. Heaven watched as her sister got out. Helena smoothed her skirt and ran her fingers through her short, perfect hair. She was not as pretty as Heaven, but she had grown into a handsome woman.

She stepped up to the door of the cabin and gave three short wraps on the wooden door. Heaven went to the door and slowly opened it. For the first time in well over a decade, the sisters were face to face. After a moment of silently looking one another over, Heaven reached out and Helena went straight into her arms for a long overdue hug.

"He's not been well for some time now," Helena said.

The sisters were sitting across from one another on the easy chairs in Heaven's living room sipping cold iced tea.

"I'm sorry to hear that," Heaven said.

"I don't expect you to come home," Helena said. "I know there was bad blood between you and father, but I thought you should know. There are a lot of things I thought you should know."

"I don't need to know anything," Heaven said. "I'm happy with my work, happy here in this little home I've made for myself."

"But you know you've made a fortune… for all of us," Helena said. "You have enough in your accounts to buy a mansion or a penthouse in New York. Would you ever consider coming back home to New York?" Helena asked.

"No!" Heaven answered quickly. "I've no desire to revisit the past. New York isn't home anymore."

"Dad getting sick has made me think hard about my life. I guess somehow I thought he was indestructible and would live forever. I thought you were too. After mother died…"

"I don't want to talk about mother," Heaven cut her off.

"I know it hurts. I wish we could talk about it or about our childhood. I wanted to come to see you to tell you that I've had a lot of time to think. The company is running so smoothly now, and I have long days when I can take a breath. Those days, sitting with dad in doctor's offices waiting for them to see him to give him some idea of what his next steps are, I've had time to consider the past," Helena paused.

"The past is as clear as mud for me," Heaven said. "It's like a fog and I'm okay with that. I just want to be at peace."

"Well, some of it is crystal clear to me and I needed to come to tell you that I'm sorry. I bailed on you. All I thought about was myself. Finishing college, getting married, making the business a huge success was all I thought about. You were a little girl and you lost your mother."

"So, did you," Heaven said.

"Not the way you did. I was older and never close to her. She was your world. I was so jealous of you," Helena said.

"Why?" Heaven asked.

"Because she loved you so much. You were prettier. You still are," she said with a smile. "I wanted her to love me that way, to see me as beautiful like she was. You're so much like her."

At that last statement, Heaven felt a shiver run up her spine.

"Let's change the subject," Heaven asked and rose to go to the kitchen. "You must be hungry. Are you going to stay the night? We can go into town. There are some great restaurants here."

"No," Helena said. "I'm flying to Atlanta this evening. I have a meeting with the buyer for a big clothing chain in the southeast. It's going to be a big deal for all of us."

"I understand. Thank you, by the way," Heaven said. "I know that we would be nowhere without your business sense."

"I would have nothing to sell if it wasn't for your designs, Heaven."

"Father is a good designer too," Heaven answered.

"He was never the designer you are," Helena responded. "He's done some good work over the years, but he's not the genius you are."

"I'm working on something new but I'm not quite there yet. Would you like to see what I have so far?" Heaven asked timidly. She was always nervous to show her new work and even more so where Helena was concerned.

For the next hour, Heaven showed Helena what she was working on. Helena loved the work, and the two sisters talked about next steps to marketing to a whole new group of women.

"What if we called the line, 'Be Mine' Angel Wedding Wear?" Helena suggested.

"Yes," Heaven said exhilarated by the idea and the praise from her sister.

"Well, I hate to have to say it, but it's time for me to head back to the airport. I have to return my rental car and get set for my flight. Thank you for letting me come, Heaven," Helena said.

"I'm glad you did," Heaven responded.

The two sisters stood in Heaven's doorway locked in a long embrace. After a few moments, they broke their hold on one another and Helena walked to her car. With a final wave, she pulled out of the driveway and was gone. Heaven sighed deeply, went back into the cabin and straight to her bed. She fell asleep and did not wake until the next morning.

Over the next several months, Heaven finished her work on "Be Mine," and sent all of her designs to her sister and brother-in-law to start the line in motion.

Once the work was done, she had a strange and sudden urge to travel south for the winter. It was cold in Chapel Hill and she needed sun on her face. She packed a few bags and one day, more than two years since she'd arrived back at the cabin, she was in the car and driving toward Florida.

Chapter 28

1992

"Ryan asked me to marry him and I said yes," Helena told her father and sister.

They were in the middle of dinner at their favorite Italian restaurant. Helena had just turned 20 years old. It was the end of the summer just before her senior year of college. Ryan was nearly five years her senior, but Helena was more mature than most girls her age. The two had met at a reception for one of Helena's professors who Ryan had also studied with when getting his undergraduate degree. Their connection was immediate, and they were rarely apart after that first meeting.

Ryan had finished his MBA and was working in Manhattan for a small but prestigious marketing firm. He liked the work but not the people he worked with.

"And when I finish my degree, Ryan and I would like to take over the marketing and sales for the company, Daddy," Helena announced.

Both Heaven and Jordan were speechless. They had met Ryan and liked him very much, but neither of them expected a marriage announcement so soon. Helena was a strong-willed young lady and clearly she had made up her mind about her future.

"Well, I guess congratulations are in order," Jordan said finally.

"That's wonderful, Helena," Heaven added. "I know you guys will be very happy. Ryan seems like a great guy."

"He is, and thank you both, but what I really care about is your agreement to have us take over the business dealings for Angel Wear. I have no interest in designing, or for that matter any talent, but I showed Heaven's designs to Ryan and he was very excited. He thinks with both of you designing and he and I doing the marketing, dealing with the buyers, doing the books and sales, we can grow the company in leaps and bounds."

"I admit that you're far better with at all of that than I am, Helena," Jordan said. "I've been trying to cover all of it while you were in college but having you on board full time would make life a lot easier."

"Thank you, father. But this isn't just about making things easier for you. I'm happy to be able to do that. This is about growth." Helena turned to her younger sister. "Heaven, you have a gift. You were born to be an artist. Your designs are fresh and unique and a great counterpoint to Father's clean, classy lines. Together, you two can be unbeatable. We need to step up our game and Ryan and I are prepared to go full steam ahead."

"What about college?" Jordan asked. "You have a year left. I don't want you quitting."

"I spoke with my advisors and they're willing to let me consider working for the company as a big part of my senior studies. I'll have to be on campus three days a week and I can jam all my final requirement courses in, but I'll be back here Wednesday afternoons through Sundays."

"Will you and Ryan live with father and I?" Heaven asked.

"No, Ryan rented an apartment here in Brooklyn. We'll be about a mile from here," Helena said.

"I guess you have it all worked out," Jordan said.

"Yes!" Helena answered.

Heaven sat in silence. It seemed that her future was planned out. She loved designing but she was just a junior in high school. Neither her sister nor her father asked her if she wanted to be a clothing designer. They both just assumed she would do as she was told.

And so, she did.

***

Heaven sat at her drawing table. It was a rainy Saturday afternoon. She was flattered that her sister and father thought she had what it took to be a professional designer. She wanted to take designing clothes more seriously. Up to now, she had designed clothes geared to young people. Heaven was just sixteen and her designs were clean, modern, and perfect for teenaged girls. But as she sat there thinking about what her future would be as a designer, all she could think about was the way her mother had danced.

She could still see her on stage, her movements so different from the other dancers. Heaven missed her every single day and often saw her in her dreams.

She watched the raindrops pelting against the big leaded windowpanes of the Brooklyn apartment she'd grown up in, she began to draw. It was as if her hand was not her own. She drew a flowing outfit, not meant for young girls but for women who wanted to show their sensual side; their sexuality. The designs were complicated in that they were layered and had pieces that could be removed and manipulated but in a way, they were simple. They were both elegant and racy. She could see her mother in every piece she drew. She could see her on stage, moving in that way that only she could, removing the materials of the outer skirt in her new design, twisting and turning, legs flashing, bodice tight around the breast with cuts and angles that exuded sex and lust while somehow remaining classy with an air of innocence.

She drew all afternoon and into the evening. She told her dad to leave her dinner next to her, but she didn't touch it. It sat there getting cold for hours while she was immersed in the work. She looked up from her drawing table and realized it was dark out but in front of her were dozens of designs, one better than the other. Heaven stood up, walked into her bedroom and collapsed. She woke ten hours later and went straight to her drawing table. She was surprised to see both her father and her sister sitting at her area with her drawings splayed out in front of them. They were engrossed in conversation and didn't see her enter at first.

"What are you guys doing?" Heaven asked jolting them from their discussion.

"Heaven! My goodness," Jordan said. "This work is… it's…"

"It's incredible," Helena finished her father's sentence. "Where did these ideas come from? They're so sophisticated."

"I don't know," Heaven said shyly. She would not tell either of them that they were reflective of her mother and her dancing. She doubted they would understand and the fact that her father had not spoken about her mother for years, not even to mention her name, did not bode well for any reference to her mother with her designs.

"Well, frankly, they're beyond anything I could have imagined from you at your age. I expected you would work with Father and learn the craft from him. Your designs have always been excellent for someone your age, and Ryan and I thought we might really develop the junior miss line with your work, but these are a different animal altogether," Helena said.

"Thank you," Heaven managed. She was flabbergasted at the praise from her sister. Helena had grown cold since their mother's death. She was a good sister and helped Heaven as much as she could, but there was little communication between them. They didn't share a sisterly bond or warm touching moments. They had never consoled one another over the loss of their mother. Helena, like Jordan, never mentioned their mom. She avoided the subject and shut Heaven down on the couple of occasions she tried to talk to

Helena about Angelique. Heaven carried the guilt of knowing she was the one who told her father about the club in Atlantic City. She would always wonder if she hadn't, would her mother have lived. She didn't know what had happened when Jordan went down there that day, only that her mother was dead shortly after that trip. Maybe something happened between them that caused her mother to kill herself. She assumed it was suicide, but she couldn't even confirm that. No one would talk about it, especially not Jordan, who was the only person who knew the truth.

Jordan was joyless and sullen and had been so since that fateful day when he came home to announce that Angelique was dead. Watching his face light up over her designs, Heaven felt a burst of pride and even happiness that her work had gotten a rise out of him. And her sister's reaction made her feel a connection to both of them in a way she had not felt in a long time.

Over the next several months, Heaven continued to work on designs that became more and more sophisticated. Her father mentored her in the areas of construction of the clothes. He was an expert in the understanding of fabrics, what worked for what design, what material would be easiest to work with, and what colors of fabric would clash or compliment each other.

She was a sponge, and their relationship seemed to be growing. She felt closer to him than she had ever felt in her life and it filled a little bit of the giant hole in her heart left by the loss of her mother.

"I don't want to go back to school," Heaven declared during the Christmas holiday. "I don't see the point in it. I've looked into getting my GED and I want to take the test and be done with it."

"Why?" Jordan asked. "Don't you like school? You only have a year and half and you'll graduate. A high school diploma is very important to have?"

"I know what I want to do with my life and I'm already doing it. Helena has one more semester until she graduates and she's here far more than she's on campus. Ryan is doing amazing things and we're growing faster than anyone could have imagined. I love this, dad," she said smiling up at him. "I want to be here all day working with you and with my sister and Ryan. This is my future and I'm already in it. Why waste time on gym classes, and algebra, and silly talk about whose boyfriend cheated on who?"

"Okay, then!" Jordan smiled and gave his youngest daughter a hug. She looked so much like his wife. The older she got the greater the resemblance. It was hard for him to look at her, and yet hard not to.

"Let's tell Helena you won't be going back. I'm sure she'll have plans for you."

Over the next four months, Heaven and her father worked tirelessly, sometimes late into the evening. Helena planned a huge show to introduce the new line of Heaven's work. They had never been able to change the brand name despite the fact that Angel Wear reminded all of them of Angelique. It was too established. But with Heaven's designs, they could create divisions under the blanket that was Angel Wear. They called the line and the fashion show, "Heaven's Heat by Angel Wear." They invited every major buyer on the east coast, and Ryan managed to get sponsors to cover most of the cost of the venue, the models, and even the cocktail after party.

Things were wonderful. Until they weren't.

Chapter 29

2012

Palm trees decked in Christmas lights lined the Dale Mabry as Ura arrived in Tampa. She pulled into a motel that looked familiar to her and parked the Caddy near the front entrance. She went into the clean, pleasant lobby and up to the front desk. The man behind the counter had his back to her and was on the phone.

"Yes, Ma'am, I'll get housekeeping to bring you fresh towels right away," he said into the phone. He clicked a button on the phone and spoke into the receiver again. "Maria, please bring some towels to room 223. Thanks." He hung the phone up and turned to see the new person who was waiting for his attention. His mouth flew open at the site of her. "Ura! Oh, my goodness. Is it really you? We haven't seen you in years."

"Yes," Ura replied. "I'm Ura. You'll have to forgive me, but do I know you?"

"Oh, of course, why would you remember me?" the little man said sheepishly. "It's been what, fifteen years or more since the last time you stayed here. I'm Jonathan. I was the night clerk when you were here last. Still here!" he said then smiled broadly, "But I'm the general manager now."

"I'm so sorry, Jonathan. I guess it has been a long time. I'm sorry my memory isn't very good, but I guess I remembered this place. It did seem familiar, and I need a place to stay for a few weeks. Do you have any rooms available?"

"For you!? Absolutely. How's a room with a king bed right near the pool sound?"

"It sounds perfect. I'll take it."

"Wonderful. Welcome back, Ms. Ura. We're very happy you chose to stay with us again. We've made a lot of improvements to the old place," he said proudly and began getting her room keys and paperwork. "What model car are you driving these days?"

"Gold Caddy," she said.

"Not the same one?"

"Yes. I love her too much to sell her," Ura said. "Mechanics love me. I give them lots of work keeping her in good shape, but she runs like the day I got her."

After a few more pleasantries, Ura got her room key and went out to move her car to the door of her room. It was a first-floor room near the back of the property, and the room had sliding glass doors out to the sparkling clean, heated pool. The area around the pool was decked out in Christmas lights and décor. Even though it was December, the guests would swim in the warm water of the pool and sit on lounge chairs enjoying the afternoon sun. It was often 80 degrees or more, even as Christmas approached. Ura remembered how much she loved winter in Florida. The weather could turn cold, with temperatures dropping into the forties but even when that happened, typically, it would bounce back in a day or two and everyone would go from jeans and hoodies to shorts and flip flops.

Heaven pulled her bags from the trunk of the car and into her room. It was clean and neat with a comfortable king-sized bed as promised. There was a decent sized TV, and the bathroom was updated. She suddenly had a flash of a memory of being there before. The bath was not as modern as it was now and the TV was a bigger clunkier model, but she felt that feeling she often had; that déjà vu. It made her feel queasy and uncomfortable. She undressed, put a few of her things away in the drawers and closet, and turned on the TV to catch the evening news. The TV anchors were also familiar faces which was at once comforting and confusing. She'd been here before. In this town, in this motel, with the same man at the front desk, but she only remembered parts of it, like looking out a window made of shattered glass. She could see bits and pieces of her life here. She knew she had a life in this place, but she could not seem to see it clearly.

In a little while, she closed her eyes and fell into a deep sleep. She had odd dreams about a handsome man, a little girl, and a room where people were drinking, and laughing, and enjoying themselves. She woke nearly twelve hours later, hungry and disoriented. It was 11 am on a Saturday morning and all she could think about was a hot cup of coffee and a big breakfast. She dressed quickly and headed out into the warm, pleasant day. A few blocks away, she found a Waffle House. She pulled the Caddy into a space and went inside.

She was sitting at a table by herself drinking a cup of steaming hot coffee and waiting for her food to be prepared when the door swung open. A handsome man in his forties, his hair greying a little at the temples, entered the restaurant holding the hand of a little girl of about five or six. Ura felt her heart leap from her chest. Dennis! It was Dennis walking through the door, and in a flash she remembered that they would come to this Waffle House every Saturday for a late morning brunch. The little girl with him was hers. *Hope,* Ura thought. *That's my daughter, Hope.* She sat motionless staring at them as they waited to be seated, a flood of memories returning to her. Dennis was laughing at something Hope said and was looking down at her and not at Ura. Finally, as he looked up from the child, his gaze moved around the room and caught site of Ura. For a moment, he froze. His mouth dropped open, and it seemed as if his knees buckled a little and he adjusted his stance so as not to fall over.

"Ura?" He stood there staring as if he were seeing a ghost. "Ura. What are you doing here?"

"Hi," she said quietly. She slowly stood and walked over to her husband and daughter. She bent down and looked at Hope. "Hello," she said.

"Hello," Hope returned but tightened her grip on her father's hand.

"Do you remember me?" Ura asked the little girl.

"Yes, I think so. Are you my mommy?"

Ura's heart ached. "Yes," was all she said.

Dennis was speechless. He looked at his wife and slowly moved toward the table she'd been sitting at. Ura watched him for a moment.

"Let's sit down," he said turning to her.

Ura followed him to the booth and scooted back into her seat. Dennis and Hope slid into the booth to sit across from her. After an awkward moment of silence, he reached across the table and offered her his hand. She looked at it for a second, then reached across and grabbed his hand and held it tight, tears welling up in her beautiful green eyes.

"Welcome home," Dennis said.

"Can I have a chocolate chip waffle, Daddy?" Hope asked. Her innocent simple question broke the tension and both Dennis and Ura laughed.

"Absolutely," Dennis said.

***

"She's disoriented, confused. It seems like she remembers everything one minute and then seems to forget most things the next." Dennis was sitting in the office with Tony explaining his situation. Ura had been back for about a week. She was still sleeping at the motel but was spending most of her time with Dennis and Hope. "She says she'll move back to the house this weekend. She thinks she needs a little time and space to gather herself. When she's with Hope, she seems like her old self, but when she's alone with me, she's shy and awkward," Dennis said.

"Do you think she's sick, Den?" Tony asked.

"Yes. Yes well, at least something's not right. I don't think she remembers where she's been all this time. The first time she left, I thought she was just going through something she couldn't share with me, maybe running from something or someone, even the law possibly. When she came back, things were so good for so long. We were very happy. I didn't think she would leave again. I didn't think she would leave Hope for sure."

"None of us did, either, buddy. We've all been heartsick about it for a long time. Leaving your husband is one thing, but leaving a three-year-old daughter well... I have to say, I've been pretty damn mad at her for the last couple of years. You're my best friend, Dennis. You're my brother from another mother. And Hope is more than just my goddaughter. I feel like she's my own kid."

"Well, you practically raised her, Tony. She loves you so much and so do I. This whole adventure of a life would have sucked without you, man." Dennis said. He looked at his best friend pleadingly. "What am I gonna do?"

"Get her some help. If you think this is a mental issue, and you love her, get her to see someone."

"I don't know if she will."

"Dennis, you need to get to the bottom of this. She can't keep tearing your life apart. She needs to stay put, not just for you, but for Hope," Tony said.

Ura moved back into the house with Dennis and Hope. She slowly seemed to be getting back to her old self, at least the person that Dennis knew her to be. She spent time with Hope and learned to cook all her favorite dishes. Dennis tried to broach the subject of Ura's mental state, but he didn't know where to start. He wanted to believe that she was fine, that she had a logical reason for her disappearing acts. His heart said leave it alone, but his head said protect yourself, and Hope. If Ura left again, he worried that Hope would be hurt badly. What would he say to her? How would he explain it? He was afraid to bring up her latest disappearance and return. He just wanted her to stay with him. He wanted to keep her safe. He wanted his family to be whole.

She'd been back living in the house for over a month, and while they slept in the same bed, they hadn't been intimate, yet. Dennis longed to touch her, to make love to her, but he was afraid to scare her off. He didn't want to pressure her, but he ached to be with her.

"Can I ask you something?" he asked as he lay next to her one night. They had put Hope to bed and were in their master bedroom. Ura turned to face him, her left elbow bent to hold up her head, she locked eyes with him.

"Of course," she said.

"Do you plan to stay this time?"

"I never planned to leave, ever. I don't know why I do or even where I go. I get lost. But I seem to always find my way back, my way home." She reached over and touched his arm. "I love you, Dennis. I don't know what's wrong with me, but I do know that."

Dennis pulled Ura into his arms and kissed her lightly on the mouth. She returned his kiss with far more intensity. That was all it took. In a matter of minutes, they were undressing one another and making love the way they always had. It was as if time had stopped and their world was once again perfect.

"I've missed you so much," Dennis said as he took a breath. He kissed her face, her eyes, her neck. He ran his hands over every inch of her soft creamy skin. He wanted to touch every inch of her as if doing so would convince him she was really there.

Ura began to remember details. His hands, his lips, were so familiar. She knew this man better than anyone in the world, and she never wanted any other man to touch her this way. She had a flash of a memory of another man, a sweet young man in a motel room. She remembered it the way one would remember a pleasant dream, but she knew he was not this man; not her man, not Dennis.

Dennis took his time with her. He insisted on pleasuring her, making love to her slowly and fully. His hands were strong but smooth like soft leather as they moved over her body. Ura sighed as he ran his fingers gently over her arms and legs. Once she was fully relaxed, Ura moaned as he spread her legs apart to dance his fingers over her wetness, and she ached to feel him inside her. He obliged by slipping one finger then two into her, making her arch her back to meet his thick fingers. He slid his fingers in and out of her, then slid down between her open legs to use his tongue to make slow, deliberate circles around her clitoris, while his fingers continued their rhythmic thrusts.

Ura lifted her hips to meet his mouth and hand. She was lost in him and knew that this was everything. She was exactly where she belonged. Slowly, Dennis brought her to a place of total abandon. When she finally climaxed, she shuddered with release and continued to have little after shocks of joy every few seconds. Dennis moved to take her in his arms loving the little jolts of ecstasy he had given her. She buried her head in his chest and after a moment began to cry. She allowed herself to sob and the relief of letting go was monumental for both of them.

They made love every night from then on and Dennis started to relax. Life felt like it was going back to normal and he began to believe that she would never leave him again.

It was 2 pm when the doorbell rang. Ura was alone in the house. Dennis was picking Hope up from her afternoon dance class and Ura was preparing to marinate some chicken for their dinner that night. She ran from the kitchen to the front door and looked out through the peep hole. There was a man in a rumpled black suit standing at the door.

"Can I help you," she said upon opening the door a crack but leaving the chain lock in place.

"I'm looking for a Heaven Kenney," he said.

Hearing the name Heaven, sent a jolt through Ura's body. She knew someone named Heaven. Who was she?

"I don't think I know who that is," Ura answered.

"Is that your gold Cadillac in the driveway ma'am?" he asked.

"Yes, it is," Ura answered.

"It's registered to a Heaven Kenney. If that is your car, are you sure you're not her?"

"Why are you looking for this Heaven person?" she asked starting to panic.

"Her sister Helena is looking for her. She hired me to find her. I ran a trace on her car and this address came up as related to the license plate."

"Why are you looking for this woman?" Ura asked.

"Her sister needs to speak with her on an urgent family matter. I have a picture of her. She sure does look like you." He pulled a picture out of his pocket and held it up to Ura. "You sure you aren't her?"

Ura shook her head no, but the woman in the picture could have been her twin. Her head began to hurt.

"Well, if you do know her, or know where she is, you might want to tell her to contact her sister or brother-in-law," he said.

"I will, thanks. I'm not feeling well," she said. "Please excuse me." She closed the door and went to the living room to sit down on the couch. Her head was pounding. *Ura, Heaven, sister, Ryan, Helena.* Names were reeling in her mind. *Jordan, father, mother. Angelique, Angel Wear.* She passed out cold.

***

"Jordan is very sick," Ryan said. "It doesn't look good Heaven. We don't think he has much time. He's in Mount Sinai in Manhattan. You need to come soon."

Heaven was at a rest stop on I 95 just outside of Jacksonville, Florida. She had called Ryan on the cell phone number he'd given her the last time she talked to him.

"I'll be there tomorrow," she said and hung up the pay phone she was calling from.

Heaven arrived at the hospital at 8 pm the following night. She drove straight through, only stopping for food, gas, and to relieve herself.

"What room is Jordan Kenney in?" she asked at the desk.

"He's in intensive care, fourth floor. Only immediate family allowed in."

"I'm his daughter," she replied.

She was given a pass and directions and headed directly up to his room. She took an elevator and wound her way down the dim halls. She turned a final corner and came to the door of Jordan's room. The floor was quiet except for the sound of whirring machinery and medical equipment. Heaven stood in the frame of the door staring into the room. Jordan was laying in the hospital bed, tubes sticking out of his arms, attached to the machines that surrounded the bed. She froze. He wasn't awake but she could hear his ragged breath. He looked small and frail and very old.

In that moment, she was suddenly seventeen years old again, and she began to shake. Images flashed vividly in her head. She turned on her heel, retraced her steps and left the hospital.

***

As the site of the Portland City limits came into view, Selena felt herself relax. In that moment, she remembered that she should have gotten her period several days ago.

Meanwhile 3,000 miles away, Jordan Kenney left the earth behind.

Chapter 30

Jordan and Heaven – 1994 – 95

"Happy birthday, dear Heaven. Happy birthday to you," Helena and Jordan sang as the eighteen candles burned on the pretty pink iced cake; one candle for each year of Heaven's life and one extra to grow on.

She tried to manage a smile, but she wasn't feeling very good and didn't feel like celebrating.

Helena noticed that her sister was under the weather, but she didn't say anything. Heaven had become sullen and even more distant than usual. She blew out the candles on the cake and Helena gave her the knife to make the first cut for good luck. After the cake was served, Heaven excused herself and went to her room.

"What's eating her?" Helena asked Jordan.

"Beat's me," he answered, and began clearing plates but did not look at his oldest daughter. He shuffled off to the kitchen, dishes in hand.

"You'd think she would be over the moon today. How many kids get a gold Cadillac for their seventeenth birthday?" she said but her father did not respond.

Helena went to the studio to look at the new designs Heaven and Jordan had been working on. She was surprised at the growing sophistication of Heaven's designs, but she was a bit concerned about the darkness of them as well. Heaven's designs had always been light and appealed mainly to the younger market. Lately, her work was far more adult in nature. Helena had showed them to Ryan and they both believed the new work could be a huge hit in the same space as Victoria Secret's line. These new designs would work for women wanting to look uber sexy at a nightclub. They were exotic and bold; not indecent, but close to it. There weren't something one would expect to come from the mind of a 17-year-old. Ryan coined the phrase, "Exotica," which was what they decided to call the entire new line.

Where is this coming from, Helena thought as she thumbed through the new designs on Heaven's desk. She closed the door to the studio and knocked on Heaven's bedroom door.

"Hey, I'm heading out," Helena said through the door.

"Okay," Heaven replied but did not come out.

Helena stood there a moment not sure if she should attempt to enter or talk to Heaven further. She decided it probably wouldn't do much good and she headed back to the kitchen. She said a quick goodbye to her father who was at the sink doing dishes. He didn't turn around but just waved his hand at her.

My family, Helena thought as she left. *If it wasn't for business, I don't know if I would even talk to either of them. Thank God for Ryan.*

Once Helena had left, Jordan went to Heaven's room. He knocked once, then opened the door and entered. She was laying on her side on her single bed, her face to the wall. She heard him come in and pretended to be sleeping. "You awake, Heaven," Jordan asked but she did not respond. He slipped over to her bed and gently sat down next to her. Slowly, he began rubbing her back and after a few minutes, slid his hand under her soft cotton tee shirt and continued the action, but now with his hands sliding in circles on her soft, smooth skin. She did not move, and slowly he moved to lay down next to her, circling his right arm around her. In a matter of minutes, Jordan was fast asleep and breathing deeply.

Heaven lay there awake and alert.

The new line was a hit and Helena began pushing Heaven even harder to create more of the exotic designs she had been working on for the last several months since her birthday.

"She's only a kid," Ryan said to Helena one morning over coffee. "I know you want the company to continue to grow, but maybe we're pushing Heaven too hard." He was afraid the success and money were going to his wife's head.

"She's fine. She loves the work."

"Yes, I know but she doesn't even go to school anymore, Helena," Ryan said.

"Jordan is homeschooling her. She just passed her GED exam. What would she need school for? She's making amazing money as a designer and this is just the tip of the iceberg. She'll be a millionaire by the time she's twenty-five. We all will be."

"There's more to life than money, baby," Ryan said.

"I know, but money can sure make life easier. Heaven is fine. Trust me," she answered.

"Okay, but let's keep an eye on her. Deal?" he said

"Deal," Helena responded but she was not in the least worried. All she could think about was how great things were going and how much money was flooding in with all the orders and new stores clamoring for their clothing.

Heaven stepped into the shower. The warm water felt good on her skin. She let it fall over her body and her long, beautiful hair. Her thoughts turned to her mother as it often did. She longed for her touch even after all these years. She closed her eyes and ran the movie in her mind that soothed her aching heart. She saw her mother, beautiful and alive, dancing. Always dancing. She imagined her dancing on the sand of a tropical beach, crystal blue water dancing with her, dancing behind her in the bright sunshine. She saw herself sitting on the sand at her mother's feet loving every movement and the joy she saw clearly on her mother's face. As the water fell over Heaven's naked body, she imagined her mother moving around behind her and dropping to her knees to hug Heaven tightly. She could almost feel her mother's arms around her, and she leaned back a little to press her back against the warmth of her mother's chest.

But the chest she was leaning against was hard, not the soft bosom of her mother, and the arms wrapped around her were not her mothers warm embrace. They were the hard sinew of her father's arms. She woke from the daze of her dream to realize that Jordan had stepped into the shower with her. She realized that he was naked and aroused. She felt his hardness against her.

"You look just like her," he whispered in her ear. "Do you know that?" He cupped her bare breasts in his hands and moaned. "Angelique, why?" he cried out as he entered her from behind. Heaven's mind went blank as she stood under the warm stream of water and something in her snapped irrevocably.

Heaven was backstage at the Angel Wear Fashion show that Helena and Ryan had put together to show off the new designs. A young woman sidled up next to her. She was a model and at first glance could have been a cousin of Heaven's or even a sister. She had the same hair and eye color and was about the same height.

"I love your work," she said to Heaven.

"Thank you," Heaven said turning look at the girl. It was not unlike looking in a mirror that was slightly askew.

"I'm so excited to be wearing your clothing. I love it," the model said. "My name is Ura, by the way."

"Nice to meet you, Ura," Heaven said. *What a beautiful name*, she thought.

Helena walked out onto the stage to the thunderous applause. "Ladies and Gentlemen, we are so glad you were all here to get the first glimpse of our new line, Exotica. Angel Wear is fortunate to have one of the youngest, most talented designers in the world. In fact, tomorrow is her eighteenth birthday. You call her Heaven, but I call her sister. Would you like to meet her?" Helena shouted. Cries in the affirmative called back to her. "Heaven, please join me on stage," Helena said into the hand-held microphone she carried. That was Heaven's cue to step out onto the stage, but she did not appear. Helena repeated herself but to no avail. "She's shy. Let me go fetch her," she said and rushed from the stage. "Where is she?" Helena asked Ryan who stood in the wings.

"I have no idea. She was here a minute ago."

Helena went back out on stage and apologized to the crowd saying that Heaven was so excited she was too overwhelmed to come out. The crowd dispersed and Helena and Ryan searched the entire backstage area. Finally, Ryan thought to check the parking lot. The gold Caddy was gone. He came back in to tell Jordan and Helena that Heaven seemed to have left. The models and make up people were packing up, and the clothes were being placed in garment bags.

"Hey, my purse is missing," said Ura.

"What?" Helena asked.

"I put my purse down under my make-up table and it's gone," the model replied.

"I'm sorry, but it will turn up. We know everyone here. No one would take your purse," Helena said. But she had bigger things to worry about. *Where the hell is Heaven?* She thought.

***

Ura turned the big Gold Caddy onto the entrance ramp of the Jersey Turnpike heading south. By midnight, she was crossing the Delaware Memorial Bridge. She drove until she passed the exits for Washington D.C. At around 2:30 am she stopped at a roadside motel and took a room for the night.

The next morning, she continued to head south, toward Florida, toward the sun.

Chapter 31

2013

Christine was behind the bar, as usual, when Selena walked in shaking the rain from her hair. "Can a girl get a ginger ale in this place?" Selena said with her tough New York accent.

Chris looked up, and for a moment, was stunned into silence until she realized this was no aberration. She was really looking at Selena, clear as day, standing in the doorway of her bar, dripping rainwater onto the carpet.

"Holy shit!" was all Chris could manage.

Denny was in the DJ booth, and a girl that Selena didn't recognize was dancing on the stage. There were some men at the bar, a few others and some women scattered at the tables near the stage. It was 2 pm on a Tuesday so the bar was mostly quiet. Selena was hoping Chris and Denny would still be there and she wasn't disappointed. Chris rushed out from behind the bar and ran full tilt at Selena lifting her off the ground and twirling her around whooping as she did.

"Where in the hell have you been?" she asked finally putting Selena down.

"Oh, you know. Here, there, everywhere. What's it to ya?" Selena asked, then burst into laughter and hugged her friend hard.

Denny, hearing the commotion, left the sound booth and came over to see what was going on. She stopped in her tracks and looked at Selena. "Well, look what the cat dragged in," she said then came toward Selena. "Welcome back," she said, and gave her a warm hug.

"Good to be back," Selena responded, then stepped back to take a look at Denny taking both her hands in her own. Selena immediately noticed a shiny ring on fourth finger of Denny's left hand. "And, what is this?" she said, running her thumb over the impressive diamond.

"We went nuts and got married while you were gone," Chris said flashing a band on her ring finger with tiny diamonds embedded in the gold that circled her finger.

"YAY!" Selena yelled, and grabbed them both, pulling them in for a tight group hug. "I'm so happy for you guys!"

"Don't get too excited. We just had a commitment ceremony for now. But they're talking about it becoming legal in the next year or two," Chris said. "We're hopeful, and Denny has been volunteering with the Human Rights people. They're lobbying hard for equality." Chris was clearly proud of Denny and put an arm around her waist. It was obvious to Selena that her two friends had grown a lot since she last saw them.

"It'll happen. It has to," Selena said.

Selena sat at the bar and Denny went back and forth to the sound booth to handle the music while the three women spent the rest of the afternoon catching Selena up on all the news of the bar and the city she had grown to love so much. Selena didn't offer much about where she'd been or why she'd left. She dodged their questions because the truth was she didn't really know where she'd been. She just knew she was happy to be there, happy to be with the two of them, and even happier that they had settled down so well with one another. She could tell they were truly in love. *Some things just take time,* she thought as she watched the two women move around one another sharing smiles and light touches. Denny seemed to have grown into her own. Over the course of their conversation, Selena discovered that Denny had quit dancing altogether and was running the sound part time but mostly handling the bar's day to day financial business. She was also going to school and was considering a career in law. Chris was bursting with pride over Denny's accomplishments and it was obvious she loved the younger woman a great deal.

"So, what now?" Chris asked, finally.

"I have no idea. I just know I'm here and plan to stay here for a while," Selena answered her.

"We could use you around here, if you're looking for work," Denny said.

"I'd like to dance, if that's possible," Selena asked.

"Duh!" Chris said laughing. "When can you start?"

"Tomorrow!"

"Done," Chris answered. And just like that, Selena was back in the swing of her life in Portland.

"Okay. I'll be back tomorrow around 4. Is that okay?" Selena asked.

"Perfect." Denny responded. "I'll dig up some of your old music."

"Great," Selena said. She hugged them both goodbye and left them at the bar.

Once Selena had exited, Denny turned to Chris. "She was pregnant when she left. What do you think happened to the child?"

"Maybe she left her kid with the father," Chris answered. "She didn't mention it, and I don't think we should either."

"I hope she didn't lose it," Denny said.

"I know how much you love kids, baby, but we'd better let Selena tell us what she wants to about this, if and when she wants to."

Denny just nodded her head in agreement and went back to her DJ booth.

***

"That's the fourth Jelly donut you've eaten today, Selena. What the hell?" Chris asked. She didn't want to say anything, but in the little more than a month since Selena had returned, Chris noticed her number one dance attraction was gaining weight. Selena seemed to be sporting a little belly that was starting to pooch out.

"I can't stop eatin' em," Selena moaned. She felt near to tears for the second time that day and she was embarrassed about her donut addiction. Truth was, Selena suspected that her need to eat donuts had very little to do with her need for sugar and a lot more to do with the fact that her period had ceased to come. Also, the queasy stomach in the morning had progressed to tossing her cookies when she woke up. It all felt oddly familiar, yet she couldn't see how. She was pretty sure these things led to one thing. She was pregnant. But how, with whose baby? Memories started to pop into her head. She remembered seeing a Doctor Wu while she was in Portland the last time she was there. Flashes of pictures made her dizzy. A house somewhere in Texas and a woman who made her feel like part of a family. A man whose face she couldn't quite make out, his hands big and warm around her waist.

Selena felt like she was losing her mind. Finally, she asked Denny if she knew of a Dr. Wu.

"Yes, you went to her last time you were here. Don't you remember?" Denny said perplexed. She was worried about Selena. She seemed distracted and sometimes confused. Denny was afraid to say anything about Selena's last pregnancy. What if she had lost the child, miscarried? "Dr. Wu moved to Seattle though, but I go to the woman that took over her practice. Do you want me to make an appointment for you to see her, Selena?" Denny asked.

"Yes," Selena was confused. *Why had she seen the doctor the last time?* "I'm not sure, but I think I may be pregnant. It's that or I'm having some kind of problem. Either way, I need to see a doctor."

Two days later, the new doctor confirmed Selena's suspicion. She was indeed pregnant. Selena had been renting a room not far from the bar but as she got closer to having the baby, Chris and Denny insisted that she move in with them. They had recently moved into an old house with a big backyard and there was plenty of room for Selena and the baby. Selena was often ill near the time the baby was due and Denny took over. She took Selena to every doctor's appointment and was her Lamaze partner. Chris picked up the slack at the bar and all the other girls pitched in to help.

"Denny!" Selena screamed. She was having sharp pains and knew it might be time to head to the hospital. Denny rushed into Selena's room and helped her from the bed. "I think I'm havin' a baby," Selena said.

"Yeah, I think you're right," Denny said laughing. "Let's go do that. Let's go have your baby."

They navigated Denny's little Kia through the streets of Portland and pulled up to the emergency entrance of the hospital. Denny called Chris and she left the bar and was already there waiting at the door for them to pull up. Chris helped Selena from the car and Denny went to park while they went in to get Selena some attention. After four long hours, Selena finally gave birth to a perfect little baby girl.

"So, what are you going to call her?" Chris asked once mother and child were resting calmly. Selena was holding the tiny little baby, swaddled in a pink blanket, in her arms. Chris and Denny flanked her bedside.

"Faith!" Selena said. "I want to call her Faith, because that's what she and I will need to have in this life."

Selena was happy. She had no idea who this little girl's father was, but she was determined that she would have a great life. She had faith that it would be that way.

***

Life was peaceful for the next year. Faith grew quickly and she was a beautiful child. She was fair in her coloring but with deep chestnut hair and green eyes. She took her first steps in the backyard at Chris and Denny's house and her first birthday party was a major bash. Chris closed the bar on the Sunday before Faith's birthday and invited the entire staff and all of the regulars. There were so many presents that Denny threatened that they would have to buy a bigger house.

"Oh, no!" Chris said. "We can barely afford this old money pit."

A few months after the party, a major announcement came. Gay marriage laws had changed, and it was now legal for LGBTQ people to marry legally in Oregon. Chris threw a huge party at the bar, and at one point in the night, she made the DJ who was working that night stop the music. She pulled Denny up on the stage and in front of the entire bar got down on one knee.

"Denny," she said. "I know we've had a commitment ceremony, and you're wearing my ring and I'm wearing yours, but I want to know, here, in front of just about everyone we know, will you marry me?"

"Duh!" Denny said, and pulled Chris up into her arms for a long and passionate kiss. Three weeks later, Selena, with Faith in her arms, stood next to Denny as her maid of honor, as she married Chris. It was nothing short of total joy for all of them.

***

"I'm sorry, baby." Chris said to Denny stroking her hair gently.

"Why did this happen to us?" she asked as she lay in her hospital bed. A moment later, Selena walked in the room. Little Faith was holding her mother's hand until she saw Denny.

"Auntie Den," she cried out, pulling away from her mother to rush to her aunt's bedside. Faith was a little more than two years old, and she loved her aunts. Selena had moved into a little apartment with her daughter, but they saw the girls nearly every day, and Denny watched Faith every Thursday and Friday nights so Selena could dance at the bar.

"I'm so sorry, honey," Selena said to Denny squeezing her hand. "I know how much you wanted this baby."

Denny had lost the baby after four months. The doctors told her that carrying a baby to full term was risky for her and they had spent a lot of money on fertility drugs and insemination all to have it end in sadness.

"Maybe one day, they'll let us adopt, honey," Chris said, but she knew that was pretty much a pipe dream. She wanted to give her young wife the baby she wanted but Chris had had a hysterectomy in her thirties after some medical issues that surfaced. She couldn't have a baby even if she wanted to and she surely didn't want to. Now, it seemed that Denny couldn't either and lesbians were not at the top of the list for adopting children.

"Yeah, maybe," Denny said sadly, and turned over to face the window. Chris sat holding her hand and Selena stood rubbing her back. Little Faith pulled herself up onto the bed with a little help from Selena and curled up at her aunt's feet. They all stayed that way for a long while and soon both Faith and Denny were asleep.

***

After losing the baby, Denny threw herself into work and her efforts to advocate for gay rights.

"I want to throw a rally at the bar," she announced one afternoon.

"What kind of rally?" Chris asked.

"The HRC is pushing for adoption rights for LGBTQ couples. They need a place to hold a rally to make people aware and to get signatures. I thought we could do it here. Maybe on a Sunday, get a few food trucks in out in the parking lot, get a band. They need to raise funds for the Human Rights Campaign. We could make it fun and ask people to donate at the same time."

"Go for it, baby!" Chris said. That was all that Denny needed. She went full tilt into motion and got Selena and some of the other girls to help plan and co-ordinate the event.

The day of the event, there were tables and chairs set up in the parking lot, a stage for the band, and four food trucks rolled in, each of which promised to donate twenty percent of their profit for the day to the HRC.

Selena was walking through the parking lot, pushing Faith in her little stroller. Denny had asked her to check in with all the vendors and food truck people to make sure they had everything they needed and were ready for the rally. As she approached one of the trucks, she felt a strange sense of déjà vu. This particular truck was very colorful and had big green frogs on it. The trucks wrapper sported the name of the business, "The Peace Frog." They touted great coffee and exceptional homemade baked goods. The truck's slogan was an innuendo of pot smoking, "Get Baked at The Peace Frog." The double entendre indicating eating baked goods and getting "baked" smoking pot. Just as Selena got to the window of the truck, a big, dark-haired, young man turned to look out bringing her nearly face to face with him.

"Heaven?" he said in disbelief. "Heaven!" he shouted. "HOLY COW! Is it really you?" The young man rushed from the truck and grabbed Selena, pulling her into a bear hug.

"Woah there, buddy!" Selena said in her New York accent as she wiggled from his grip. "What's this about?"

Lono, hearing her heavy accent, stepped back confused. "Aren't you my friend, Heaven from Chapel Hill?" he asked.

"Name's Selena, and I've never been to Chapel Hill," she answered but she felt a twang of confusion. Why did the name, Heaven, sound so familiar? And hadn't she been to Chapel Hill once? Why did that sound so nice? "Sorry. I'm just checkin' to see if you food truck guys need anything. You good?" she asked finally.

"Yeah, yeah, we're good. I'm sorry, you're a dead ringer for my friend Heaven. I haven't seen her in years, but I was so sure. Weird." Lono said then spied the little girl in the stroller. "Who's this little angel?" he asked.

"Faith," Selena said. "My little girl." Selena felt a sudden warmth come over her. She knew this was a good man and she felt oddly close to him. "I like your truck. I hope you make a killin' today. I'll come back later for coffee and a muffin."

"Sure. On the house when you do. I'm sorry about the inappropriate hug," he said laughing. "So weird. I'd have sworn…"

"No worries, man," Selena said, and with a sad smile, walked away from Lono who stood and watched her move to the next truck.

That's Heaven, he thought. *I know it is. I'd know her anywhere.* "What the heck is she up to?" he said aloud as he stepped back up into his truck. *I'm gonna ask her when she comes back.*

But she didn't.

Selena's head was swimming as she walked around the rest of the parking lot. When she got to the bar, she stepped inside to the cool dim lighting. Her head had begun to hurt so badly she could barely see. She plopped down into a chair at one of the tables and dropped her head down on it. A few minutes later, Chris came in to set up the bar and saw her sitting there. Faith, still strapped into her little stroller, was napping.

"Hey, you okay?" Chris asked Selena.

"Headache. Really bad one."

"Why don't you take Faith backstage and lay down on the couch for a bit. She's out cold anyway. Maybe you both need a nap."

"Okay," Selena said, and slowly got up. She pushed the stroller into the room behind the stage. There were no shows while the rally was going on, so no one was back there. She lay down on the couch and pulled the stroller near to her. She fell into a deep but troubled sleep. When she woke, Faith and her stroller were gone. At first, Selena felt disoriented and didn't know where she was. Then she realized her child wasn't with her and she panicked. As she rose from the couch, Denny came in with Faith in tow.

"Hey, sleepy head. You okay?" Denny asked.

"Yeah, I'm better," Selena said but it was only slightly true. She was still having shooting pains in her head. She yelped as she tried to rise.

"Okay, that's it. We need to get you home." Denny said.

"How's the rally going?" Selena asked.

"It's almost over, and it went really well. Let's call you an Uber to take you home. I can keep Faith if you want to rest."

Selena's head was splitting. The thought of trying to take care of Faith the way she felt was daunting.

"Really? She won't be in the way?"

"Are you serious? Faith is never in my way. Go home," Denny said.

***

The headaches were getting worse. Selena lay in bed for days at a time with blinding pain causing the walls to dance. She hallucinated often and woke in a pool of her own sweat from dreams or visions of things she couldn't distinguish as real or not. The words, faith, hope, and charity kept running through her mind. Names, Dennis, Denny, Selena, Tilly, Heaven, Jordan, Angelique; she couldn't stop the flood of noise in her mind. *Where are they?* Selena thought. *I need to find them.*

The girls had taken Faith with them, and Denny came over to Selena's apartment three or four times a day. Often, she would find Selena sleeping, but tossing and talking in her sleep.

"Honey, she's talking in different accents. She seems to know me one minute and then she looks at me like I'm a total stranger the next. It's like she's going crazy or something," Denny said to Chris one afternoon after leaving Selena. "I woke her up and put a cold towel on her head. She seemed fine by the time I left, but she's in a lot of pain. The headaches are getting worse. I think we need to get her to a doctor."

"If this doesn't get better in the next day or so, we need to bring her over here. She shouldn't be alone," Chris said.

"Yes. I asked her if she wanted to come with me, but she was exhausted and said she just wanted to sleep. She thanked me for taking care of Faith, as if that's a chore," Denny said, looking over at the little girl sitting on their living room floor playing happily with the dress up doll Denny had bought for her.

"Well, let's give Selena another day and then we'll go over there and get her to the doctor together if she isn't any better. She can't fight both of us," Chris said, and gave her wife a kiss on the forehead. "I have to get back to the bar. You and Faith need anything before I go?"

"Not a thing," Denny said smiling. "We're going to watch 'Surf's Up,' again."

"Again?" Chris asked.

"The kid loves surfing penguins, what's not to love?" Denny laughed.

***

Late in the afternoon the next day, Denny and Chris went to check on Selena, but she wasn't there. On her kitchen table was a letter addressed to Chris and Denny. Inside there was one sheet of white lined paper.

All that was written on it were just a few simple words.

Take care of Faith. She's yours now.

I love you all,

Selena.

Chapter 32

2015 – 2018

When Tillie got to the Palace Adult Entertainment Club, she saw that a lot had changed. The place looked sharp, with new signs out front that touted burlesque shows and a businessman's lunch buffet claiming the best food and drinks in town.

"I hardly recognized this place," Tillie said in her big Texas accent. Andy was behind the bar when she walked in. He tilted his head the way he always had as a kid, and all at once, they recognized one another.

"Tillie? Is that really you?" Andy asked.

"This can't be little, Andy." Tillie said in response. "What happened to you. You went and grew up," she said laughing.

Andy came around from behind the bar and gave her a warm hug. "Guess I did. Can't stay little forever. How the hell have you been? Where the hell have you been?" he asked, smiling broadly at the woman he had loved so much as a boy. "I've missed you woman. You look amazing. Hardly aged a day."

"Oh, boy, you're layin' it on thick, there. I'm an old lady now," Tillie replied.

"That'll never happen. You're more beautiful than ever."

"I'll take that. How are things? How's the bar?" she asked.

"Bar is doin' great, as you can see," he answered. The place was much classier and upscale than it had been when Tillie was there last. There was a long buffet of hot and cold dishes set up against one wall and the place was filled with men and women in suits and ties, eating and drinking, while two very pretty girls danced on the stage to entertain them through their lunch.

"People come in for lunch and bring clients too. It's kinda crazy, but I'll take it. We're kickin' butt, Til."

"I'm proud of you, Andy," she said. "How's your dad, doin'? He still runnin' the place?"

"Dad works for me now. We got him into a rehab for a while, but it didn't take altogether. He's slowed down on the drinking a lot, but he has his battles. Bonnie's been great with him. They got married a couple of years ago, and she keeps him in line. I don't know why she loves him so much, but I'm grateful that she does."

"That's great, Andy. She always did love Beau. She's a good woman. But tell me, how'd ya get the place so spruced up," Tillie asked. "It looks amazing."

"Funny story," Andy said. "I got asked to be in a lottery pool with a couple of my pals, and who would have thought it, we actually won. My share was almost a million dollars. I invested a bunch of it in renovating the bar and classing the place up and it worked. We're a hit!"

"So, you're a millionaire!" Tillie said. "And a right handsome one. I bet the girls are all over that."

"Not a millionaire anymore. I'm a bar owner though, and of much classier bar," he laughed. "No time for girls either. Besides, you were always my best girl. Tell me you're back for good," he said and squeezed her arm.

"I don't know. I just know I had some unfinished business and needed to come here. Had to see you and had to work out something. I felt like I left somethin' behind here. Need to come settle it."

"Are you still dancing? You're still as fit and pretty as you ever were. Any chance you'll come work with me?" Andy asked.

"If you'll have me," she replied.

"When can you start?"

"Anytime. I'm all yours," Tillie said.

***

Tillie had been dancing at Andy's bar for nearly a year, and while things were great, she felt an emptiness. Andy was like the son she never had, and they were far more than employer and employee. Bonnie and Tillie reconnected, and Tillie even lent a hand with Beau on days when he was a little too much to handle. She never mentioned the trouble he'd caused with her that day. Beau was subdued and had mellowed out with age. His fight with alcoholism had finally taken its toll and he mostly stayed away from the bar except to help clean up or check ID's on weekend nights when it got busy.

Tillie danced on the weekend nights and was still a huge draw for the bar. She helped organize the burlesque shows they did on Saturday nights which had become so popular that there was a reservation list month's out to get in.

Tillie had also taken on the role of hiring and firing the dancers. She had to let one particularly popular girl go because she caught her doing cocaine in the dressing room and came to find out she'd been trying to solicit customers to buy from her.

"This sucks! She was one of our best draws," Andy said. "Can't have the reputation we're selling drugs here. They'll shut us down for good."

"I know. I had to let her go. She was pretty darn pissed. I'll find someone to replace her. We're always getting' girls in here applying to dance," Tillie said.

A few days later a girl walked in and asked to speak to someone about dancing at the bar. Tillie was in the office and the bartender sent the girl in to see her.

"What's your name, sugar?" Tillie asked her.

"Cee," she replied. She was stunning, with chestnut colored hair and sea blue eyes. She looked to be about 5'8" tall and had a perfect figure.

She's got the looks for it, Tillie thought. She seemed oddly familiar to her. "How old are you? You have to be over eighteen to dance here.

"I'm nineteen, ma'am," she replied.

"Have you ever danced before?" Tilly asked.

"I've been working over at the Starlight lounge for about four months now but they're not the kind of bar I want to dance in. They just want tits and ass on a pole there. I want to do more than that. I saw the burlesque show here three weeks ago. That's the kind of dancing I want to do."

"Well, you're certainly pretty enough," Tillie replied. "Come in for an audition tomorrow at 11 am. Bring two songs. We open at 11:30 for lunch. I'll give you ten minutes to impress us. Fair enough?"

"Fair enough," she answered then excused herself and left the office.

The next morning, the young lady showed up at 10:55 am. She had two songs cued up on her iPad and gave them to the D.J. then stepped up onto the empty stage. Andy and Tillie sat at a table a few feet from them stage as the music started.

Cee was wearing a long overcoat and as the song began, she began to remove the coat. Every movement was slow and seductive, and as she took the coat off, Tillie looked over at Andy. His eyes were glued to the beautiful creature who was owning the stage. She was sultry and moved like a gazelle. She disrobed as she danced and was absolutely fantastic. Moreover, there was something very familiar in her moves. Tillie's head felt a little light. Where had she seen movement like this before? In a flash, she saw a picture in her head of a little girl in the wings of a stage watching a woman move across it just the Cee was moving now. *Where was that? When was it?* And in the next moment, the thought vanished.

The song ended and the next one began, but Tillie waved to the DJ to stop.

The young woman stopped moving as the music ended. "I thought you said I could do two songs. If you don't like these I…"

"No need for a second song. You're hired," Tillie said. "Come in for dance rehearsals on Sunday at 10 am. I'll have the schedule up by then. You'll get six regular shifts, and when you're up to speed, we'll feature you in the Saturday night Burlesque show. I doubt that will take long."

"Just like that?" Charity asked.

"Just like that," Tillie replied, and looked at Andy who was still unable to speak. "Thoughts?" she said to him.

"Welcome aboard… What did you say your name was?" Andy asked the beautiful young woman on the stage.

"Charity!" she responded. "But everyone just calls me Cee."

Tillie felt as though her heart has stopped for a moment. She looked at the girl on the stage and felt a chill run down her spine. *What's wrong with me*, she thought.

"I'd rather we call you Charity," Andy said. "Better stage name. It suits you," he said smiling broadly at her.

"Fine with me," Charity said. "I'm just glad for the chance. Rents due soon," she said laughing. Andy stepped up to the stage and put his hand out to help her down.

"Glad to have you here," he said holding her hand and her gaze for a moment longer than expected. Then he shook himself from his stupor. "Nice to meet you, Charity." Then he turned to Tillie. "I'm going to check on the kitchen. I'll leave you two to work out details and paperwork." With that he turned and left.

"Wow, is he the owner?" Charity asked.

"He sure is?" Tillie said with pride.

"But he's so young," Charity said. *And handsome*, she thought.

Charity became a fan favorite quickly, and moreover a favorite of Andy's. It was obvious that he was smitten with her and went out of his way to be around whenever she was. Eventually, he mustered up the courage to ask her out, and she said yes without hesitation. If there was such a thing as love at first site, it might have applied.

Tillie found herself oddly compelled to get close to Charity as well. She tried to convince herself that it was because of her fondness for Andy and he was so obviously falling for this girl. But deep down she felt another connection to Charity that tugged at her heart. Charity was becoming far more than a dancer at the bar. She was always willing to help. She loved working with Tillie on the costumes and had a natural, almost uncanny ability to know what fabrics would work best and what colors blended or clashed. Tillie saw her as a protégé, and taught her everything she could about clothes, hair, and make-up. Charity had real style. One day, Tillie and Charity were working on some costumes for the Burlesque show, sitting backstage chatting like old pals.

"You sew really well, Cee," Tillie said using Charities nickname. "Did you take sewing class in school?"

"No, my mom taught me," Charity said.

"Well, thank her for me. She's made quite the seamstress of you."

"That would be a long-distance phone call for sure," Charity said with a wry laugh.

"Your folks don't live in the area?"

"They don't live in any area. Car crash when I was fifteen. I was adopted. When they died, I went back into the system. They had no relatives. We were a real threesome," she said with a catch in her throat.

"Oh, I'm so sorry to hear that," Tillie replied. "So, you got sent to an orphanage or foster parents?"

"Fosters, three sets, till the last one. The husband got a little handsy with me, so I left."

"Left? Where did you go?" Tillie asked.

"I was almost seventeen, so I got a job waiting tables. Lied about my age. I lived in my car for a few months, then I met Maureen, my roommate. You've met her," Charity said.

"Yes, nice girl," Tillie said.

"Yup. She saved my life. She had a little apartment and worked at the same café I did. She got suspicious and followed me after work one night and realized I was sleeping in my beater vehicle. She knocked on the window. Nearly gave me a heart attack. She insisted I come stay with her. We set up a little bed in an alcove off her living room. It was tight but we got along really well. Once I started dancing and making more money, we moved into a 2-bedroom apartment. She's like a sister to me."

"What does Maureen do for work?" Tillie asked.

"She's studying to be a nurse, and she still works at the café nights and weekends."

"Did you ever think about going to college?" Tillie asked.

"I never finished high school, Tillie. I did get my GED though. Maureen helped me study."

"You're a smart girl. You can't dance your whole life, Charity," Tillie said. "What would you study if you had the chance?"

"I like business. I love seeing how Andy deals with the bar and the bills and schedules, but I love fashion too. Is there a job that includes both?"

"Fashion is a big business. I think you could be a designer or maybe a buyer for a big chain. There's a lot to it," Tillie said.

"Sounds like you know a lot about it," Charity said. "Were you in the fashion business or have you always been a dancer?"

"I… I guess I just like fashion," Tillie said, suddenly confused by the question. "Anyway, you should think about school. You'd do great. I know it."

"Thanks, but I don't have the time or the money for school. I'll be dancing for a long time, I think," Charity said, and went back to focusing on her sewing with a sigh.

"Charity, will you marry me?" Andy sat at his office desk practicing the way he would say those words. He had the ring in his hand and nearly dropped it. "Shit!" he said. "I'm gonna make an ass of myself."

"How are you gonna do that?" Tillie said, walking through the door as he was making his declaration.

"Okay, I need your advice," he said.

"Shoot," Tillie replied. "What's on your mind?"

"Promise not to freak out or try to talk me out of it?" Andy pleaded.

"I'll do ma best. Unless you're fixin' to do something really dumb."

"I'm gonna ask Charity to marry me," Andy said, and thrust the ring toward Tillie.

"Wow, that's a big deal, Andy. Are you sure about this? She's a bit young to get married, not that you aren't but…"

"I know, I'm a few years older, and I hope wiser, but she's so mature. She's been on her own for a long time now. I want to give her a great life, Tillie. I love her."

"You think she wants to marry you?"

"I think so. At least I sure hope so," Andy said.

"I love you, you know that, right Andy? I just think you're being a little hasty. Charity is nineteen years old. She should go to school, get out of dancing."

"She won't have to dance once we're married. She can just be my wife," Andy said.

"I hope that's enough," Tillie said, and squeezed his shoulder. "I'm going to work on costumes."

Two days later, Tillie was sewing a gown in the little room behind the stage when Charity came running in to find her. Charity was waved her hand under Tillie's nose.

"Look!" she said holding up her left hand. She had a shiny diamond mounted on a gold band on her ring finger. "Andy asked me to marry him," she squealed happily.

"That's great, honey. I'm happy for you," Tillie said, but she her voice lacked enthusiasm.

"You don't sound too excited about it," Charity said.

"I am, it's just that…"

"What?"

"You're nineteen, Charity. I know you love Andy. Hell, I love Andy. He's a great guy, but marriage can wait. What about school? Have you given that any more thought?" Tillie asked.

"Where would I get the money to go to school?"

"What if I gave you the money?"

"What? Why would you do that?" Charity asked.

"You're a very special girl, Charity. You could be something in this world. If you'll go to college, I'll pay for it. But there's a catch. You stop dancing, and you wait to marry Andy till you graduate."

"I love dancing, and I love Andy. I don't understand why you want me to quit either of them," Charity said.

"Honey, I've been dancing as long as I can remember. I don't want you to be me in twenty years. Quit dancing, put marriage on hold till you're through with school, then marry Andy. If it's true love, he'll wait, and you'll be marrying him from a much better place in life, not because he's the best option you have."

"This is crazy generous, Tillie. I'm in shock. I'd like to talk to Andy about it and think some. Is that okay?"

"Absolutely."

Three days later, Andy and Charity asked Tillie to meet them for coffee at a nearby café.

"We've talked things over, and we have a proposal for you," Charity started the conversation. "I do want to go to school. I looked into some programs, and I'm going to apply for community college to start with to get my business degree. I'm looking into internships with some local clothes designers and I might even be able to do some runway modeling in exchange for learning the business."

"You've really given this some attention," Tillie said. "I'm proud of you."

"I want to take you up on your offer to help me with school and Andy wants to help cover the cost too. So, here's what I've decided. I'm going to stop dancing except for the Saturday night burlesque shows. You're right. I don't want to be a dancer my whole life. I want more. But I also want Andy."

"And I want everything for her, not just to be a housewife," Andy piped in.

"So, I'm going to start school in the fall, and Andy and I will wait to get married till next spring. Then I'll help take over a lot of the finances and business at the bar so he can concentrate on marketing and production. We want to build a life together and we both want to pursue the things that interest us. Andy might even go back and get a business degree himself someday."

"I like your plan." Tillie said. "And I'll be happy to help fund your dreams, whatever they might be."

"I don't know why you want to be so generous, but I love you for it," Charity said.

"My pleasure," Tillie said.

The following May, Charity wrapped up her first full year of school and the wedding was planned. A week before the ceremony, she and Andy went to see Tillie at the little house she rented.

"We have a big announcement and wanted you to be the first to know," Andy said.

"We're pregnant!" Charity blurted out.

"Wow!" Tilly said. "This is good news, right? What about school?"

"I'm due in November. I'm going to take some courses over the summer and take only the fall semester off. Then I go back for the spring semester and get my AA. We're on track. I promise."

"Well, then, give me a hug." Tillie said, and pulled them both to her.

"One more thing. We want you to be the baby's godmother," Andy said.

"Oh, no! You need someone younger."

"We want you. You're not exactly ancient you know," Andy said.

"Sometimes I feel like I've lived a dozen lifetimes," Tillie said. "I'll be happy to be her godmother."

"What if *'she's'* a boy?" Andy said.

"She won't be." Tillie said wryly. "I'll bet money on a girl."

A few weeks later, the doctor confirmed Tillie's suspicions. Andy and Charity were having a girl.

Tilly sat in the first pew at the church, tears streaming down her face as Andy and Charity said their vows. Maureen was the maid of honor and Andy's best friend Chad stood up as best man. After the ceremony, they all went back to the bar which was closed for the reception. Andy had his mother and son dance with Bonnie and when it came time for the father daughter dance, Charity took the mic and made an announcement.

"Most of you know that I lost my parents as a teenager. I've been lucky to find a new family here with Andy and his dad and of course, Bonnie. But there's one person who has stepped up in my life in the most unexpected and selfless ways and done more for me than I could have ever dreamed of. I never knew my real parents, my real mother. I was adopted by two wonderful people and lost them too soon, but I got lucky. Another mom showed up in my life to help me, guide me, and encourage me to be the best version of myself, and I owe her my life. If she doesn't mind, I'd like to do a daughter, mother dance with that person. Tillie, will you join me for a dance?"

Tillie stood and moved to the dance floor. She was stunned and deeply moved. The DJ began the song, *You Are the Wind Beneath My Wings,* by Bette Midler.

As the song progressed and with Charity's head on her shoulder, Tillie's mind began to swirl. She saw a younger version of herself handing a baby to a woman in an office. She saw a handsome man holding the hand of a little girl, palm trees swaying behind them, the mountains behind a shining city, two women each holding one hand of a small child, a baby girl. Tillie heard names, Ura, Selena, Heaven, Dennis.

She began to repeat the words, "Charity, Hope, Faith; Faith, Hope, Charity," under her breath.

"Are you okay?" Charity asked her.

Suddenly, Tillie pulled away from Charity. "I love you, Charity. I've always loved you, my daughter. Be happy," she said. Then she squeezed her tightly, let go, and ran from the dance floor leaving a confused Charity standing there in shock.

***

The gold caddy was heading east. She turned the radio on and hummed along as she drove. The signs on Route 10 showed the mileage to New Orleans and then further on, Florida.

She took a deep breath.

"Home."

Chapter 33

Arriving Back in Tampa

She had sharp hunger pains and realized she hadn't eaten anything since breakfast. That was more than eight hours prior. As she pulled into Tampa, she had a craving for a blood rare steak topped with smoked oysters and a salad with blue cheese dressing and lots of vegetables. She saw a sign for a steak house and steered the Caddy in the direction of just such a meal.

"Ms. Ura," the waiter said, when he saw her. "It's been a lifetime. How have you been?"

"I'm sorry, do I know you," she replied.

"Isn't your name, Ura? I mean, it's been a while and your hair is a different color, but I would have sworn…"

"I'm not sure who Ura is but I would love a steak," she said and smiled broadly at the waiter.

"Of course, ma'am. What can I get you?"

"I'll have the sirloin, rare with smoked oysters on top, and a salad with blue cheese dressing and lots of vegetables. Also, can I have a Killian's Red, on draft if you have it."

The waiter looked at her in complete disbelief. Why was Ura pretending she didn't know him? This was the exact meal she and her husband Dennis had eaten nearly every

Tuesday for years. *What's this about,* he thought. "Of course, right away, and I'll bring you some warm bread and ice water."

"Thanks!" she replied.

Once he placed the order and brought her salad, beer, and bread, the waiter made a call.

"Where the Girls Are, Dennis speaking."

"Hi, Dennis, It's Jamie, from the Green Tavern. Sorry to bother you but I thought I should call."

"What's wrong, Jamie?" Dennis and Hope had continued the tradition and ate at the Green Tavern almost every Tuesday night. Jamie had become almost part of the family.

"A woman came in this evening and she's sitting at one of my tables. It's been a while, but I would have sworn she was your wife, Ms. Ura. She's older of course, and her hair is flaming red, nearly orange, but she's a dead ringer for her."

"Did you speak with her?" Dennis asked excitement building in his voice.

"I did. I even called her Ura, but she said she didn't know anyone named Ura and she wasn't who I thought she was."

"Can you stall her? Keep her there for a bit? I'm on my way," Dennis said.

"Of course," Jamie replied and hung up.

I'm sorry the steak is taking so long," Jamie said. "The kitchen is backed up tonight. Food will be out in a few minutes."

"That's okay. I'm not in a rush," she said.

Jamie had asked the cook to wait to fire up the steak for her. He nervously watched the door for Dennis's arrival. Ten minutes after his call, Dennis came rushing into the tavern.

"Where is she?" he asked spotting Jamie near the door.

"At your usual table," Jamie said.

Dennis took a deep breath and walked slowly to the next room. He peaked in and saw the back of a woman with a full head of bright red hair. He moved toward her table and, as if she sensed his presence, she turned to face him. If she wasn't Ura, she was her double. Even though he hadn't seen her in many years, he knew that face, every curve, those lips, those eyes; this was his wife.

"Hello," he said carefully, as if he might scare her away or she might disappear into thin air.

"Hello," she replied, and smiled at him. "Do I know you?" her accent was thickly southern.

"I don't know," Dennis said, confused by the sound of her voice. It was Ura's voice, but not her accent. Ura had no accent to speak of. "My name is Dennis, what's yours?"

"Tillie. Please to meet you Dennis. Can I help you with somethin'?"

"Jamie told me you favored someone I knew, someone very important to me. Her name was Ura."

"Yes, he mentioned her. I don't know her, do I?" She seemed perplexed and a look crossed her face as if she were trying to remember something.

"She's my wife, and she's a dancer, a very good dancer. You look just like her."

"That's odd. I'm a dancer too. I was coming to Tampa to find work," she said.

"I own a dance bar," Dennis said. "Ura was our lead dancer too."

"Are you hiring dancers?" she asked.

"As a matter of fact, I am. Do you mind if I join you? We can talk while you eat and maybe you would like to come see my bar."

"I'd like that. Please sit. Tell me all about your bar."

For the next half an hour, she ate her steak and Dennis told her about *Where the Girls Are*. He told her about the shows they did, and she told him about Texas and how she worked in a bar there. She was vague and seemed a little confused about the details.

As she finished her steak and the last sip of her beer, Dennis spoke carefully, hoping not to scare her off.

"Would you like to follow me to the bar and meet some of the other girls?"

"I think that would be okay," she answered. "Is it far from here?"

"Less than a mile away," Dennis answered.

When they got out to the parking lot, as they rounded the building, Dennis saw the gold caddy. It was the same car Ura always drove. It was old but in remarkable shape. In that instant, any tiny doubt that this was his wife dissipated.

"I'll pull up and you can follow behind me," he said, but he was petrified that she would disappear again. *Please, God! Make her stay on my heels,* he begged silently.

His prayer was heard.

They pulled into the parking lot at the bar and Dennis jumped out to open the door for the woman he knew was his wife. On the drive, he called Tony to tell him to follow his lead. He hadn't enough time to fill him in, but he knew his friend would roll with the punches. Most of the girls who worked at the bar were new and it was Sunday evening. No one dancing would remember Ura.

"C'mon in," Dennis said opening the door for her.

As they walked in, Tony came right over. "Welcome," he said. "What's this pretty lady's name?" he asked Dennis with a slight nod of his head as if to say, I'm with you, pal.

"Name is Tillie," she drawled.

"Well, nice to meet you… Tillie," Tony said. "Can I get you a drink?"

"Absolutely!" She felt oddly comfortable with these two men.

"What'll it be?" Tony asked.

"Can you make a decent margarita?"

"That's different," Tony said under his breath, and went behind the bar to mix the drink. "I need one myself."

"Would you like to see our backstage and meet a couple of the girls?" Dennis asked. *Could she have some form of amnesia?* he thought. *Maybe seeing familiar things will bring back some memories. He was so sure this was Ura. It's her face, figure, car for god sake. What could have happened to her?*

"Sure," she smiled broadly.

He took her backstage and showed her the dressing room. They said hello to the two girls who were backstage getting ready to go on later.

"This sure looks like a nice clean bar. It's a lot like my old bar.

"Oh, really? Where was that?" Dennis asked.

Her face clouded over for a second. "Umm, Texas, I think." Suddenly her accent was gone. "No, That's not right."

"Well, it doesn't really matter," Dennis said. "You're here now. I can't wait to see you dance. Do you want to dance a couple of numbers?"

"You mean now?" she asked.

"Whenever you're ready," Dennis said. *Maybe if she starts dancing on her own stage she'll remember who she is.* Dennis was so confused. He felt as though he was losing his mind. This was surely his wife and she was sick.

"Yeah, well, I dunno. I mean. I guess I can give it a shot." Suddenly she sounded like she was from New York. "What the heck. Let's do it."

"I'll get the DJ to cue up a song for you," Dennis said. "I think I know just the song. Wait in the wings. I'll announce you, okay, Tillie?"

"Tillie? My name's Selena," she said.

"Oh, yes, of course, Selena. I'm sorry, I was thinking of a friend of mine," Dennis said. *Jesus! What the hell is going on here?* He thought, his mind racing. "Give me five minutes and I'll call you up."

Dennis went up to the DJ booth. "Charlie," he said. "Cue up Al Green's, Let's Stay Together. I'm going to bring someone up for a song."

"Sure, you got it."

Dennis grabbed the cordless mic and went up to the stage. He motioned to Charlie to fade out the song that was playing then whispered to the girl who was dancing that he needed her to take a short break and she exited.

"Hi guys," Dennis said to the crowd. It was a Sunday evening and the bar was well attended but not full. Suddenly Dennis had their attention. I want to introduce a friend of mine. She's going to dance to a favorite song of mine. It's the song that made me fall in love at first site nearly twenty years ago right in this very bar. Please welcome Selena to the stage."

He looked over at the woman who he knew was his wife, his Ura. She seemed frozen for a moment, then the song started, and it was as if she woke up from a dream. She stepped out on the stage and it was like a mirror of first time she had done so. She started moving the way she had so many years before.

Dennis moved toward the bar and Tony came out from behind the bar to join him. "Jesus, brother. Did we just go back in time?" Tony said.

On the stage, the sultry creature that had stolen Dennis's heart so long ago was moving to the music. She owned every corner of the stage and was playing to the audience. Every eye was on her and people began throwing money onto the stage, but she didn't even notice. She turned to the back wall which was all mirror. She watched herself as she slid down, opening her legs in an almost frog like stance then slowly coming back up to slide her hips back and forth. She put her hands against the mirror and bent forward so that she was face to face with her own image. All of a sudden, she stopped dancing and stood staring at herself.

She slowly pulled the bright red wig from her head and let it slide to the floor then turned to face the audience.

Dennis moved to the foot of the stage and she walked forward. He opened his arms as she approached him and when she was inches away, she looked down at him and said, "Dennis, where is Hope?" With that, she collapsed into his waiting arms.

Chapter 34

Answers

The ambulance raced into the night, flashing red lights and sounding its horn, as they drove to the hospital. Dennis held his wife's hand. She was stiff and unresponsive.

"What's happening?" he asked the EMT?

"We don't know yet, sir. She seems to be in a coma. Her vitals are good though. It may be some sort of psychotic episode. Does she suffer from some sort of PTSD?"

"I'm not sure what that is?" Dennis answered.

"Post-Traumatic Stress Disorder," he answered.

"I have no idea. She's come in and out of our lives for years. She would be okay then she would just disappear. She's been gone for years and suddenly, tonight, she just showed up, but she was acting like she was someone else."

"Well, hang tight sir. We're almost there. She's stable," the EMT said and went back to monitoring his patient.

"We're going to run a series of test," the doctor told Dennis. "We've got her in emergency right now, but we'll move her to a room in a couple of hours. "Can you tell me what happened right before she collapsed?"

"It's a bit more complicated than that, doc," Dennis started. "My wife has been coming and going in our lives for years.

She seems stable for a bit then one day will simply disappear. For a long while, I thought she was in some kind of trouble with the law. The last time she left, I was so busy raising our daughter, I didn't allow myself to wonder anymore. She's been gone for so long now, just seeing her was a major shocker. She acted like she didn't know me and claimed her name was Tillie. She even had a Texan drawl. When we went to the bar, she later said her name was Selena, and her accent changed to New Yorker. She started dancing, and then was staring at the mirror at the back of the stage. She took her wig off, walked up to me and asked about Hope, then passed out into my arms."

"Has she ever changed personalities in front of you like that before?" the doctor asked.

"No. She's been Ura for as long as I've known her."

"Have you ever tried to find her when she went missing?"

"No," Dennis admitted sheep faced. "The first time she left, I just thought she might have decided she didn't want to be with me. When she came back, we were so happy, and then Hope was born. I had my hands full with a child and a business to run. I was angry at her, but I loved her so much that when she came back again, I simply let her take up where she left off. I guess I just took her in stride. I've never loved another woman beside her. Is she sick, Doc? What's wrong with her?"

"She may have some form of dissociative disorder."

"I have no idea what that means," Dennis replied.

"Well, people who have had extreme trauma in their life, usually early on, can dissociate. It's a kind of mental disorder, and they usually disconnect from loved ones and surroundings. They can lack continuity between thoughts, memories, surroundings, and even their identity. People with dissociative disorders escape reality, often involuntarily, to help keep difficult memories from hurting them. They can suffer amnesia and even have sets of alternate identities depending on the type of dissociative disorder that's has manifested. Extreme stress can temporarily worsen symptoms. Your wife has probably suffered some sort of trauma and something would trigger her to dissociate and disappear, perhaps taking on alternate identities and forgetting the part of her that's Ura, if that's even who she really is."

"What do you mean, who she really is?" Dennis asked.

"What do you know about her as Ura? Where did she grow up? Have you ever met any of her family members?"

"No. She's always been so closed mouthed about her past. I assumed it was something she didn't want to think about. Maybe a bad family life. She never even told me her last name. She'd make a joke about her name. Said it was just Ura, like Cher, one name."

"You must really love her," the doctor said.

"You can't even imagine, Doc. So, what now? How can we help her?"

"There's treatment for dissociative disorders. They'll be a lot of talk therapy to find out what set this in motion, what traumatic event or events and then there are some great new medications and methods. If this is indeed her problem, while it can be difficult, many people learn new ways of coping with what's happened to them and can eventually lead healthy, normal, and productive lives."

"So, there's hope?"

"Absolutely. But I think you need to find out more about who she really is. I would do some fast sleuthing if I were you."

"On it! I guess, it's long overdue for me to find out who my wife really is."

"Yes. The more we know about her past, the sooner we can help her get answers and get better," the doctor said. "For now, go home and get some rest. We'll call you when she wakes."

Dennis nodded in agreement, but he had no intention of resting. He pulled his cell phone from his pocket and called his best friend.

"Tony," Dennis said. "I need a favor."

"Anything. How is Ura? What can I do?" Tony had gone to get Hope from her babysitter and had taken her to his house. A few years back, Tony had married an Italian woman named Sophia and they had a little girl of their own. Hope was sleeping safely in his spare room. "Hope is all settled in. Do you need me to come to the hospital?"

"No, I just need the name of that detective friend of yours."

"Judith Parks? Why?" Tony asked.

"Because it's about time I find out who my wife is."

"I'll share her contact with you in minute. Let me know what else I can do pal"

"Just keep Hope with you. That's all I need for now, but I'm gonna need all of you, I suspect. I'll explain later," Dennis said, then hung up. A second later, he got the text from Tony that shared the info. He called Judith right away and set her in motion to figure out the mystery that was Ura.

"Her name is Heaven Kenney." The detective said when she reached Dennis on his cell phone. "She was born and raised in New York and is a famous fashion designer. Her father was Jordan Kenney who started their design company that is run by her sister Helena and her husband, Ryan. Jordan passed away a few years back. I contacted her sister. They haven't seen her for several years. Apparently, she owns a little cottage in Chapel Hill, North Carolina. Helena went there to see if she was hiding out, but the place was locked up tight, and hadn't seem to have been lived in for a long while," Judith said.

"So, she made up the name Ura?" Dennis asked.

"Or she thinks she's Ura some of the time," Judith answered. "I researched the disorder she may have. They actually think they're the people they more or less become."

"And she's a famous fashion designer? But how?"

"Her sister said that she started designing in her teens. She took off at around 18 years old the first time. She would disappear for a year or more and then show up with a whole new line of clothing. They gave her large sums of money when she asked for it and paid any credit cards she rung up. They're on the up and up. They have a bank account they've kept all these years with her share of the profits and now they're selling the whole shooting match for a ton of money. She hasn't created a new design for more than five years now, but her clothes are timeless, apparently. They're still being sold worldwide. She's worth millions."

"Holy shit!" Dennis said.

"Helena wants to see her. She'd like you to call her," the detective said.

"I would love to speak to her. I'll call her right away. How did you figure this out so quickly?" Dennis asked.

"The car. She's had that car since she was seventeen years old. I checked the VIN on it. Wasn't hard from there."

"I don't know how to thank you," Dennis said.

"Just a check will do," Judith said, and laughed. "Glad I could help."

"She's awake, Mr. Brooks. You can see her now," the nurse said.

Dennis had been sitting in the waiting room for most of the last three days. Other than going home to change and shower, he had been waiting for Heaven to wake up. He stood slowly, a little nervous to see his wife, the woman he knew as Ura. Now, he had to come to terms with a whole new person, one whose past was unknown and whose future was uncertain. Would she recognize him? Would she know who she really was? What other lives had she been living? He followed the nurse into the hospital room. Heaven was sitting up, looking dazed but wide awake.

"Hi," Dennis managed.

"Hi," she responded.

"Do you know who I am?" he asked.

"They told me you're my husband," Heaven said.

"Yup. That's me," Dennis said trying to sound cheery. "Do you remember me at all?"

"I do. I know your face. It's a very kind face. I just don't remember a lot of other things. Can you tell me some things I should know?"

"Well, for starters, we have a little girl. Her name is Hope. She going to be thirteen in a couple of months, and she looks a great deal like you. She's wonderful. I think you'll like her."

"When was the last time I saw her?"

"About six years ago. When you're feeling better, I'll bring her to see you. Would you like that?"

"I'm sure I would."

"Your sister would like to see you as well. I spoke to her yesterday."

"Helena?"

"Yes, you remembered her. That's good," Dennis replied. "Is it okay for her to come see you?"

"I think that might be nice."

For the next hour, Dennis told Heaven about her life with him in Tampa. He told her funny stories about the bar and Hope. He made her laugh a little, and by the end of the hour, she allowed Dennis to reach over and hold her hand. The doctor came in and said it was time to go. He motioned to Dennis to meet him outside the room.

"She's doing remarkably well. We want to keep her in here for a few more days then we need to move her to a treatment facility. There's a very good one in Orlando. One of the best for working with people with Dissociative Disorder. I think that's the best option for her."

"Whatever you think, doctor. Orlando is less than two hours away. Will I be able to visit her?" Dennis asked.

"Eventually. Maybe not for the first couple of weeks, but in time, she will be able to come home if the treatment works. They'll start her on some meds and set her up with talk therapy every day. At some point, once she starts to improve, she'll be able to see a regular psychiatrist weekly and move toward a normal life."

"What if she doesn't want to come home to Hope and I?" Dennis asked.

"That I can't answer, Dennis," the doctor said. "All I can tell you is that she can get better in time. What life she wants to live once she does, will be up to her."

"Heaven," Helena said gently as Heaven stirred in her bed, beginning to wake. "It's me, Helena." Helena had flown in from New York. Dennis filled her in on the issues and she was happy and relieved that Heaven was safe and alive.

"Helena? You're here?" Heaven said sleepily. "How did you get here?"

"Dennis called me. He said you were in the hospital. I got on a plane right away. I'm so happy to see you, sis." Helena's eyes were filling with tears. "I'm so sorry."

"What for?" Heaven asked.

"Everything. I think I understood how difficult things were for you as a kid. I was so focused on the business, making money, and being successful. Nothing else mattered. Ryan had a heart attack two years ago. He's better now, but it made me realize how little all of this mattered. I almost lost him, and I had no idea where you were. The two most important people in my life, one was gone, and the other nearly gone. I can't tell you how sorry I am, and how much I want to make things up to you."

"You've nothing to make up to me. I'm glad you're here," Heaven said.

"And I'm not going anywhere. They said they're moving you to a great place in Orlando that can help you. Ryan and I are renting an apartment nearby for however long you need to be there. I'll be there every visiting day and for anything you need. I told Dennis they're will be rooms for him and for Hope if they want to come anytime."

"Really?" Heaven sounded like a little girl with her response. "You would do that?"

"Already in the works. I'm never losing you again. Okay?"

"Okay. I'm glad," Heaven said.

In the next few days, Heaven and Helena talked for as many hours as the doctors would allow. Dennis came to see her at least twice a day. The plans were made to move Heaven to the treatment facility, and on the last day she was in the hospital, she asked to see Hope. Dennis brought her in after explaining that her mom was not well but that she was going to get better little by little.

"Don't be afraid," Dennis said to Hope. "She's still your mom. She's just had a rough time of things and she wants to see you."

"I'm okay," Hope said. "I want to see her."

They entered the hospital room. Heaven was sitting up in bed. Her hair was combed, and she looked rested. Her face broke into a huge smile at the sight of her daughter. "Hello," she said tentatively.

"Hi, mom." Hope went to her mother's side. "I've missed you."

In a matter of minutes, they were talking and laughing. Dennis stood to the side, tears glistening in his eyes. After a while, the nurse came in to say it was time for Heaven to rest. Dennis asked her to take Hope to the waiting room. "I need a moment with Heaven," he said.

Once the room was clear and he was alone with his wife, he went to her side.

"She's beautiful," Heaven said. "Thank you!"

"For what?" Dennis asked.

"For her. For taking such good care of her. For everything," Heaven said. "Why are you still here?"

"They said I could stay for a few minutes."

"That's not what I mean. I mean why are you still here in my life? From what I've learned over the past week or so, I've disappeared on you, left you to raise Hope alone. I don't know what's wrong with me or where I've been. They tell me the doctors can help me figure it all out. It may not be pretty. I would understand if you never wanted to see me again," Heaven said. "It may be a long time before I'm a whole person, if ever."

"Heaven, you need to know something. Your name doesn't matter. Where you've been or what you've done doesn't change things. I have only loved one woman, and that's you. I've always been here, and I will always be here. Deal?"

"Deal!"

"I love you," he said.

"I'm counting on it," she answered.

"I have waited half my life for you. I'm not leaving you now." Dennis said, then leaned down to kiss his wife.

Epilogue

Heaven Turns Fifty - 2027

"Surprise!" the group yelled in unison as the lights came on in the expansive living room of their Chapel Hill home.

The gathering for Heaven's 50th birthday celebration was a miracle in and of itself.

"Dennis! How did you… when did you?" Heaven stammered at the sight of all of them. Her beloved Dennis, gently taking her elbow, wielded her into the room.

There they all were. Charity, with Andy and their two little girls, Hope, looking so grown up, filming the entire event on her high-tech phone, and little Faith, holding fast to both of her mother's hands. They had all come to celebrate Heaven and Dennis and the difficult journey that got them all to the place they were; a place of love, kindness, and understanding.

Helena and Ryan and their little twin boys drove over from their beach house on the Carolina coast to be there for the occasion. Even Lono was there, having traveled from Portland with Chris, Denny, and Faith.

Tony, or as the girls called him, Uncle Tony, and many of the girls from the bar, some old faces and some new helped fill the room.

And there were people who were not there in body but in spirit, people that Heaven's memory had stitched together in her years of therapy. Some of them she might never see again in person, but she would find them in her dreams.

The others, her children and the people that loved and guided them while her mind had taken her elsewhere, her grandchildren, and her many friends were all standing there before her, beaming at the sight of her. Her blonde hair was half as much white now and her figure wasn't quite the perfect hourglass it had been in her youth, but her green eyes still shone brightly as the tears cascaded down her cheeks.

"I went on a trip with my mother many years ago and I recall thinking that I was the luckiest girl in the world," Heaven said. "Now I know that I am the luckiest woman alive!"

Acknowledgements

-   I want to express my gratitude to Lil Barcaski for her help to bring this deeply heartwarming story to the completion as I had envisioned.

-   GWN publishing.

-   LongBar Creatives Solutions and Cyndi Long for the beautiful book cover.

About the Author

Cheryl Yax is a dynamic personality who is living her life to the fullest! Cheryl has had an exciting life and has enjoyed careers as a flight attendant, dietary manager, marketing business consultant, real estate investor, and so much more!

Cheryl has been working on writing this book for over twenty years and had a driving desire to see it to completion as her 60th birthday present to herself.

Lil Barcaski – Writing Assistant

Lil is an accomplished writing coach and a published author. She is also the VP at LongBar Creative Solutions, a full-service business consultancy and parent company for GWN Publishing. Lil is presently working on a novel based on a true story of a serial killer in Missouri in 1978 and two non-fiction books.

Will there be another book about Heaven and her family and friends? Only time will tell.